nothing is heavy

vicki jarrett

LINENPRESS

Published by Linen Press, Edinburgh 2012

1 Newton Farm Cottages
Miller Hill
Dalkeith
Midlothian
EH22 1SA

www.linenpressbooks.co.uk

Cover photograph: © Rebekah Burgess | Dreamstime.com
Cover design: Zebedee Design, Edinburgh & Vicki Jarrett
Typeset in Sabon by Zebedee Design, Edinburgh

Printed and bound in Great Britain by CPI Antony Rowe

ISBN 978-0-9570050-3-7

For my family

You've got to jump off the cliff and build
your wings on the way down.

Ray Bradbury 1920-2012

ONE

largely potato-based

The angel was wearing L-plates. Her wings were bent, her halo hung at an angle and she swayed on her feet like she was standing on the deck of a ship.

From behind the counter of the Deep Sea, Beth watched and waited. If this is a messenger from God, she thought, then He is having a laugh.

The angel put an arm out to steady herself. Her hand connected with the person coming into the shop behind her and she grabbed a handful of his jacket and hung on. They staggered against one another, making it hard to tell whether they were fighting or holding each other up. A trace of perfume and spilled beer drifted across the counter but was quickly swallowed by the clouds of hot chip fat. The familiar smell barely registered with Beth anymore, unless in the wake of some passing interruption.

The guy wrapped an arm around the angel's waist and tried to kiss her, crumpling the L-plate safety-pinned to her back, just below her wings. She leant back, avoiding his face. 'Will you quit it?' she said.

'Aw c'mon, Angel. You might get run over by a bus tomorrow.'

To give him his due, thought Beth, he's not wrong. That could happen. 'Salt?' she asked. Neither of them heard her. They were too wrapped up in each other. She shook some salt onto the chips anyway and stacked the parcels on the

7

counter, feeling their heavy warmth settle within the paper. The angel was laughing now and nodding. Her halo wobbled as the guy pulled her close again. They kissed messily then stood grinning at each other, their faces shining and wet under the fluorescent shop lights.

'That'll be three pound fifty,' Beth said, raising her voice just a little.

The guy dug out some change and crashed it down on the counter. Then they picked up their chips and were gone.

Outside, through the plate glass window, Beth could see a whole flock of angels. A host. They all had pink wings and haloes and greeted the couple with cheers. The girl responded by winding her arms around the guy's neck and kissing him again. He held the chips safely out of reach with one hand and slid the other under the angel's tutu. This time her halo came loose altogether and fell to the pavement. The host squealed and clapped. Three of them linked arms and started to dance along the pavement, skipping from side to side. *Off to see the wizard.* The rest followed. Beth watched them recede into the neon-painted darkness of just one more Saturday night.

Tonight, like other weekend nights, was busy in the Deep Sea, especially after pub closing time when the street acted as a funnel for the drunk and lost to drain out of the city centre. They trailed through looking for food, taxis, somewhere still open to drink, someone to talk to, fight with, kiss. Beth managed, despite running the place on her own.

Before leaving her to it after the dinner-time rush, Gianni had made sure she had plenty of stock. The double fridges through the back were bulging with fish, pies, sausages, chicken, black puddings and enough batter to drown a horse, plus three huge vats of chipped potatoes submerged in cold water. She'd haul these through to the front shop one at a time as she needed them.

'You're all set,' Gianni had said running a comb through

his black hair, smoothing it down and checking his reflection in the mirror. He'd changed into a clean shirt, top two buttons left undone, silver St Christopher pendant showing. 'Phone me if the place burns down. Otherwise, don't disturb. Okay?' She assured him she wouldn't. 'Feeling lucky tonight!' he'd said, and swung out of the shop in a cloud of hopeful aftershave. He was headed for the pubs and clubs of the city centre in search of his second wife. He said he knew she was there somewhere, it was only a question of looking. The final interviews, however, would always be conducted by his mother.

Beth had met Gianni's mamma a few times and shuddered at the memory. Luisa dressed in black and dyed her hair to match, rehearsing the role of widow while Tony, her husband, rehearsed the role of corpse. Tony had retired years ago although his name was still painted on the old chip van parked round the back. A framed photo of the van in its heyday, dazzling white and decorated with cartoon fish and burgers, hung on the back wall like a favoured relation from a more optimistic past. Now it was virtually a museum piece, its sides scabbed with rust. *Tony's Chi* clung on in pale blue letters above the cab. They still used it for ferrying stock around and for parking outside the football and poaching some trade from the flashier trailer shops.

Last time she'd seen her, Luisa had pinched Beth's arm and said she was too thin and that it wasn't good for business. People would think there was something wrong with the food. She reminded Beth of the witch in Hansel and Gretel. Or was it the wicked step-mother? Or perhaps some cross between the two? Maybe it was just that she didn't understand mothers. A possibility since she'd never had one.

Her childhood, as far as she could remember, had been largely potato-based. She didn't think about it often. When she did, she could hardly remember the faces of the grandparents who had raised her. Her memory had recast them in fuzzy black and white and their features were fading at the edges. She tried not to think about them too much, in case she wore out what was left. What she remembered best was the potatoes: boiled, mashed, chipped, roasted, no meal complete without them. The smell of the peelings in the sink, the slimy starch of them between her fingers when she scooped them out of the plug hole and squeezed the water out. Even now, the turned-earth smell of peeled potatoes took her back to a time when her life was, if not exactly idyllic, then at least only partly screwed up. She'd never had a completely clean slate, coming into life with the debit column already carrying a couple of entries: her father before she was born and her mother shortly afterwards. Her gran had done her best but her heart hadn't been in it. Her grandad had been a vague presence, as men of his generation were in the lives of children. And then they were gone.

She half-filled one of the long-handled wire baskets with the rest of the uncooked chips from the second vat of the night and shook the excess water off over the sink. Working alone suited her fine. She operated on auto-pilot and didn't have to think about much of anything. She sank the basket into the fryer, watched the chips taken by the brown foaming bubbles, listened to the busy hiss of hot fat.

Junction Street was topped by a broad intersection at its northern end, the meeting point for three main roads heading out of town. From there it narrowed into a single hardened artery reaching south. The street was home to the Deep Sea and half a dozen other fast food places, arcades, late-opening bars and night clubs. But the twenty-first century reached only as high as the lampposts. From there on up, the buildings were the same dirty stone tenements that had lined the street for over a hundred years: not that old compared to the rest of the city but old enough to harbour a few ghosts. Some of the buildings had been altered over the years: stories added, others taken away, creating an uneven jumble of flat and pitched rooftops that reached upwards, back into the darkness.

Beth watched Saturday night flash past the window. People moved in waves back and forth, closing in then parting again, like theatre scenery being wheeled on and off. Her own face reflected back at her from the glass, broken into pieces by the lights from outside: one eye dissolved in the red flare of a traffic light, her mouth taken by a speeding taxi. She closed her eyes and listened. Underneath the churn of traffic there was the familiar stream of human noise: shouts and screams, the clatter of running feet, snatches of song, wild laughter. Unchanged in the two years she had worked there. Unchanged probably since the year dot. It's always been like this, she thought, the only difference now is better lighting.

She opened her eyes as an ambulance tore past, sirens howling, heading for the troublesome heart of the city. Sirens were part of the soundtrack of Junction Street. The fire station was nearby and the engines would regularly burst out of a side street and speed off, jumping the lights on the wrong side. And there were always police cars. More around closing time as arguments became things to be settled with fists. That was the third ambulance tonight. Beth had been counting. Not out of concern, or sympathy, or even morbid curiosity. It was just something to do. Tonight's scoreboard said: 3 ambulances, 4 police cars, 1 fire engine, 2 stag parties, 1 hen night, 46 bags of chips, 25 fish, 17 smoked sausages, 3 indecent proposals and 2 death threats. No partridges or pear trees, yet. But she was trying to keep an open mind.

She gave the basket a shake. The chips were starting to turn golden but weren't quite cooked yet. A horn blast pulled her attention back to the street. She blinked a couple of times, not sure she was really seeing what she thought she was seeing.

A large monkey leapt from the path of a red and white bus and onto the traffic island. He turned and made a distinctly human gesture at the bus driver.

Usually stag parties restricted themselves to stupid hats and matching t-shirts, sometimes kilts and tammies. But now she thought of it, there had been a group last week wearing grass skirts, garlands of flowers and huge, plastic breasts. They'd barely been able to stand upright for laughing at each other. Maybe a monkey wasn't all that surprising, apart from the fact that he was alone. A missing link.

The bus pulled away and the monkey stood for a while, a forlorn look about him as if unsure what to do next. Beth saw him perk up when he spotted the chip shop. He crossed the road in a knuckle-dragging lope and came inside. His hair was matted and his rubber face looked strangely sad as he hopped about, scratching his armpits and making monkey noises. She watched him. What did he think he was doing? Eventually he slowed, then stopped and asked for a bag of chips.

'Oh go on. Smile,' he said, 'it might never happen!'

She glared at him.

'You're a right miserable cow, you know that?'

'One seventy-five.'

The monkey took his chips and went outside.

Why didn't he take the head and hands off at least? It'd make eating a whole lot easier. She watched as he fumbled with the wrapper and was jostled from behind by a guy of about twenty in a white tracksuit. There were a few others, all gold chains and dangerously clean trainers. One shoved the monkey, making him stumble, and another snatched the bag out of his hand, spun on his heel and started walking backwards, eating and laughing. The monkey protested and was rewarded with a thrown chip which bounced off his rubber nose. One of the group gave him another shove before they shouldered off up the street laughing and chucking chips at each other. The monkey stood there, his hairy shoulders slumped. He might be an idiot, she thought, but he didn't deserve that. She wrapped another bag and took it to the door.

'Here.' She held it out towards him.

It took a few seconds for the penny to drop. 'For me? Wow, that's really . . . Look. I'm sorry about the whole cow thing. I mean, I shouldn't have—'

Beth closed the door and went back to work. From the corner of her eye, she was aware of him standing there, letting his free chips go cold before he turned and walked away. She looked up then and watched as he crossed the road and shambled towards the entrance of Fantasy Island.

A new addition since the old night club had burned down last year, the lap-dancing bar had brought a different kind of custom to Junction Street. She watched the men who approached the entrance, alone and in groups. Not out of any particular interest but it was something else to do when she got bored with counting things. She played: 'Will they, won't they?' to pass the time and wasn't often wrong. The groups acted differently from the single men with shouts and laughter, a few shoves, a bit of play fighting. Usually, the more noise they made, the less likely they were to go inside. The men who went in alone arrived by taxi and entered quickly, disappearing into the dark space between two neon palm trees. She couldn't fathom what it was all about. Were they all really so hopeless that they couldn't find anyone who'd take their clothes off for free?

She had the monkey down as a 'Won't'. He looked far too interested in his chips. He ignored the doorway, but slowed to look at the glowing pink and blue trees along the frontage. Silhouettes of women with exaggerated curves and minute waists hung from the trees like fruit. She remembered reading somewhere that a real human being with the build of a Barbie doll would be unable to walk upright without her spine crumbling and her tiny ankles shattering. If she wanted to get anywhere, she would have to crawl, on her hands and knees.

TWO

not a bird to be trifled with

Amber snapped out a bubble and chewed the gum back into
her mouth. Bending over the waist-high wall that ran along
the edge of Fantasy Island's rooftop, she watched a pigeon
flap out from the eaves and cross the short distance to the
next building. Where she stood, the club's flat top was hemmed
in by a sagging assortment of tiled gables laden with chimney
stacks and aerials. Down below, people hurried by, their breath
puffing out in little clouds. She leant on her forearms and
adjusted her grip on the outer edge of the wall. It was too
cold for this, but work was work, and money was money.
She kept her legs braced, pelvis tilted back and up, and rocked
back and forth on the balls of her feet. John's voice sounded
muffled, coming from above and behind her.

'You want it, don't you?'

John was pretty easy as a customer, but he did like to talk.
'Oh yeah, uh huh, I want it, I want it so much.' She should
really charge extra for talking. Have a rate-per-word, like a
journalist or something. She blew another bubble and gave
an annoyed *tsk* when a long strand of hair stuck to her lip.
She pulled at it with one hand, letting her weight rest against
the wall.

'Oh Jesus, you love it, you dirty bitch.'

'Hmm . . . hmm.' Fucksake. How long was he going to
take? He was certainly getting his fifty quid's worth tonight.
She should have charged more, but it all counted, all went

14

into the fund. Her nest egg was building up nicely. She did some mental arithmetic, totting up her week's earnings in time with John's forward thrusts; at this rate, it'd take another six months before she had enough.

John gave a little whimper. Finally. Then he relaxed against her, crushing her onto the wall. She felt the old stones give a little and watched a puff of mortar sift downwards through the streetlights. Christ, the wall was going to give way and they'd both be head first into the street.

'Get off, will you?'

John grunted and picked himself up, stepped back and pulled the johnny off, threw it behind a chimney stack and zipped his trousers. She straightened her skirt and held out her hand. He gave her some notes which she counted before stuffing into the side pocket of her jacket. He pulled out a pack of cigarettes.

'Smoke?' he asked. Now their business was done, his voice had softened and he sounded like he was passing the time of day after buying a paper.

'Yeah. Thanks.'

He lit two cigarettes and handed her one. 'You know it doesn't have to be like this,' he said. She drew on her cigarette and ignored him. John wasn't a stupid man, but he did seem to be a bit thick when it came to this particular argument. 'Why don't you stop making life hard on yourself?' he persisted. 'You know I'd take good care of you.'

'I told you. I'm not for sale.'

John spat smoke and laughed. 'Is that right?' He looked her up and down and widened his eyes in mock surprise.

'You know what I mean. This,' she waved a brusque hand at her outfit, taking in the short skirt, the platform shoes, 'is only temporary. I've got other plans.'

'Shame,' he said and turned away from her. 'Because business is looking up.'

'Fantastic. You can give us all a raise and fix the hot water in that shit-hole you call a dressing room.'

He laughed like she'd made a joke. 'If this deal comes off, you can have a Jacuzzi in there.'

'Coke again, is it?'

He nodded and blew smoke out the side of his mouth. 'That's where the money is.'

She nodded. John was harmless enough, as far as his type went. At least you knew where you were with him. What he wanted from her was someone he could dress in designer gear and use as an accessory, with the bonus of being able to fuck her for free whenever he felt like it. Considering the amount of business he'd given her recently, he probably reckoned it'd be cheaper to put her on the domestic payroll. If she took him up on the offer, he'd no doubt want her to stop taking other customers and stop dancing too. She wouldn't miss either of those things but there was no way she wanted to belong to anyone, full time. She wasn't sticking around. This wasn't her life; it was just a job. A means to an end.

John ground his cigarette out on the wall and flicked the butt over the edge. 'You're a smart girl, Amber. This is the last time I'll make the offer. Just think about it is all I'm saying.' He walked to the hatch leading to the cramped stairwell that spiralled back down into the body of the club and disappeared inside.

After a few moments, she heard the lower door bang closed behind him. She'd had worse bosses. Compared to some of the bastards in this business, John was a fucking prince. He paid a decent hourly rate and allowed the girls to keep their tips as long as they managed to push a few bottles of overpriced fizz to the punters. In some clubs, the management actually had the neck to charge the girls for their time on stage – a cost they had to make back in tips and bar tabs before making a penny for themselves. On a slow night you could end up owing the club money. Fuck that.

She finished her cigarette. On the wall below, a CCTV camera mounted on a bracket swivelled back and forth, taking in the street and all its tiny dramas. She followed its gaze. Everyone was going somewhere, some of them staggering and weaving, but none the less on their way. Junction Street was like a giant tarmac conveyor belt between leaving and arriving. It wasn't somewhere you stopped.

Tucked between the photo shop and the bookies, Phoenix Tattoo was in darkness. It had been a decade since she'd first walked in there, never imagining that all these years later she'd be back in Junction Street again. But life hadn't worked out the way she'd planned.

When she'd first gone in, Mac had squinted at her drawing, pulled a hinged lamp out from the wall and smoothed the paper out with his big hands. A strand of white hair escaped from its band and fell over his eyes. He hooked it behind his ear. Amber guessed he must be in his fifties or even sixties. Tall and wiry, with intelligent grey eyes, he wore a long-sleeved shirt, the cuffs rolled up, showing sinewy forearms covered with ancient blue-black tattoos. He whistled through his teeth and looked at her. 'That's a lot of work. A lot of time.'

'I know.'

'It'll hurt. Especially over the bone.' He gave her an appraising look. 'And you don't look like you've got a lot of padding.'

'Not a problem.'

They'd looked at the sketch together. In black biro she'd drawn an outline of her back with her design penned over it. The wings spread from between her shoulder blades and fanned out to the tops of her arms. Below, they tapered to meet at the base of her spine. She had filled in some feathers along the outer edges, a few with the barbs radiating out in fine lines from the shaft, but she hadn't completed the drawing.

'Okay. You want it exactly like you've done here?'

'That size but I'm hoping you can fill in more detail.'

He smiled. 'Sure. I can do that. I'm guessing you see the feathers as more eagle than sparrow?'

'I want the feathers like this,' she said and pulled a hardback book from her shoulder bag. It was a large book, thick as a phone directory but narrower, and well worn. The front cover was filled edge to edge with a drawing of an owl. This was not a bird to be trifled with. Its curved talons gripped a torn stump of wood, the head turned sideways on the body so that the eyes glared straight out; alien and pitiless circles of black, like water at the bottom of a deep well. The razor hook of a beak was a ready weapon, an implicit threat. She felt a familiar swoop of dread looking into the bird's implacable features but forced the fear down and raised her chin. It was time to put childhood nightmares behind her and claim the strength and the power of those wings for herself.

Mac was nodding, examining the tortoiseshell layering; the short, wide feathers of the upper portion tucked over the longer, darker, primary feathers that were the colour of a lion's mane. 'Can I keep this for reference till we're done?' he asked. He looked up and caught her reluctant expression. 'If you don't trust me enough to look after your book then we're in trouble. You'll have to trust me with something far more valuable if you want me to do this work.'

She frowned at him, puzzled.

'Your skin,' he said gently, 'is worth more than any book.'

She nodded, making an instant judgement. 'I trust you enough.'

'Good,' he said. 'I'd like to be able to go on trust as well, but I'm afraid you're going to have to show me some ID.' He shrugged apologetically. 'Have to stay legal or I lose my licence.'

'Of course.' She handed over the copy she'd made of her birth certificate.

'Hey, happy birthday.' Mac folded it and handed it back to her. 'This your eighteenth present to yourself then?'

'Thanks. Yeah, something like that.'

The first time he saw her naked back he'd paused and

18

traced a finger down her scar and out over the constellation of blue dots already inked there. 'Do you want me to cover these?' was all he ever asked. She'd told him Yes and they hadn't discussed it again.

She'd spent hours, over weeks, straddling a reversed chair, leaning forwards, listening to the buzz of the needle. Mac hadn't been lying – it hurt like fuck but it was a good kind of pain and after a while it wasn't pain at all, just a sharp, prickling heat. She was reclaiming her body and each line, each drop of ink that went into her new wings made her stronger.

Now, ten years later, on the opposite side of the street, she winced as a thin blade of pain slid under her shoulder sending tingles down her left arm. Ignoring it wasn't going to work this time. She fished in her pockets and pulled out a blister pack of pills, popped a couple out, dry swallowed them and steadied herself against the wall, closing her eyes and focusing on her breathing.

A sudden scuffing noise broke her concentration and she felt the stones shift a little under her weight. She opened her eyes in time to see a piece of slate detach itself from the short gable below and slip out, like a card from a deck, and fall towards the street. She followed its descent in slow motion.

Down below, a guy in a monkey suit was walking in front of the club, looking at the dangling neon women, his head tilted to one side. The slate was heading straight for him. All she could do was watch. Even if she called out to warn him, he'd probably just look up and get it right in the face. At the last moment he seemed to speed up and the slate shattered on the pavement behind, missing him by inches. He jumped, scattering a few of his chips on the pavement before turning and looking up towards the top of the building. Amber backed away from the edge into the deeper shadows.

John's voice echoed up from the stairwell behind her. 'Hey, Amber, c'mon. Get your arse down here. You're on.'

'Okay, okay. Keep your hair on,' she called as she swung through the hatch onto the stairs.

She dumped her coat and most of the rest of her clothes in the cramped box that passed as a changing room for as many as six girls at a time. It was empty now. The walls were bare brickwork and a long mirror ran the length of one wall above a low wooden shelf cluttered with makeup and cans of hairspray. A jumbled rack of costumes and coats was pushed up against the far end, the floor beneath strewn with assorted shoes and boots. To the right was a door without a lock leading to a single toilet and wash-hand basin. She looked at herself in the mirror and swiped a finger under her eyes to tidy her smudged eyeliner. She rummaged amongst the rubble on the shelf till she found an antiperspirant spray and directed a blast into each armpit then fluffed her hair up. That'd have to do.

Wearing a halter top and g-string, she left the dressing room and walked along the short corridor into the club room. The stage was a raised platform at the rear with a metal pole in the middle, fixed to the low ceiling. She paused at the bar to collect a dishcloth then climbed up. She gave the pole a business-like wipe-down then threw the cloth to the back of the stage. Fran had been on before her, leaving it greasy with that bloody stupid body glitter she insisted on wearing. Wasn't a problem for Fran since she didn't really work the pole, just minced around and rubbed up against it like a stray cat. But if you wanted to try any proper moves, a greasy pole with no grip was a good way to break your neck.

She took hold of the cold metal with one hand, hooked a knee round, leant back and swung wide. She pivoted round on one six-inch Perspex platform shoe, letting her head fall back and her hair swing. She scanned the upside-down room. The bar wasn't particularly full: half a dozen single guys, one subdued looking stag party and a small group of businessmen with flushed faces and loose ties. A couple of girls were working the room, their pink skin marking them out among the dark suits like a different species. Sophie, a student with eye-watering debts, trying to get through the final year of a degree in Spanish and Business Studies. Fran, single mother, two kids and a day job in a bakery, struggling to hold on to the house since her husband died in an accident at work. They were a different species all right: the clothed and the naked, those with money and those without.

She let her mind drift and went through her set thinking about all the places she was going to see when she eventually got out of here. New York, definitely. She liked cities. But there would be other places too. Jungles and deserts, waterfalls and mountains, Machu Pichu, the Grand Canyon, Iceland. She played the alphabet game: 'I bought my ticket and I went to . . .' starting with A and trying not to stop in the same country twice. Ayer's Rock, Buenos Aires, Casablanca, Delhi, East Berlin . . . She got to Vietnam without dropping a destination by the time she came to the end of her number. She stooped to retrieve her g-string and left the stage.

In the changing room she put on a short strappy dress that was virtually transparent. Better get out on the floor and talk to those businessmen; they looked like the biggest spenders.

John was sitting by the bar and beckoned her over. 'Drink?' he asked.

'Go on then. A quick one. Don't want anyone thinking I'm getting preferential treatment.'

John looked over at the other two girls. 'So what if you are?'

It wasn't that she gave a toss what the other girls thought but she didn't want to encourage John. She should have turned him down but the pills hadn't kicked in yet and she needed a drink. A swift double should do the trick.

As John talked, she noticed two men enter the bar and take a table in one of the booths at the back. The way the older man's gaze swept the room, skipping over the girls but snagging on the suits told her these were no ordinary punters. He had short silver hair and deeply tanned skin and was dressed in an expensive suit. Hard to guess at his age. He was slim and moved with a lightness that made his body seem younger than his face. The other guy looked like trouble straight off: young and overly muscular with a narrow shaved head. The bouncers would normally have knocked him back, but not in his present company. Silverhair didn't look like someone you'd want to cross. His eyes came to rest where she was sitting with John at the bar. He ignored her but acknowledged John with a nod just as one of the doormen appeared at their side. 'A Mr Murdoch here to see you,' he said to John in a low voice.

John stood up and put his drink on the bar. 'Sorry, doll. Catch up with you later. Business.' His face looked waxy under a thin covering of sweat. 'Why don't you go and see if the girls want anything from the chippy?' he said. 'Go on, off you go.' He squeezed her arm then made his way towards the two strangers. Amber watched him shake their hands, smiling far more than he usually did. She'd never seen him look nervous. He regularly dealt with some dodgy people but these two looked different. They looked like seriously bad news.

Wearing an almost floor length greatcoat over her tiny dress, she stood in the doorway of the dancers' dressing room holding a list.

'Two small chips, just salt, one portion of onion rings and a single sausage. Hey, Fran? You going to eat that or is it for your new act?' She laughed and ducked as Fran launched a copy of *Hello!* at her. It flapped overhead and landed behind her in the corridor. She picked it up and rolled it into a tube in her hands.

'You are a sick, sick puppy!' Fran laughed. 'You're just jealous of my healthy relationship with food.' She turned her back, put one foot on a chair and leant over to adjust the straps on her shoes, presenting an irresistible target. Amber took aim, released the rolled up magazine, then bolted, closing the door on Fran's shouted threats, calling back, 'Won't be long,' as she swept down the corridor.

She pulled the coat tight around her body, went down the narrow stairway and out between the neon trees. Compared to the dimly-lit fug inside, the exhaust fumes and cold gusts blowing along the street felt fresh. She pulled her collar up and headed for the green man. She wasn't taking any unnecessary risks. Not in these shoes. She pressed the button and waited.

THREE

held and held

The good news, the junior doctor at the hospital had told Beth after the crash two years ago, was that apart from a few cuts to her hands and knees and a couple of cracked ribs, she would be just fine. She watched the exhausted-looking young woman and waited for her to move on to the bad news. The doctor cleared her throat. She looked like she hadn't slept for a week and her breath smelled of stale coffee. 'Your friends . . .' her voice tailed off. She looked at the floor for a long moment then came to with a start as if prodded in the ribs by an invisible finger. 'There was nothing we could . . .' Beth waved a hand to make her stop. It wouldn't do either of them any good to draw the whole thing out. She'd seen the wreckage and what it contained. She doubted she would ever stop seeing it. The doctor looked relieved, then guilty. 'I'm sorry,' she said and put a hand on Beth's arm. It lay there for a few futile seconds before the doctor sighed and withdrew it.

'The other car,' Beth's voice was hoarse, her throat felt raw and she was suddenly very thirsty. 'Are they okay?'

The doctor frowned. 'She. There was only one person in the other vehicle. We can't tell much until she wakes up and she hasn't. Yet.'

Beth nodded and the doctor turned and left the room, the rubber soles of her shoes wringing strangulated squeaks from the floor as she walked.

She was being kept in for observation overnight because of the concussion but would probably be discharged in the morning. Alone. The enormity of this fact hovered somewhere just on the edge of her field of vision. She was still able to regard her loss from the outside, as if it was something separate from her and she was in no hurry to start processing the reality of it. She remembered how it had been when her grandparents had died: the initial numbness which wore off to be replaced by a tripping sensation, stumbling into realisation then out again. That could go on for days, months, even years. And that was just the beginning. She didn't want to even start, didn't want to accept that once again, she'd lost everyone who mattered to her.

She longed for the blessed relief of curling up under the duvet, fitting herself around the curve of Danny's back as he slept on his side, and she tripped; she wondered whether Al would have finished off that bottle of Bushmills before she got back to the flat, and tripped again; hoped Craig would be taking a day off from his latest attempt to reinvent the drum solo because her headache couldn't take the racket; trip, trip, trip. Each mis-step pushed her closer towards the fog bank that was waiting for her. She wasn't ready. She tried to clear her head.

There was a jug of water and a tumbler on her bedside table. She drank three full glasses one after another. The water was tepid and metallic tasting and did nothing to soothe her throat or satisfy her thirst. She lay flat on the bed, pulled the stiff cotton sheet up to her chin and stared without blinking at the fluorescent strip above her bed until the light started to vibrate. The water gurgled as it rolled around her stomach. She tried not to close her eyes. Every time she did, the vertical, white after-image of the light on the inside of her eyelids became the white line in the middle of the road and the evening's events played out all over again. She didn't want to remember. But then she thought of how the memory of her grandparents had become eroded with time: how hard it was now to recall their

25

faces, the colour of her grandad's eyes, the sound of her gran's voice. It was all being eaten away. If she let it, time would take everything from her, the passing days would swarm like locusts over her memories and strip them bare. Perhaps she'd got it all wrong: trying to preserve her memories by storing them away, like an old photo album stuffed at the back of a bookcase. What if the knack of memory was a muscle that needed building up? She'd have to start by allowing herself to recall everything that had happened last night, in every detail. She closed her eyes and let it come.

The gig had been brilliant. A medium sized venue just out of town; it'd been packed, the atmosphere friendly and receptive. Plenty of drink had been taken but there were no hecklers or bottle-throwing piss-heads. The crowd seemed genuinely into hearing a band instead of merely tolerating the interruption to their chat up lines. For once the band had all been on form on the same night and the songs came together exactly as they were supposed to. There was even possible interest from a small Indie label; Al had been accosted while they carted their gear off stage by a skinny guy who looked in danger of being overpowered by his own beard. He'd shaken Al's hand for a full minute, asked for a contact number and said he was going straight back to talk to his partner and he'd be calling them *soon as*.

They were euphoric when they eventually piled back into the van, Danny behind the wheel and the rest of the band – her, Al and Craig – crammed in the back amongst the instruments. They had worked out a system of stacking the gear and themselves so that the instruments didn't get damaged because they couldn't afford to replace any of them, but it was far from comfortable. It didn't matter that night though. Al had a bottle of brandy and was passing it around. Craig, as usual had sparked up his first pre-rolled, post-gig number and no one else would be getting a smoke till it was at least half way down.

Beth didn't mind. She didn't feel like blunting the edges just yet. She was buzzing, her head fizzing, her body still twitching with adrenalin. Mostly she thought of performance as a necessary evil and kept her head down, avoided eye contact with the audience. She wanted the music, was hopelessly in love with the sounds the band made playing together but if they'd never performed in public she wouldn't have cared. It was the guys who wanted the band to go places. But tonight had been different. She'd felt lifted on a wave of goodwill and had let herself go with it, as if some previously unknown version of herself was born to do this, to connect. And she'd loved it. Maybe, she thought, this was the start of some whole new phase of her life. During the harmonies she'd looked up at Danny and smiled and seen him grinning back at her, surprise and pleasure all over his face. They'd been more than friends for the last few months but were taking things slowly, both of them wary of tangled loyalties. They couldn't keep it secret since all four band members lived together in the same flat, but so far at least, Al and Craig had accepted the new situation with good humour.

'That was it!' Al was grinning wide enough to split his face as Danny coaxed the old van out of the pub car park and onto the main road. 'That was the best gig ever. That was *the* gig. That was the one. Telling you.' He took another swig from his bottle of brandy.

'So it's all downhill from here is what you're saying?' said Craig from behind a thick wall of smoke.

'Don't be such a twat,' Al snapped back at him.

'I'm just winding you up. You are way too easy.'

As usual, Al was wired and volatile after the gig. In this mood, he could easily be pushed into anger and Craig knew just which buttons to press to do that. Beth used to wonder how the band had managed to stay together as long as it had: three years before she came along and four since. Al and Craig were like an old married couple who couldn't help sniping at each other but underneath was a fierce loyalty.

'Don't start right?' Al almost shouted. 'We played a fucking blinder tonight and even you can't deny that.'

'Okay, okay. Got me,' Craig raised his hands in a gesture of surrender. He'd had his fun now and was pulling back before Al got properly pissed off. 'It was pretty good.' This was high praise from Craig, who rarely got above *fine* or *alright. Pretty good* was out the park fantastic.

Al tapped Danny on the shoulder with the bottle and as he accepted it he caught Beth's eye, holding the look just long enough for her to know there'd be more than eye contact on offer later. She smiled. Danny took a mouthful of brandy. 'You were well up for it tonight,' he said, talking to her over his shoulder as he negotiated a roundabout. 'Almost looked like you were enjoying yourself.'

Beth laughed. 'Yeah, well. Maybe.' It was still too fresh, too fragile. She didn't want to analyse it, to talk it to death just yet.

Danny passed the bottle over to Craig and accepted the joint in return.

'Do you reckon that record company guy will call?' Craig asked Al.

'Course he will. The guy loved us. He'll be begging for us to sign. Trust me.'

As if on cue, Danny's mobile started to ring, the tinny strains of *Ride of the Valkyries* coming from somewhere in his jeans.

'Jesus. That'll be him,' shouted Al. 'Gimme the phone. Quick!'

Danny was steering with his knees and struggling to liberate the phone when he dropped the joint in his lap. 'Shit shit shit,' he muttered, extracting the phone and throwing it back to Al before scrabbling between his legs for the smoking joint.

'Look,' said Beth. Through the windscreen she could see headlights coming towards them. On the same side of the road. 'Look.' The inside of the van was flooding with a cold white light. She watched as it turned Danny into a dark silhouette, a shadow puppet.

'Hello!' shouted Al into the phone, and that was the last thing she heard before everything went quiet. And white. And that seemed to last a long time.

The next thing she knew she had grass in her mouth and was lying on her back looking up at the stars. She wondered how she got there, wondered if she could move, whether her body was still there at all. But it wasn't urgent. Everything was wonderfully peaceful, as if she'd just woken up from the most refreshing sleep and all was well with the universe. There was nothing she needed to know right now. The stars were impossibly beautiful and so close she would be able to touch them if she reached up. They were singing to her, hundreds of voices joined in the same exquisite harmony that held and held, swelling to fill the heavens with its message. The universe was infinitely generous and constant and she was part of it. She was safe and loved. She belonged.

But then, without warning, the music faltered, wavered and died, blown away by a cold wind that was also wiping the stars from the sky. No, they weren't gone, they blinked out then reappeared. Something was obscuring them, something blacker than the sky was circling high above her, something huge, something with wings, descending.

She squeezed her eyes shut and turned her head, searching for that feeling of peace, desperate to hold on to it, to shield herself from whatever was coming for her. But it was too late. It had already slipped away. Reality came crashing down on top of her. She gasped for breath and noticed that she was shivering. She stood up shakily and looked around. Further up the road a red estate car had spun across the carriageway and come to rest on the verge. Its front end was twisted and steam curled upwards from the bonnet. The air smelled of burnt rubber and engine oil. In the opposite direction she saw their van, or what was left of it. It looked as if it had been picked up and crumpled in a great fist, like a badly written letter, or an empty wrapper. It was upside down and one of the wheels was still spinning. She walked towards it, her stomach tightening, her throat closing.

The back of the van was towards her, the doors hanging open. She peered into the darkness.

'Guys?' It came out as a whisper.

Nothing. Just creaks and small clunks of settling wreckage. She moved closer and stared into the mess then groped her way forwards. Her hand closed around a trainer. There was a foot inside and the foot led to a leg in frayed denim. Craig. She tugged at his ankle but nothing happened. He was pinned down by something heavy. In blind frustration she grabbed hold of his foot and pulled harder and the trainer came off in her hand. She dropped it and clambered further into the back of the van. The biggest amp was on its side just about where Craig's head should have been. She flinched as her knee went down in something wet and warm. To her left she saw a corner of Al's leather jacket poking through tangled metal. She clutched at it but it was dripping wet and slipped through her fingers. Panic began to take hold of her and she scrambled backwards out of the van and looked at her hands. They were dark with blood. Her head was spinning and the effort of getting air into and out of her lungs seemed almost impossible.

Danny. Oh god. Where was Danny? She stumbled round to the front of the van then stopped with a jolt and staggered back a pace, rebounding as if she'd walked into a wall. He was half in half out of the shattered windscreen, his limbs arranged in ways they never should have been. Bits of bloody glass were scattered all around him like glittering confetti. His head was turned to the side. She bent down and gently pushed his hair back. She needed to see his face. Tiny red gems fell from his dark fringe and rattled across the bonnet. Danny's face was white as marble, his eyes wide open, unblinking, unseeing. He was already gone.

'No,' she said. But it didn't do any good. She felt her body buckling and went down hard on her hands and knees on the glass-scattered tarmac. She started to crawl. When she reached the verge she threw up. There hadn't been much in her stomach but what there was pushed its way up her throat and spurted out through her mouth and nose. And it kept on coming until it felt like it was coming out of her eyes, the pores of her face, the roots of her hair, like her body was doing its best to turn itself inside out.

She opened her eyes, sat up in her hospital bed and made a clumsy grab for the jug on her bedside table, knocking the tumbler to the floor where it bounced instead of breaking. She refilled the jug back to the top with the contents of her stomach.

A nurse came. Beth apologised but the nurse smiled and whispered, 'Don't worry about it. Nice catch, by the way.' She took the jug away and fetched a doctor who shone a pen light into her eyes. 'I think we'll hang on to you a little longer and schedule a scan before you go. Just to be on the safe side. Probably nothing to worry about.' She put her pen light back in her top pocket and forced a smile that only made her look more tired. 'I'm sure you'll be fine.'

Her stay in the hospital was extended. And extended again. She couldn't hold food down, her body rejecting all attempts at feeding as if balking at the concept of survival, and the promised scan kept being rescheduled. She was moved to an open ward. On the second day, at the end of visitors' hour, a nurse stopped by her bed and frowned at her bedside cabinet, her uneasiness at the lack of cards, flowers or unwanted fruit evident. 'Is there really no one you could call?' she asked.

Beth shook her head and looked away.

Her life revolved almost entirely around Danny and the band. Before them, she'd kept herself to herself. There was no one out there now beyond the hospital walls who would miss her. She sat through visiting hours and watched the other patients gingerly embrace their families, hold hands on top of the sheets, talk, and even laugh together. She had the sensation she was seeing them through glass, from the outside looking in.

Apart from the police taking a statement from her, she had only one visitor: Cameron, Craig's dad and owner of the flat they all shared. Beth had met him a couple of times previously. He was a barrel-chested, amplified man who worked in event management and who walked into every room as if surveying it for where to put the lights and speakers, how to arrange the seating and organise the people. But the Cameron who stood at her bedside was different: his whole body contracted to half its normal bulk, as if the old Cameron had been cracked in half like a Russian doll and this smaller, darker version substituted for the brightly painted original. He opened his mouth to speak but choked and swallowed without forming any words. Then he looked around as if he didn't know where he was or how he got there. Before she could say anything, he turned and walked away, his outline growing smaller until he disappeared from view.

Danny's family were in Ireland, and according to the police, his remains were to be flown over there. Al only had his dad. The authorities were trying to track him down, his last known whereabouts on the hippy trail somewhere in Nepal. One way or another, they were all claimed and there was nothing she could do.

On the third day, she asked the doctor whether the woman from the other car had woken up and was told No. She was stable but unresponsive. Beth had gone over and over her recollection of the crash but the seconds between light flooding the cab and her waking up on the verge seemed to have been edited out. She remembered she'd been leaning over the front seat, trying to warn Danny but all she'd been able to say was, 'Look.' Had she made a grab for the steering wheel herself at the last minute? And if not, why not? Whichever way she looked at it, her own actions, or the lack of them, were what caused the vehicles to meet head on. The impact must have somehow thrown her clear, fired her straight through the windscreen, leaving her with little more than scratches. Guilt lay on her chest like a stone slab.

Whatever the exact logistics of the wreck, one thing was certain: the other driver was not to blame. And now she owed the woman an explanation and an apology, even if she couldn't hear it. She asked if she could see her.

At first the doctor made half-hearted noises about *protocols* and *procedures* but eventually shrugged and said, 'I don't suppose it matters. No one else has been in to see her.'

In a private room, Beth sat in a chair by the bed and listened to the soft machine noises of the room: a breathy hum; the occasional muted beep; the woman's slow, regular breathing. Venetian blinds admitted a watery light from outside. Digital displays and monitors glowed like green and orange lanterns on a distant shore. The atmosphere was strangely soothing. She gazed at the woman's face. She was middle-aged. There were crows' feet at the corners of her eyes and deeper lines running from her nose down either side of her mouth, like brackets. Her hair was dark – what could be seen of it poking out from beneath the bandages covering the top of her head. Her expression was one of absolute serenity. This woman was safe in that place of universal acceptance that Beth had visited all too briefly while lying on the roadside verge. But this woman hadn't woken up yet. Possibly never would. Beth envied her.

There was a plastic hospital band on her wrist. Beth leant in to read the name written on it in blue biro. HELEN N was as much as she could make out. She sat for a long time in silence. The need to explain the circumstances of the crash, to apologise and beg forgiveness, ebbed away on the gentle tide of Helen's breath. There was no need for any of it. An irresistible feeling of familiarity was growing within her; not the spooked feeling of déjà vu, but an easy intimacy that loosened her aching muscles and quieted her mind.

It couldn't be of course. Logically she knew it was only a coincidence that this woman had the same name as her mother; the mother who had given birth to her from the stillness of her own coma before letting go and drifting away. And it was simply a fluke that, from the photographs Beth had seen, her mother could have looked just like Helen in middle age. A dead ringer. She knew all that. The information was recorded in her mental filing system, as though on index cards.

But the longer she sat there, the less relevant the facts seemed. What, or who, was stopping her from taking those index cards and shuffling the pack? A monitor tweeted softly and the light in the room dimmed further as the day turned to night outside the hospital windows. *Nothing* and *No one* were the answers to her question.

She reached out and placed her hand over the warm, still hand of the comatose woman. 'It's all right, Mum,' she said. 'I'm here now.'

FOUR

glowing like a fairground carousel

George looked at the grey fragments behind him on the pavement and frowned. A roof slate. Could have bloody killed him. He peered up towards the rooftops. It was hard to see anything beyond the glare of the streetlights. He thought he caught the ghost of something pale in the darkness but it was gone before he could make it out.

'Could've bloody killed me!' This time he said it out loud. Either his brush with death had gone completely unnoticed by the other pedestrians or they just weren't bothered. A pair of middle-aged women stopped laughing as they neared him, looked at him sidelong and took a wide berth, weaving away on their heels, arms linked. He was just another lunatic talking to himself in the street. His heart hammered in his chest like it was trying to remind him about something. What? That he was still alive? That was worth remembering. He tried to slow his breathing and looked across the road.

The girl in the chip shop had her head down, cooking and wrapping food, moving back and forth between the counter and the fryers in her little oasis of light as if she was on rails, hardly ever looking up. Her movements reminded him of a kids' program he'd watched as a child. It had a fancy town hall clock with two clockwork figures, male and female, who would emerge and complete the same intricate, choreographed movements every hour, every day, always the same. He walked a little further up the street and sat down on the stone steps of the bank, to have a rest and gather himself a bit.

He looked at the neon girls and the palm trees. He came this way pretty much every day on his way to work and he'd never really looked at them before. Earlier that night, when the stag party was still in full swing, he'd been talking to one of Davey's old army mates from down south who worked for a company that made neon signs. 'It's funny, really,' the guy had said. 'People think the signs are machine-made, but what you're looking at there is proper craft. Every sign, every bend of every letter is done by hand. It's all hand and eye. Genuine craftsmanship. Times Square in New York, yeah?' George nodded. He'd never been there but he'd seen it in enough films to feel like he had: mile-high buildings dizzy with giant TV screens, flashing displays crammed edge-to-edge with blinking neon. 'Course there's a lot of digital crap now but it's the original neon I'm talking about. All of them, every one, handmade.' Then the guy had got technical. Stuff about the different gases and coatings on the inside of the tubes they used for effects and colours. George lost track somewhere between argon and mercury.

The girls weren't the only neon in the street. There were other signs, including one above the Deep Sea, a vivid red fish surrounded by curled waves of cobalt blue sea. Other signs were less artistic. Further up the street a rival takeaway promised CHIPSPIZZAKEBABSOPEN, a quick-print shop lit up LOWLOW PRICES and an amusement arcade made claims to INSTANT CASH PRIZES WINWINWIN. The messages weren't inspiring but knowing someone had toiled over it all and handled every curve, gave the street a softer, more home-made feel.

George slotted another chip through the mouth hole of the monkey mask and chewed. At first the mask had itched like a bastard but he was getting used to it, getting to kind of like it actually. It saved having to explain the mark on his forehead to everyone: the big, stupid L-shape that'd been stamped there like a brand since morning. He hadn't taken the mask off all evening even though it rubbed the raw skin there and made it sting. At least it covered his embarrassment. Davey thought he was making a point about the costume mix-up but George had joked about getting his money's worth from the hire price and Davey had let it go. Tomorrow was Sunday so there was time for the mark to fade before work on Monday morning. Davey was a pretty relaxed boss. They'd known each other since school and he never pulled rank as employer but he'd be unlikely to tolerate George wearing a monkey mask while serving customers. Anyway, the costume had to be returned to the hire shop on Monday.

He shouldn't have let Davey talk him into coming along to Stewart's stag do. He rarely enjoyed these things but Davey wasn't easy to turn down. 'Monkeys, man. We're all dressing as monkeys,' he'd said. 'You know Stewart's really hairy, right?' George pointed out, not for the first time, that he didn't know Stewart. 'Aye you do,' said Davey. George shrugged. It wasn't worth arguing with Davey when he was sure of something, even when he was wrong. Especially when he was wrong. 'Anyway,' Davey said, 'it's a piss take on that. Be funny as fuck.' He sat back and nodded at George as if he'd just agreed with him.

George had taken him seriously and had ended up looking like a complete arse. The rest of them, half a dozen or so guys he knew vaguely from Monday five-a-side football, or other nights out, had turned up wearing big mutton-chop sideburns, chest wigs and open necked shirts. A caricature seventies disco look, complete with oversized medallions. Davey snorted with laughter and raised his hands apologetically when he saw George approaching in full costume. 'Oh Christ, I'm really sorry, mate, forgot to tell you. We scaled the idea down a bit. No one could find a proper monkey suit. Well, apart from you, obviously.'

Considering the L on his forehead, George was grateful for the excuse to keep his face covered. The guys would have a field day if they saw it.

That morning he'd woken up on the sofa, his head hurting. When he finally sat up, he realised he'd been sleeping with his forehead pressed against the sharp corner of a framed photo. It was of Zoe and him on holiday together, back when things were still good between them. They had their arms round each other, surrounded by a cloudless blue sky that had looked like it would go on forever. She was smiling, in a summer dress, sunlight streaming through her blonde hair, her skin golden. And there he was, a lazy grin on his face, taking it all for granted. Could that really be three summers ago? He rubbed the skin on his forehead and winced. That would explain the dream he'd been having where he'd been mistaken for a post box by an endless stream of people with pointy parcels. Still dressed from the day before, he grabbed his jacket and headed out to the corner shop without looking in a mirror.

Milk, rolls, pack of bacon and a paper. Since Zoe had left, he'd slipped into the habit of shopping for each meal as it came along. The 'weekly shop' had always been her department and taking it over in an organised way, instead of popping into whatever shop he was passing and picking up a pot noodle, was like admitting she wasn't ever coming back. He knew his diet was rubbish so sometimes he bought fruit then forgot to eat it. He liked his morning routine though, liked to get some fresh air into his lungs, see what the day looked like, how it tasted, before trying to get to grips with it. He also liked a bit of banter with Arshad at the corner shop. Arshad was in his seventies but couldn't bring himself to retire. All his children were off training to be doctors and lawyers; not one of them wanted to take over the shop. 'I will be leaving only in my box!' Arshad laughed, showing his indestructible gums. Some days he didn't say much at all but

George's day was always better for a cheery *Good Morning*. It mattered.

But this morning, Arshad only stared, his gaze fixed above George's eyes. George checked his eyebrows. Still there. His forehead was more tender than he'd realised, and it wasn't simply part of his hangover. Arshad nodded and pointed to a carousel of birthday cards and sweeties with a small mirror mounted at the top. George looked at his reflection. His face was pale and baggy from last night's drink, his eyes were bloodshot, and a great bloody livid red L, like a learner driver's sign, was stamped right into the middle of his forehead. It was more than an indentation. He must have been rubbing his head back and forth against the photo frame in his sleep. The skin inside the L was scraped raw. He groaned and tugged his hair down over the mark as best he could.

When he got home, a group of kids were sitting on the wall outside his block of flats, drinking cider and practising swearing. He kept his head down but the wind that always howled between the tall buildings caught his hair and plastered it back just as he was passing. There was a long two seconds of silence while even the wind seemed to hold its breath as the kids stared. Then they were falling about and putting their thumbs and forefingers to their own foreheads, making L shapes and shouting, 'Looozer', dancing round him gleefully as he hurried away. The itchy mask was preferable to more of that.

Apart from the costume mix-up, the stag do had been a disappointing if not unusual night out. He had watched Davey being knocked back by half a dozen women as he grew drunker, more morose, and finally maudlin. George knew before the night was out that Davey would be hugging him and telling him, 'Ah luv you, you know that, I really really fuckin luv you, you are the best mate in the world ever, and I really mean that, I know you don't believe me and you think

I'm drunk, and I am drunk, but honest mate, you're my best mate and I really do luv you.'

But before that could happen, George had become separated from the rest of the group and was left wandering around on his own, almost being run over by a bus, having his chips robbed, and barely avoiding death from a falling roof slate. A person could get paranoid.

'Hey hey! Monkey boy! Where you been? I thought they'd taken you back to the zoo.' Davey sat down next to him on the steps of the bank and put an arm round his shoulders. One of his sideburns was missing and the other was peeling off and hung down in a flap at the side of his neck. 'Glad I found you,' he said and belched. 'Those guys are a bunch of wankers. Chip?' Davey offered his crumpled bag to George before noticing he had one of his own. 'Oh, you've got some. Cool.'

Davey could be a bit much a lot of the time, but right now, weaving along the street together, bouncing off each other's shoulders like bumper cars, George knew there was no one else he'd rather be with. Davey could be an arsehole, but he was an honest arsehole. There was no side to him. If he was pissed off, you knew he was pissed off. If he was happy you knew he was happy. It would never occur to Davey not to express exactly what he was thinking. Right now he was moving into his expansive philosophical phase of drunkenness and George was only half listening, watching the reflected neon of the city roll under his feet on a wet wheel of tarmac. Davey was waving a chip in the air, making a point.

'It's just fucking and eating. I'm telling you. Folk like to dress it up all fancy and bang on about ideas, or love, or culture or any of the other bollocks – science, religion – all of it man, just smokescreens. Take it apart far enough and the only things driving any of it are fucking and eating. We're just animals man, all of us. The rest is bullshit.'

'Hmm,' said George through a mouthful of potato. Davey

often had some theory or other at this stage in the evening. He would be very passionate about it, aggressive even, and then forget the details the next day and deny ever having said or thought anything of the sort.

'Are you listening to me? This is important. Fucking and eating – what do you reckon?' Davey had stopped now and was fumbling with a packet of cigarettes. Responding to Davey in this frame of mind was a tricky business. You couldn't brush him off, or worse, agree with him. You had to argue with him, but just the right amount.

'I dunno, Davey. What about all this?' Their journey had brought them into a wide street with clean sandstone buildings. George gestured around them taking in the concert hall with its green domed roof, softly lit like a docile spaceship; the cinema over the road; the open square and the statues. 'We wouldn't have all this if everything was like you're saying.'

Davey snorted. 'All what? All this *civilisation*? All this fucking *art*,' he spat the word out as if it tasted bad.

'What about music?' George said. He had Davey there. No way he could argue with that. For Davey, music was a religion. More than once, George had had to convince him that it wasn't morally wrong to sell a guitar to someone who knew absolutely nothing about Blind Lemon Jefferson. Somebody had to keep the shop in profit, even if the boss had other priorities.

Davey grinned. 'Ah ha!' he said, a cigarette bouncing between his lips as he chewed and chased the tip with his lighter. He got it lit, took a long drag and blew out a column of smoke. 'It's simple, Georgie-monkey-man. Just folk trying to communicate, impress each other. Like birdsong, y'know? What sounds all spiritual to us is really them shouting: This is my fucking tree, right, come over here and I'll peck your bastard eyes out, I am hard as fuck and I will fucking kick your arse, you scrawny wee shite, oh and by the way wummin birds, I am a fantastic shag, fancy a quick one, come on!' Davey delivered this translation in a loud voice while flapping his elbows like an overexcited chicken. A young couple sniggered as they walked past. 'Doesn't mean it doesn't sound fucking beautiful, doesn't mean it can't move you. You know I love my music. But I'm under no delusions.'

'What about love then?' George regretted it as soon as it was out of his mouth. It just fell out like something he'd forgotten to swallow, something wet and half-chewed. He hoped Davey hadn't heard him. He could do without another lecture on being a soft bastard.

'Fucking! Definitely. C'mon!' said Davey, as if it was the most obvious thing in the world. He spread his arms wide, looked up to the sky and nodded, acknowledging divine agreement; as if God was on his side, and since that was two against one, George should concede the point. But he didn't.

'You love your mum, right? You love your brother? You might even love your mates.'

Davey frowned. The fake sideburn had peeled off the side of his face and was now stuck on his neck, looking like a fat pubic caterpillar. 'Course there's all that. But take away the cuddly stuff, love, or whatever, and it's just shiny wrapping paper.'

George knew Davey didn't really believe in his own theory. He was running out of steam and carried on arguing because he enjoyed it. It was his idea of a good time. He'd argue against gravity if he could get a rise out of someone.

'So, which is it then? Do you want to eat me or fuck me?'

'Both!' Davey laughed, his mouth wide open and full of chewed potato, smoke funnelling from his nostrils.

George had had better offers. Not lately, right enough, but he had.

Davey threw his cigarette into the gutter and put his hand up for a high five. George slapped his palm. Once Davey's hand was up like that, you had to, unless you wanted it to come down on your head.

'Is that not a bit dismal though? Everything reduced to those two things?'

Davey shrugged. 'Personally, I don't see the problem. They're my two favourite things in the world. You take stuff too seriously, you know that?' he said, screwing up his empty chip wrapper. He threw the paper ball in the air, tried to head it into a litter bin and missed. George picked it up and dropped it in.

Taking things seriously was what Zoe had accused him of not doing enough of. Admittedly that was only one item on an exhaustive list of complaints she'd delivered over the months before she left, but she had seemed pretty clear on that point. He sighed. The sort of feelings he'd had for Zoe weren't all about sex and food. Okay, so a lot of them were, but not all of them. He thought again about the framed photo he'd slept with the night before. It was one of the few shared items she'd left behind. In it, she was already starting to look like a stranger. Perhaps she'd been one all along. He sometimes got the feeling that the Zoe he'd been living with was some person he'd made up in his own head; someone who looked a lot like Zoe but wasn't really her at all. The real Zoe? Maybe he'd never even met her. The stupid thing was – he still missed the made-up version.

Davey was staring at him. 'You're doing it again!'

'What?'

'I can hear your brain working from here. Just quit it, okay? Find another sea for your fish and all that, yeah?'

'I wasn't thinking about her,' George lied.

'Don't lie to me. I know you. You can't pull the sheep over my eyes.' Davey came towards him, arms outspread, and George found himself engulfed in a sudden hug. 'You are my best mate. Y'know that?' said Davey, his voice taking on the strangled tone of the final phase of drunkenness, the one that came just before unconsciousness.

He peeled one heavy arm away and put his own around Davey's waist, propping him up. 'Yeah. I know. Time we got you home.' It wasn't far to Davey's flat. George walked him to the door and helped him with his keys, guided him down the hall to his bed where Davey toppled over and started snoring almost before he hit the mattress.

Now what? George wasn't tired, wasn't even properly drunk, which was annoying considering the amount of effort he'd put into the task. He went and helped himself to a beer from the fridge, settled into Davey's ridiculously massive armchair and grabbed the TV remote.

When he woke up, the beer can was still full. On the TV a man with a bright orange suntan was shouting, 'Cheap as chips!' to camera and brandishing fistfuls of notes. George punched the Off button, stood up and stretched. He looked at his watch. Another hour of his life had slipped by without anyone noticing, not even him. Another sixty minutes had relocated from his future to become part of his past – a place where nothing could ever change. Was this the way the rest of his life would pass? Time flowing around him like he was a rock stuck in the middle of a river? A loud snort and a crash from along the hall interrupted his thoughts.

In the bedroom, George picked the alarm clock up off the floor, righted the bedside cabinet and moved it out of range of Davey's flailing arms. Davey rolled over again, shouting something unintelligible into his pillow. George retrieved the duvet, spread it over his friend and pulled it up around his shoulders.

Back outside, he felt completely sober. He knew he couldn't be, technically, but his brain felt cleansed and he was fully awake. He didn't much fancy going back to his own flat. All that undisturbed air filling up every room, thickening because it wasn't stirred by the movement of someone else. Walking from room to room, he had to push his way through. It was especially bad in the bedroom. He thought maybe he'd wake up one day unable to move at all, his body packed in solid air, trapped like a fly in amber.

Perhaps he should have just stayed at Davey's. Slept the night in the armchair. Too late for that now. It'd be impossible to wake Davey to answer the door. No, he'd have to go home. He walked slowly past an all-night garage, glowing like a fairground carousel against the dark buildings surrounding it. The cashier wore a green polo shirt and baseball cap and was slumped behind the counter, reading a newspaper. George thought again of the girl in the chip shop.

It was the first time he'd noticed a woman in a long time and he'd called her a miserable cow. He shook his head. What a total idiot. But she'd looked so sad, he'd wanted to make her laugh, but then something in her expression had triggered a memory of the way Zoe had looked at him near the end; a look that could suck all the juice out of you, leave your insides all shrivelled up and small, like a raisin at the back of a kitchen cupboard. But that girl could have any number of reasons for looking like that and they were nothing to do with him. *Smile! It might never happen?* He heard himself saying it again and winced. She didn't deserve that. And then she'd been kind to him. She didn't look the sort who did that very often. He pictured her serious face and guarded eyes. She looked nothing like Zoe. She was as dark as Zoe had been fair. His mother had said Zoe was from Viking stock, with her broad shoulders, straw blonde hair and grey eyes. It suddenly came to him who the girl in the chip shop reminded him of. It was an album cover, Patti Smith, *Horses*, that Mapplethorpe shot of Smith in black and white, an unsettling combination of presence and distance, subject and audience, looking right back at you. She looked complicated. He sighed. Wasn't life complicated enough? He knew where she worked. He could always go back and apologise properly another day.

And then he noticed the stand of flowers. They'd been taken inside the garage for the night and leaned drunkenly in black buckets; a few meagre bundles of tired stalks with little smudges of pink petals. Carnations probably. Flowers like that would strike completely the wrong note if given to a long term girlfriend, or your mum on her birthday. But as a spontaneous apology to a complete stranger who almost certainly wouldn't be expecting it? Perhaps they could outperform themselves. It wouldn't even matter if she threw them away because it would be a good thing for him to do. A random act of kindness, and he did owe her one.

FIVE

something greyish underneath

Beth eyed the food in the hot-cabinet and wondered if she'd need to do another basket of chips before closing. It was getting late and the busy time was over. Soon she could start thinking about closing up and mopping the floor. Give it ten more minutes. She thought about the empty flat waiting for her, about the bottle of Jack Daniels and the television, about the numbness the combination produced. Television showed a different world to the one she watched on the big screen of the shop window: the weather was better, everyone was good looking and hardly anyone seemed to worry about money. But at least she could turn the television off. More often than not though, she'd fall asleep in the chair, glass in her hand, while the shiny people carried on, unheeded in their fuzzy pastel box.

It was warm inside the shop but turning cold outside. Autumn had edged away from summer and was turning towards winter. Two years after the crash, and she was still waiting to be fine in the way the doctor at the hospital had been so sure about. Probably she'd meant the everyday fine of being generally well and healthy. But Beth couldn't be absolutely sure. 'Define fine,' she should have said, but of course at the time she hadn't been thinking about definitions. It was only later that she decided she needed a specific meaning for the word, otherwise how would she know whether she was or not? There were twenty-six possible definitions in her

Chambers dictionary. Only two of them fitted her: *very slim or slender* and *consisting of minute particles*. Most of the others implied some sort of excellence or clarity. She was pleased to have found two she could use because it meant she could tell herself and anyone else who asked that she was fine and not feel as if she was lying or being offhand. Everything was just fine, if you defined fine the right way. If you defined fine hard enough, you could subtract the whole word from itself, de-fine it, and have nothing.

The door swung open. 'Hey, smiler! How's it going?'

Amber was one of her regular visitors from Fantasy Island. She would pop over for a break and something to eat, sometimes bringing a list of requests from the other dancers, and if the shop was empty she'd stay a while and they'd talk. Or more accurately, Amber would talk and Beth would occasionally respond, but it wasn't strictly necessary. They didn't talk about anything real. They didn't know each other's history or where they lived or anything much about what they did when they weren't working. It seemed to suit them both that way.

'Pretty dead in here tonight. You?'

'Oh, y'know,' Amber shrugged, laughing. 'Pervs, saddos and wankers. The usual.' She pushed her hair back and grinned. Amber was constant movement, like a reflection in rippling water. She never stood still but moved her feet on the spot and talked with her hands, red nails flashing, specks of light catching on her glittery eye shadow. She had a throaty voice and a laugh that made Beth feel glad of her company.

She liked that Amber made no pretence about what she did, including her freelance work. In fact, she didn't seem to recognise that it might bother some people. She thought it was hilarious that some of the other girls in the club insisted on calling themselves exotic dancers. 'We're strippers. That's all there is to it. I mean, sure, you have to put some art into it. But the punters wouldn't be there at all if you weren't going to get your kit off. That's the whole point. If they wanted to see dancers, they'd be down the road watching a bunch of posh anorexics tiptoeing around pretending to be ducks or whatever.'

Beth had seen posters for the ballet outside the theatre. 'Swan Lake?'

'Yeah, that's the one. Now that really is perverse. Could have done that myself if I wanted to though.' Amber arched her arms above her head and raised one leg, straight and high, then toppled over. 'But not in these shoes, obviously. Anyway, that game is a lot more work for a lot less money. No use to me.' She rummaged in her bag, pulled out a lipstick and bent towards a chrome strut in the display case to use as a mirror.

Beth had no idea what a ballet dancer or a stripper got paid but she was pretty sure it was more than the minimum wage she was getting. She didn't complain though. What was the point? Gianni would just find someone else. And the job suited her, although she'd wandered into it more or less by mistake.

After the accident, she'd spent a fortnight sitting in the flat staring at nothing, surviving on stale biscuits and tinned tuna until eventually she ventured out to the chippy. There was a Staff Wanted notice in the window. It seemed like something to do, somewhere to put herself. And it had worked out fine. She didn't have to take off her clothes or put on a face. People didn't want a personality; they just wanted their food. She was almost invisible, no more than an anonymous piece of human machinery between them and their dinner. And she was good at it, even in her spare time, ghosting through the supermarket to pick up tea bags and milk, drifting back to the flat. Unseen. She doubted she would show up on the film from the CCTV cameras that swept over the city night and day except as a moving smudge or an outline fading towards transparency.

The only person she spoke to about her money worries

was Helen. She'd been in for a visit that afternoon. Since the accident, the hospital visits had become part of her routine: daytime visits, evening work, night time drinking. She found the predictability reassuring. Having a routine made her feel safe.

The passage of time was subtly changing Helen's appearance but had done nothing to improve her condition. The bandages were long gone, her hair had grown, the bones of her face were more prominent, and under the sheets her body had wasted, but otherwise she was exactly as she had been the day they'd first met. Beth was her only regular visitor. Apparently the daughter had come in once but hadn't been back. It meant she got to keep Helen to herself. They could be a better mother and daughter to each other than those fate had allocated them. Beth was dutiful in her visits and Helen listened to her without interrupting. That was the way it was supposed to be, wasn't it? Helen's eyes sometimes moved under her eyelids and Beth interpreted these responses as a vocabulary of sorts.

Her visit that afternoon had been brief.

'Sorry, I can't stay long,' she'd said. 'I'm doing a few extra shifts. Don't think it's going to be enough though. You'll never guess what I got today.' She rummaged in her bag and brought out a letter, unfolded it and read out loud: 'Our client requires that the rental arrears stipulated be paid in full by the end of this calendar month. Should payment not be received, our client will have no alternative but to issue an eviction notice with immediate effect and to pursue this matter through the courts.'

She folded it up again and put it back in her bag. 'Seven grand. How the hell am I supposed to get my hands on that sort of money?'

Helen's eyes shifted slightly from side to side under her eyelids, which Beth translated as gentle disapproval.

'I know, I know,' she replied. 'Don't say *I told you so*. I should never have kept the flat on, it's far too big for just me. Or I should have rented out a couple of rooms but . . .' She paused and rubbed her temples where a headache was forming. 'I never thought Cameron would do anything like this, especially since he's not been bothered to collect any rent for nearly two years.'

Her wages barely covered food, drink and utility bills so she'd let the rent situation slide, choosing to ignore it and hoping it wouldn't matter. And it hadn't seemed to. But now Cameron had put the flat in the hands of a factor who was taking a different view. She searched Helen's face and detected another slight eye roll. 'Okay, pretty stupid. I'm working as much as I can. If I can manage to pull together a few hundred, maybe they'll give me a bit more time. I've nowhere else to go. So what do you think? Think they'll go for it?' She leaned over Helen's face, hoping for some sign of approval. There was no movement. 'Well. It's worth a try.'

Amber was putting her lipstick away and humming a tune. It sounded familiar. Beth narrowed her eyes, the shop lights suddenly seeming far too bright. Why was Amber humming *Ride of the Valkyries*? It wasn't exactly the sort of thing they'd be playing in the club. She'd never been in there but she'd put money on them not being big on Wagner. Maybe some trip-hop outfit had sampled the top line and semi-drowned it under a heavy downbeat and looped percussion. That might be possible. And who was she to say what Amber might listen to in her spare time? She shook her head, trying to dislodge the tune. Probably Amber was tone deaf and was actually humming *Lady Marmalade*, heroically out of tune.

'You got a list?' she asked, hoping the distraction would stop Amber humming.

Amber handed over her list and launched into a story about one of the other strippers and her bizarre stage act. 'I'm not kidding. She's got this whole weird junk food thing going on. It's totally manky.' Beth was fairly convinced she was making it up to get a laugh out of her, but that was okay; it was a lot more entertaining than being told to smile by a drunk monkey.

Then the door banged open. Amber stopped talking and Beth looked up. A tall man in a suit was standing in the doorway, just standing there, staring. But not at her or Amber, his eyes were wide open and seemed to be focused on something far off and surprising, something that wasn't inside the shop. He took a couple of stiff-legged steps towards the counter, dragging his shoes across the floor. And he was still staring, but that wasn't all he was doing. He was pumping blood from the top of his head like a small volcano erupting. Beth hadn't noticed straight off because the blood was going backwards, not down his face, like it did now, a sudden veil of red over one eye and down his cheek, dripping off the edge of his jaw.

Then he stopped, blinked once and opened his mouth as if to say something, but before he could, he tipped forwards, landing like a toppled dictator with his arms out either side. Silence hung in the space where he'd been standing. Amber was very still, staring down at the man on the floor, her eyes wide with shock, mouth hanging open. Beth peered over the counter. There was a pool of blood forming around the man's head in a wet halo. His eyes were still open but they weren't moving and the blood pumping from his head wasn't pumping any more, just kind of falling out, like from a tipped-up bottle. She could see the hole in his head. Looked like a bit of skull was missing from the crown, white flecks of bone stuck in his hair and something greyish underneath that could only be . . .

'Oh,' said Amber. 'Oh fuck.' She crouched down to look at him. 'John?' she said, but there was no answer.

Beth sniffed. One of Craig's girlfriends had been a nurse and had told her once that she could smell head wounds. Beth never believed her. The girl had talked a lot about the things nurses knew and other people would rather not. She said she would know, on a crowded bus, if someone had a head wound, even if everyone was wearing hats, she could smell it, a kind of sweet, decaying smell, like meat only just gone over. Now Beth believed her. Without warning, her stomach clenched into a fist and punched upwards. She couldn't help it, straight into the deep fat fryers. The fat spat and frothed back, throwing up what looked like deep-fried diced carrots to float on the surface.

Amber had straightened up and was pacing back and forth, casting frequent glances back to the body on the floor, at this guy she apparently knew. 'Oh shit. I don't believe this,' she said.

'I know,' said Beth, breathing through her mouth. She felt spaced out and wired all at once. Although only seconds had passed, it felt like the guy had been on the floor for hours and she could hardly remember a time when the three of them hadn't been this way together in the shop. She should do something to snap them all out of it, get them back into real time. She picked the shop phone off the wall.

'What are you doing?' Amber's voice snapped like a whip.

'Dialling 999. Y'know?' Beth pointed to the body on the floor but Amber just frowned at her. Beth wiped her mouth on her sleeve and looked out of the window. People were passing by outside, oblivious. Probably best they stayed that way. She put the shop phone back on the hook, came round from behind the counter and quickly lowered the blinds over the door and the windows, sealing them from outside view.

The dead guy, and she was really very sure he was dead now, hadn't moved at all. She crouched down and looked into his eyes. A slight air of puzzlement lingered around them but the lights had definitely gone out, leaked away through the hole in his head, along with what looked like about a hundred pints of blood. She went back behind the counter and picked the phone up again.

'Wait!' Amber said, coming towards her. 'Hang on. I need to think. Fuck. Just wait a minute.' She was pacing faster now, chewing her lip and holding one hand to her forehead.

'Wait for what? Why?'

Now Amber was talking to herself, muttering, and Beth couldn't make out what she was saying until she turned back towards her. 'I can do this,' she said, psyching herself up for something, still talking more to herself than to Beth.

'Do what?'

Amber seemed to come to some kind of conclusion. 'Right. Here's the thing. I've got to go. I wasn't here, okay?' She backed away towards the door.

'What?' Beth was more puzzled than angry. Surely Amber wasn't going to do a runner and leave her here with this bloke, this body, this dead body belonging to someone, some John she obviously knew?

Amber had started pulling on the door handle. Beth opened her mouth to protest but Amber lifted a flat palm to her and shook her head. 'I'll explain everything later. I promise. Just trust me for now.'

Trust? Beth dropped her gaze. Trust was a promise. She didn't do trust anymore. Whatever this was about, it was none of her business. This was all happening to other people. It was pure chance they were all there at the same time. It made no difference to the guy on the floor. He'd still be dead. 'Well, I suppose,' she said with a shrug. There was no reason to refuse. 'Whatever.'

Amber mouthed, 'Thank you' and made her exit, fast. Beth watched her running back across the road to Fantasy Island, dodging in and out of the traffic. She took the keys from under the counter and locked the door, being careful not to step in anything. There was a looping trail of blood across the tiles in the shape of a question mark with the dot being where the guy's head hit the floor, only the dot was too big now to be properly in proportion. Perhaps she shouldn't have let Amber leave. She'd known the guy after all, had called him by name. She must have her reasons.

Beth waited for five minutes before she called the police. It was a long five minutes. The sounds of the street continued as usual but inside the only sound was her own breathing.

'What's the story, John?' she whispered. But John wasn't giving anything away.

She thought police call handlers would have heard it all, but the woman Beth spoke to sounded genuinely surprised. 'Dead? You sure?'

'Well,' Beth told her, 'he's not breathing, part of his head is missing and there's a lot of blood. So, yeah, I'm sure.'

The call handler asked for the address and told Beth to stay put, that there'd be a car along straight away. She had hardly put the phone down when a car pulled up outside. She tiptoed round the blood, unlocked the door and let them in. Two uniformed police, so young and freshly laundered they looked like kids playing dress up. They stood and gaped at the body, then at Beth, before apparently remembering they were supposed to be in control of the situation. One of them radioed in and confirmed that, yes, it was a body and it certainly did appear to be dead. The other got his notebook out of his pocket with difficulty because his hands were shaking.

She did her best to help him along and gave him the facts, as much as she knew, without mentioning Amber. He nodded and scribbled. An ambulance arrived and the paramedics gave the official verdict. More police arrived and said they'd have to wait for the police doctor and scene of crime team. The shop was filling up with bodies quicker than the late rush for chips after pub closing time. One of the child policemen apologetically offered Beth a lift down to the station. It didn't seem she had any option. She handed the spare keys to the oldest looking one and asked if they could lock up when they were done. 'You get all sorts round here,' she said.

SIX

one more time and you're out on your arse

Amber mounted the stairs two at a time, flying along the narrow passage into the club before she could reconsider. The plan forming in her mind was insane, she knew that. But it was possible. She wished she had more time to think it through but that wasn't the way things worked. When a door opened on something really big, something that could change everything, you had to take your chance. These moments turned on seconds. She had to make her choice and follow it through before the door slammed in her face.

The dressing room was stuffy, the air sticky with hairspray and perfume but unoccupied. Everyone would be out front, dancing or working the tables. Amber tried to concentrate. She had to think fast.

The door from the toilet opened and Fran emerged, fag hanging from her mouth as she adjusted the fit of her gold sequined g-string, running her thumbs under the elastic and up over her hips to get the sides level. She glanced up at Amber. 'Y'know, sometimes I think my bones weren't put together right in the first place. Can't never get this fucking thing straight. Not without near on cutting myself in half,' she said, and took the fag from her mouth, blinking away a stray curl of smoke. She narrowed her eyes and looked at Amber more closely as if reassessing. 'What's up with you?' Her gaze flicked around the dressing room, looking for something and not finding it. 'And where's the food, you daft cow?'

'Oh. I . . . There wasn't any. They were closing up.'

'Uh huh?' Fran looked at her sceptically. 'Hungry, were you?'

'What?' Amber struggled to focus on what Fran was saying. She wished she'd leave her alone. She had more important things to think about.

Fran sighed and shook her head. 'Look, honey, it's none of my business but just try not to make a mess in the bog. And for Christ's sake use the air freshener when you're done.' She stubbed her cigarette out in the overflowing ashtray and shot three blasts of breath spray into her mouth. 'Right. Fish to fry.' She blew a kiss to her own reflection and waved absently at Amber then swept out of the room on her gold stilettos, pulling the door closed behind her.

Amber gave a snort of amusement. So Fran had her pegged as the binge-and-purge type. Not bloody likely. Fran was so wide of the mark it was funny. Anyway, whatever she thought, it was of no importance to the matter in hand.

She paced the empty room, nervous energy fizzing up and down her limbs like electricity. She kept seeing John, lying there on the chip shop floor. From her coat pocket she brought out the flat piece of stone she had lifted from near his head while Beth had been busy closing the blinds. It was the same material as the slates from the roof of the club; dark grey with an oily sheen. She remembered she'd seen another piece sailing down through the sky, about an hour ago, narrowly missing that idiot in the monkey suit. It wasn't too much of a stretch to picture another bit working its way loose and falling, only this time finding a target. John must have walked across the road with this thing stuck in his head. Hadn't known what hit him probably and just kept going. Did she feel guilty? She stopped pacing while she searched for that emotion. No. Definitely not. Why should she? His death was in no way her responsibility. If anything it was his own. He owned the club so the state of the roof was down to him. And if it was made worse by them banging against the wall earlier on, then that was down to him as well. She hadn't disliked John but neither was she particularly attached to him, and the world wouldn't be any the worse off for his absence. She turned the piece of slate over in her hands. Bad luck getting whacked by your own building though.

She went over what she knew. John had, in his own words, *a major bit of business* lined up, most likely with that guy Murdoch and his ferrety sidekick who were still sitting in the bar. But was John buying or selling? Either way, there might well be a large amount of coke and a large amount of money still on the premises. They could be making the delivery with John buying it and selling it on at a profit but if she had to choose, and she did have to, she'd go for John selling and Murdoch buying. As far as she knew, John never dealt directly with punters. It wasn't his style. He preferred to distance himself from the shop floor and saw himself as management, purely on the wholesale side of the business. By dealing with distributors, never the end users, he liked to think he kept his hands clean.

If John was describing this as *major* then it had to involve at least five figures, maybe six. That amount of money could bring her fund up to jackpot levels. It would be more than she'd make in a lifetime of extras and tips. She'd be stupid not to take advantage. It wouldn't be like she was robbing anyone who would even notice. The rightful owner was currently lying in a pool of blood on the other side of the street. And if she handed over the gear to Murdoch for the agreed price then nobody lost. The only problem was finding it, but how hard could that be?

As long as Beth kept her mouth shut, the police might delay making a visit to the club long enough for her to close the deal. She didn't really know the girl but keeping her mouth shut did seem to be one of her specialities: like getting blood from a stone sometimes to squeeze a conversation out of her. But even if she did keep quiet, it was only a matter of time before news of John's death filtered its way back across the street.

She looked up and her own reflection looked back at her

from the mirror. It looked her right in the eye and told her to get a fucking grip and stop wasting time. Chances like this didn't just fall out of the sky every day. This was a fucking gift.

The clock was ticking. Last chance to back out. What was she scared of? She flipped the piece of slate in the air, caught it between her flat palms and opened them up again like a book. The side facing upwards was streaked with drying blood. 'Heads say do it,' she said to her reflection.

She'd need to change first. Underneath her coat she still wore a flimsy mini-dress; not the image she wanted to project now. She found her own street clothes where she'd left them in a heap over the back of a chair: a pair of jeans, boots and a hooded top. Not exactly business-like either. The jeans and boots would do but the top was old and worn and made her look like a student. She cast around the dressing room for something more suitable and found a white shirt and black blazer on a rail at the back of the room where they kept costumes. It was part of a Britney Spears get-up, complete with school tie, short hockey skirt and straw boater. School girl fantasy. Not one of hers. Still, the shirt was plain and reasonably clean. Buttoned up under the jacket, with her hair twisted into a roll and pinned on the back of her head, she looked half way plausible.

She dusted her face with powder and checked her lipstick, testing a smile in the mirror. She picked up the piece of slate from the top of the dressing table, wrapped it in a tissue and put it back in her pocket.

Show time.

She entered the public area of the bar. The two men were at the same table up the back of the club in the semi-darkness, sipping their drinks and watching the girls. On closer inspection she noticed that only the young man was completely absorbed by the display of female flesh. Murdoch was watching everyone with equal interest while affecting an air of nonchalance.

Success or failure all hinged on this first act: whether she could convince Murdoch she was for real. The danger was he'd see through her straight away. She would have to play it very carefully. It was all about owning the role. If she believed she was that person then he would believe it too. It wasn't like she didn't have any acting experience to draw upon. She strode across the room and pulled a chair up to their table.

'Well, hello,' said Murdoch with a lazy smile that went nowhere near his eyes and put her in mind of an alligator. 'I must say, the hospitality here is really quite charming.' He was immaculately groomed: tanned skin, silver hair lacquered back from a high forehead, a whiff of sandalwood cologne, but the hard lines of his face and the flat calculation in his eyes put a stop to any notion of attractiveness. Her mouth went suddenly dry. Too late now. She was committed.

The younger man was watching her greedily. His mouth hung open, showing more fillings than teeth. He licked his lips. He wore a short-sleeved polo shirt and his skin, tight over ugly knots of muscle, was pallid and clammy-looking. A prison tan, she thought. He sidled up close to her and placed a bony hand on her leg. There was a collection of badly executed tattoos on the back of his hand and down the finger joints, attempts at words misspelled or abandoned half way through, altered later in angry attempts at obliteration. He moved the hand upwards, squeezing her leg. She made an effort to smile. His touch was disgusting but she'd tolerated worse for less reward. But this time her body wasn't part of the deal. His grin faltered as she lifted his hand firmly from her leg and put it back in his own lap.

'Please excuse Ryan,' said Murdoch, shooting the young man a mock disappointed look, 'I'm afraid he doesn't get out much.'

Amber gave a small nod of acknowledgement and got straight to business. 'John asked me to speak with you.' She addressed Murdoch directly, ignoring Ryan who had retreated to glower at her from behind his beer. 'He's been unexpectedly called away and has asked me, as his business partner, to attend to matters in his absence.'

Murdoch raised his eyebrows and sat back in his seat. 'Is that so?'

'I hope that won't be a problem.' Amber kept her voice low, level and assertive. This was the turning point. Either he believed her or . . . or from the look of him, he could quite calmly reach across the table and snap her neck like a cocktail stick. It could only have been seconds but it felt much longer as he mulled over what she'd said, scrutinising her without blinking, considerations and consequences whirring like machinery behind his eyes.

Eventually he shrugged and spread his hands in a gesture of acceptance that didn't necessarily encompass belief. 'You have the goods?' he asked.

This was all he cared about, Amber realised with relief. He didn't give a flying monkey's about John, or who she was, as long as he got what he came for. His absolute focus might have been admirable, if it hadn't been so chilling.

'Of course,' she replied, all assurance. 'And you have the money?'

Murdoch stiffened and shot her a look. 'Naturally, we are prepared to offer compensation.' He allowed his gaze to rest for a second on a briefcase next to him on the seat. It was black leather with a rigid body and protective metal edging on the corners.

'Excellent,' she said and paused. She dragged her eyes away from the briefcase but they were drawn back again as if magnetised. She felt light-headed. Her freedom was so close, within touching distance. With her goal in sight she couldn't resist taking a chance. 'Shall I just take that now?' she said, despite knowing it was unlikely Murdoch would hand over any money when he hadn't seen anything in return. Especially given he was now doing business with a stranger.

'When we get the merchandise. As usual,' he said with a

measured undertone that warned her she was close to a line it would be unwise to cross.

'Of course.' She felt her face flush and silently cursed herself. She'd nearly blown the whole thing by behaving like a total amateur. Using the word *money* had been bad enough but asking if she could take it before their business was done was unbelievably stupid. No time to beat herself up about all that now. All she could do was bluff her way on and hope he chose to let it slide. 'Why don't you two relax and enjoy the show while I check your consignment is all in order?' she said, standing up.

Murdoch gave her a curt nod.

She'd got away with it, but only just. There was no doubt he was suspicious but he had his priorities. As long as she delivered the goods, he would play along.

The door to John's office was unlocked. She let herself in and started searching. She pulled out desk drawers, rifled through the filing cabinet and pulled the cushions from the large leather couch that stood against one wall. She squeezed each one, checking for tell-tale lumps. Nothing. She stood in the middle of the room and turned around slowly. Where would he have put it? It had to be somewhere secure. There were no pictures on the walls and no other sign of a safe anywhere. So, perhaps not in this room at all.

She went back out into the corridor and was almost knocked down by Fran storming back towards the dressing room. Her hair was messed up and her lipstick was rubbed around her mouth, making her lips look swollen. 'Fucking animals,' she spat. Her voice cracked but Amber knew there was no way she would allow herself the luxury of tears. 'Private dance, *plus* extras, and they tip me a tenner. A tenner! Fucking cheap bastards. Nearly decked one of them.'

Amber reached up and brushed Fran's hair out of her eyes. 'Hey, come on. Calm down. Do that one more time and you're out on your arse. John warned you.' Amber felt a small tug of dislocation. Despite having witnessed it, John's death was too recent to feel real. The gaps he'd left behind were hidden potholes she could still stumble into. Thankfully, Fran was too angry to notice any difference. Amber followed her to the dressing room. They might be able to help each other out here, she realised. She watched Fran pull a crumpled tenner from the front of her sparkly knickers and put it away in her purse. 'Would you do me a favour?'

'I'm pretty short on good will right now. What do you want?' Fran found her lipstick and started to repair the damage.

'Couple of punters out there. Muscly guy and an older one with grey hair?'

'Yeah, what about them?'

Amber retrieved the jacket she'd be wearing earlier, pulled out the fifty quid John had given her and held it out to Fran. 'Keep them busy for as long as you can and I'll give you the rest of my tips at the end of the night as well.'

Fran whipped the money out of Amber's hand before she could blink and tucked the notes away. 'Going to tell me why?'

Amber shook her head.

'No. I didn't think so. Well, lucky for you I need the money more than I need an explanation.'

'Just distract them for a while.'

'Don't worry, sweetheart.' Fran puckered her freshly-painted lips then grinned. 'I'll make them forget what day it is.'

'Thanks. I owe you one.'

They left the dressing room together. Fran went back into the club. Amber peeked through the gap in the curtain and saw her doing her best catwalk sway towards the back of the room. Ryan was already grinning like an idiot. Murdoch wouldn't be so easily distracted but hopefully he'd allow Ryan a little leeway.

Amber began trying the handles of the other doors along the corridor. She found a storeroom and a cleaning cupboard and searched them, tearing open boxes of paper towels and jars of stuffed olives, rummaging behind crates of booze. Nothing. There was one more door to try. She held her breath and twisted the handle. It was locked. Interesting. She turned the handle again and leant her weight against the door. A good lock too. This had to be it.

She was standing in the corridor wondering how she was going to get into the room when she heard footsteps approaching.

SEVEN

rose wood 3-colour sunburst

Beth shivered and rubbed her hands together. If anything the air inside the station was colder than the October night outside. She wondered if the low temperature was a deliberate tactic to keep suspects from getting too comfortable, or to stop the police nodding off while filling in paperwork. The Desk Sergeant was wearing a scarf and had his hands wrapped around a steaming mug. He looked about to say something as they approached the desk but then sneezed, splashing tea over his hands. He swore under his breath and blew his nose into a cloth hanky.

'Plumber still not been?' asked the young PC who had brought Beth to the station. The sergeant was now dabbing at the splashes of tea on his desk with a green paper towel that lacked any absorbent qualities.

The older man looked thunderous. 'He was in all right. Chancing cowboy bastard. I've called him out again and when he gets here I'm putting the incompetent bawbag under arrest until he fixes the heating properly.' His face cleared and he looked at Beth appraisingly. 'You're here to give a statement?'

Beth shrugged and nodded.

'All right. Just have a seat over there,' he gestured to a huddle of plastic stackable seats over by the far wall. 'Someone will come and get you in a minute.'

She walked across the worn green lino and sat on one of the hard chairs. A sobbing teenage girl sat at the other end with a boy of about the same age trying to calm her down. The girl's knees were scraped and a dribble of blood was crawling down her shin, dark against her pale skin. Her shoulders shook and a trail of snot descended from her nose. 'Christ. Got a tissue?' the boy asked Beth.

Beth shook her head.

'Thanks a bunch, cow,' he said.

Beth sighed. This night wasn't getting any better.

The station was an old building with high ceilings, the walls painted in olive drab and magnolia. Half a dozen notice boards hung lopsided on the wall with posters flapping from them: Crime Stoppers and Neighbourhood Watch, How to Theft-proof your Bicycle. Doors opened and closed, uniformed policemen and plain-clothes came and went, carrying papers and brown plastic cups. A draft swirled in from the corridors, the cold current of it tugging at her ankles.

After what seemed like hours, a middle-aged man with his top shirt button undone and tie pulled sideways approached her.

'DS Page,' he said, consulting a piece of paper he was holding and extending a hand. 'And you are Elizabeth Dunn?'

Beth nodded, rose and shook his hand, assessing his grip. It was a habit her grandad had drummed into her as a child. DS Page returned a brief shake, his damp hand skidding out of hers like a bar of soap. She followed him through a series of doors and into an interview room, wiping her hand as unobtrusively as possible on the leg of her jeans.

They sat at an oval table under fluorescent lighting. A woman around Beth's age in a dark blue skirt and jacket that looked new and uncomfortable sat down beside Page and placed a manila document folder on the table. Small bag of chips and a pickled egg, thought Beth. She looked different in the suit, her black hair pulled back in a tight ponytail, but was distinctive enough to remember. She had intense, clever eyes and perfect skin. She came into the shop about once a month, always ordered the same thing, was pleasant and polite. She showed no sign of recognising Beth now, and began pressing buttons on a console built into the centre of the table. It emitted a series of bleeps and a green light came on.

Despite the cold, DS Page was sweating. He looked like he sweated a lot; the beige material of his shirt under the arms was faded and patterned with concentric tide marks, like growth rings in a tree trunk. His bald head was shiny under the lights but his blue eyes were cool. He was looking at her as if he couldn't decide whether she was in shock, guilty, or just a bit simple.

Beth knew he would be less suspicious if she appeared more upset about having someone drop dead in front of her but apart from the immediate physical reaction of throwing up, John's death hadn't touched her. In fact she felt quite calm. She was only a witness; not part of it. If she'd known the guy, there'd be some reason to be upset but, although he'd looked vaguely familiar, she was sure she'd never spoken to him. So, no, she wasn't upset, she just wasn't. And she didn't have enough faith in her acting abilities to pretend otherwise.

She'd never got the knack of pulling out the expected emotional response for the circumstance. It wasn't that she didn't feel anything, she'd just learned early on to keep her feelings to herself. Her gran, through rigid self-control, had hidden her grief over the loss of her daughter so that it wouldn't cloud Beth's childhood. As a result, Beth had grown up with the idea that displaying strong emotion was a dangerous impulse to be suppressed, equivalent to taking all your clothes off and doing cartwheels in public.

Emotional incontinence was overrated anyway, she thought; people bursting into tears on the telly all the time for trivial reasons, as if it proved they were good people, that they were 'genuine', when it demonstrated exactly the opposite. Beth sometimes thought she'd been left on the wrong planet. When she was a kid, she used to fantasise that the story about her dead parents was an elaborate cover. She didn't think they were going to reappear, or that she was a secret princess, as at least half the girls at school liked to imagine. She preferred to believe she wasn't actually human at all and didn't belong to the species any more than she belonged in a termite mound. She used to hope that one day her real family would come back for her, in a spaceship of course, to take her back to wherever it was she *did* belong. She'd grown out of the fantasy eventually. Almost completely.

DS Page was leaning across the table, watching her. 'This is DC Chan. She'll be witnessing your statement. If you're ready?' Beth nodded. DC Chan pressed another button on the console and spoke into it giving their names, the date and time, then sat back with pen and paper, letting DS Page take over. His voice was gentle, sympathetic even. 'Okay Elizabeth, I'd like you to tell me exactly what happened tonight, in your own words. Take your time. Give me as much detail as you can. Even if it seems trivial to you, it might be important to us.'

'From when the guy came into the shop?'

'How about before then? Did you see anyone suspicious in the street tonight, for instance?'

Beth smiled. Both police officers looked at her coldly. 'Sorry,' she said. 'It's Saturday night. Pretty much everyone you see on Junction Street late on is suspicious in some way. But, I didn't see anyone carrying an axe or anything, if that's what you mean.' Page blinked at her while Chan's pen scratched across the paper.

She pushed aside the vague feeling of guilt that came from being scrutinised. She wasn't under suspicion. She'd never killed anyone, at least not deliberately, not directly. Although she couldn't be sure, she was confident enough that Amber hadn't either so didn't have a problem erasing her from the scene in the shop. She gave the Amber-free version, several times. Everything happened exactly the same, except there was no one with her. Not at the start. Not running out at the end. She didn't see how it made any difference. Nothing was going to bring the guy back to life. But Page seemed to think she must have seen more than she was telling him and kept asking the same questions, with the words rearranged. The truth was, apart from the presence of Amber, she hadn't seen a damn thing.

'I keep telling you, I didn't see anything or anyone.'

Page's voice was less sympathetic now, his encouraging smile compressed into a straight line through which his words emerged dry and flat. 'So this guy just materialises out of thin air and drops dead in the middle of your shop?'

'Not my shop. I just work there.' She wondered if anyone had phoned Gianni. She'd given them his mobile number when they'd questioned her in the shop. The place hadn't burned down but probably a dead body met his strict criteria for having his night out disturbed. She hoped he hadn't been just about to introduce himself to the woman of his dreams when his phone rang. Then again, it could have saved him from propositioning some head-case who would've made his life a misery. Or the timing could have had no effect at all. The interruption, just by happening when it did, at that particular second, could've changed everything, or nothing. Beth realised with a start that Page was still talking.

'And, despite the fact that the entire front of your establishment is made of glass, you saw nothing?'

'That's right. I was working.'

'I never realised wrapping chips was so absorbing.'

She let the remark go. It was a cheap shot and seemed to make Page feel better about abandoning his line of questioning, at least for now.

'Of course, we'll be able to check your version of events on the CCTV footage,' he said, wiping sweat from his nose with the side of this thumb while watching her for a reaction.

She did her best not to provide one. If they did have a recording of the activity in the street then she'd just dropped herself in it. Amber wasn't the type to fade into the background – in person or on film – but something about Page's manner made her think he was bluffing. She'd heard that less than half the CCTV cameras in the city were actually working. Most of them were just for show, reducing crime simply by making people *think* they were being watched. Her best option was to stick to her story.

He picked up the document wallet Chan had brought and took out a handful of photographs. He slid one across the table to Beth. A tall man wearing a smart suit, coming out of Fantasy Island carrying a sports bag, about to get into a black BMW. He was broad-shouldered and blunt looking. He was also currently, as far as she knew, still lying in a pool of blood on the floor of the Deep Sea.

'Yeah, that's him,' she said.

Page slid another photograph over. This one showed two people: a well-preserved, middle-aged guy with grey hair, slightly Mediterranean, and deep set eyes that were cast in shadow. The other man was younger and his close-cut blonde hair revealed his lumpy skull to the unflattering daylight. Page tapped the photograph with an index finger. 'What about these two? Ever seen them before?'

Beth studied the photograph some more. She saw a lot of people coming in and out of the shop, a hundred faces a night if it was busy. Multiply that up by weeks, months, and years and that was a lot of faces. But she had a good memory for regulars. She'd walk past someone in the street and think, pie and chips and a can of Tango; see a face on a bus and think, fish supper and a pint of milk. It wasn't something she had any control over, just a useless reflex. This pair were definitely not regulars. But even so, they were memorable enough, especially if they came as a set, for her to be sure she hadn't seen them.

'No,' said Beth. 'Not recently, anyway.'

'You're sure?'

'Yeah, I'm sure. Who are they?'

Page started gathering the photographs together again. He exhaled noisily. 'Nobody you'd want to meet, darling. If you ever do see them, I'd steer well clear if I were you.'

She watched as he slotted the photographs back into the folder. If they belonged in the same folder, there must be some connection between them. And if Amber had known John, then did she know these guys too? Did they have something to do with John's death? There was something about the look of the older guy that put him in a whole different category from the usual small time crooks and nutters that hung about Junction Street. Could Amber be in danger as well?

'Can I go now?' she asked.

Annoyance and resignation struggled briefly for control over Page's features, then he shrugged. 'Unless you have something more to tell us?'

'Not a thing.'

'Fair enough then,' he said and signalled Chan to stop the recording. She spoke again, giving the time and date. Beth wondered how long he'd have Chan doing the speaking clock routine before she got to ask some questions of her own. Page opened the door of the interview room. 'Take this,' he said handing her a card with several phone numbers on it. 'Be sure to contact us if your memory throws anything up.'

That reminded her, they were going to have to drain the fryers right down and clean them before the shop could open for business again. Gianni was not going to be best pleased about that.

She saw herself out.

The night air was cool but welcome after the claustrophobic atmosphere of the station. A few low streaks of purplish cloud bruised an otherwise clear sky in which a new moon hung, blade thin and fragile. Beth decided to take the short walk back to Junction Street instead of getting a bus. There was a hint of frost in the air, but not cold enough to be uncomfortable. She wound her way through the back streets, avoiding the main routes where Saturday night would still be going full throttle. In these darker, less-populated streets were pubs with lower prices and better beer, popular with locals but not so attractive to those following the sexual imperative of the night.

On the corner of Howe Street, the windows of Bobby's Bar were glowing that particular shade of molten yellow only seen from the outside looking in. Live music thumped out into the street. *The Bad Books for one night only* was written in chalk on the small blackboard by the door. She stood and listened. They sounded pretty good although the vocals left a bit to be desired. The guy was obviously trying to channel Cobain but picking up interference from Orville the Duck on the way. The volume increased and a blast of warm, beery music puffed in her face as the doors swung open and a handful of people piled outside for a smoke. More punters arrived and began to make their way inside, nearly sweeping Beth along with them. She disentangled herself from the group before they passed the threshold. Part of her wanted to go with them. To just lose herself in music like she used to; let it wash over and through her until she was cleaned out. She turned and walked away fast, the sound of the band fading out behind her until she was walking in silence again, just the sound of her own feet keeping time.

Her route took her past The Music Box: a tiny shop crowded with cardboard boxes of old vinyl records that sold mostly guitars but also stocked an eclectic array of other second-hand instruments, from battered bongos to zithers. She found herself going past there more and more often these days without any particular reason. She decided tonight she would not stop and quickened her pace as she approached but nevertheless found herself slowing to gaze in the window. They did have the most beautiful guitars. The kind of guitars that should be played, not stuck in a shop window for folk to salivate over. She always felt a mixed pang of loss and satisfaction to see one of the good ones missing but liked to imagine they'd gone to good homes.

Her baby was still there. A Fender Strat, rose wood 3-colour sunburst, limited edition. Gorgeous. Not that she would buy it, even if she had the money. Why would she do that? She shook her head, arguing with herself, and losing. Of course she would do that. She'd do it in a heartbeat and she'd take it home and she'd lock the door and play until either she was fixed or just bones wrapped around the guitar. She coughed, then turned her face away and kept walking, resolving to stay away from the back streets in future.

When she turned back onto Junction Street, her feet automatically took her in the direction of the Deep Sea. Her mind on other things, she was almost surprised to see a police car parked in front, an officer in a luminous yellow jacket sitting on the bonnet. Although the shop's blinds were down, she could see the lights were still on and people were moving around inside. She hesitated on the traffic island. She wasn't going back in there. Probably Gianni had arrived by now and he was unlikely to be in a good mood. If she made an appearance, he'd only have her scrubbing the floor. She glanced to the other side of the street at Fantasy Island. She didn't much fancy going in there either, but she had to look for Amber so what was the alternative? She could just go home and keep her regular appointment with Mr Jack Daniels, forget the whole thing, wake up tomorrow and get on with another day as if nothing had happened. And why not? Nothing *had* happened to her. And she didn't owe anyone anything.

She turned in the direction of the flat, and started walking, feeling around in her pockets for her keys, then stopped. What if Amber really was in some kind of danger? If something happened to her, something that could have been averted by a simple warning, then she really didn't have any option but to deliver it.

She looked at the entrance to Fantasy Island again. Would she have to pay to get in? Or would they let her in if she explained she was looking for someone? They'd probably heard that one before, although not from too many women, she suspected. She'd just have to brass it out.

She straightened her shoulders, lifted her chin, re-crossed the street and was just about to go inside when a figure stepped into her path. The neon lights behind him gave a multi-coloured fringe to the fur covering his head and body. She took a step back. The ape had something in his hand, she couldn't tell what, but he was holding it out towards her.

EIGHT

like he had a natural place in the world

George knocked on the window of the twenty-four hour garage. It was past midnight so the doors were locked and customers had to shout their requests through a slot like a letter box, hoping to make themselves heard above the tinny radio. He pointed at the flower display. They were a sorry bunch: carnations and chrysanthemums with curled-in petals and bent stems. But they were better than nothing and it was only a gesture after all. He waved to the garage attendant, a white-haired bloke with thick glasses, wearing a green apron. He had been reading a newspaper but now seemed to be crouching below his counter, popping up every now and then to sneak a peek at George before dropping back down out of sight. George watched him for a while then waved and banged on the glass, gesturing more forcefully this time. What was the guy playing at?

Suddenly George felt his right arm gripped by a strong hand, pulled hard, then twisted behind his back. He was being mugged. Again. Unbelievable. Was he wearing a sign or something? He'd already had his chips nicked. It was when he felt the cuffs being snapped onto his wrists that he realised this was an entirely different kind of a hold up.

'Okay, King Kong,' said a deep voice, 'think you better come with us.'

A hand on George's shoulder spun him around. He was looking at a tall, broad-chested policeman. He had a short beard, showing some grey and the sort of bulk that people automatically defer to; the uniform and peaked cap just made it official. George's eyes were roughly level with the officer's square jaw and he could see the sides of his mouth twitching as he tried not to laugh. He went to step away but the hand held him fast. 'I haven't done anything. I was only trying to buy a bunch of flowers!'

The policeman looked him up and down. 'Dressed like that? Very likely. You were trying to hold up that garage. Don't try and monkey us around now.'

George looked up at him, unsure how to react. After a few moments the large man gave up the fight and released a loud guffaw, his shoulders shook but he had no problem holding on to George with one massive paw. Oh brilliant. Trust him to get arrested by the laughing policeman.

When he eventually stopped, George spoke, making the effort to sound reasonable and law-abiding. 'Search me,' he said. 'I don't have a weapon. My ID and money are in my pocket. I wasn't trying to rob anyone. I just wanted the flowers.'

The policeman was wiping tears from his eyes. His partner was inside questioning the teller who was flapping his arms around and pointing outside at George. The second policeman, about half the age and width of his colleague, had begun to write things down but he soon stopped, closed the notebook and pushed it back into his breast pocket. He was now standing with his arms folded, nodding occasionally and looking mostly at the floor, tapping one of his feet. He glanced out to the forecourt and gave a small shake of his head. The huge hand was lifted from George's shoulder.

'Okay, pal. Where's this wallet then?'

George wiggled his arms. They were starting to ache a little and there was no way he could retrieve his wallet. 'Inside pocket. Down there,' he said, and nodded towards his crotch area. 'It does up with Velcro all down the front. '

The policemen eyed George below the waist and frowned. George gave an apologetic shrug.

'Tell you what,' said the policeman, 'if I take the cuffs off, you're not going to do anything stupid are you?'

George shook his head.

'Fair enough.' The policeman spun him around again and released the handcuffs. George rubbed his wrists and rolled his shoulders. He'd never been handcuffed before and was surprised at how painful it was. How must that feel after a few hours? He'd make a rubbish criminal. He pulled the front of his suit open, the Velcro making a tearing sound, dug out his wallet and handed it over. The policeman flipped it open and pulled out George's driving licence.

'Can you take the mask off please?'

George thought it best not to argue so grasped the rubbery front of the mask and pulled it up to the top of his head. The mark on his forehead stung as the rough inner weave of the material dragged over it and the cold air hit his face.

The policeman looked up from the license, did a quick double-take and sniggered. 'What happened there then?'

'It's a long story.'

The second policeman emerged from the garage and joined them, shaking his head. 'Same bloke. Thinks he's being held up by paying customers and presses that bloody panic alarm at least once every month. Talk about crying wolf.' He looked at George. 'Or monkey, as the case may be.'

His partner let out another laugh. 'What d'you need flowers for at this time of night anyway?' he asked. 'Peace offering are they?'

'Yeah. Something like that.'

He replaced the licence and snapped the wallet closed. 'Okay, pal. We've all been there. Hang on.' The policeman walked into the shop and emerged with a particularly broken bunch of carnations. 'These do the job?'

'Yeah. Thanks.' George took the flowers.

'Just put your money through the hatch and get going. Hope it works out for you. Come on,' he said to his partner, 'we better get back to it. It's a jungle out there.'

The big one slapped George on the back, nearly knocking him over before they headed back to their car. George dug a fiver out of his wallet, pushed it through the slot and bent to shout his thanks through the small gap. The attendant snatched the money from the tray and backed away, looking as if he still thought George might be about to produce a sawn-off shotgun.

He turned back in the direction of Junction Street and started walking. A police car passed him and let off a brief deafening blast of its siren making him jump with fright and drop his carnations. The two policemen inside the car were cracking up. The big one gave George a thumbs up as they sped off. George picked up the flowers and dusted them down, brushed the grit off and plucked a fag end from between the leaves. Nobody was going to be impressed by these but after what he'd been through to get hold of them he was bloody well going to deliver them if it was the last thing he did. He pulled his mask back down, feeling better for the familiar warmth over his face.

He had the feeling this crappy night was trying to tell him something. Maybe it was exactly what he needed, something to push against. He adjusted the fit of the rubber over his features and smiled underneath. Things would start changing from this point forward, he decided. His run of bad luck was over and good things would start happening from now on. He set off again with renewed determination. For the first time in too long, he was absolutely sure of what he wanted to do.

When Zoe had left, it was as if she'd taken his sense of certainty with her, packed it up with most of the furniture, all of the crockery, her clothes and medical textbooks. For the two years since then, he'd been drifting along, veering from heartbreak to confusion and back again. He still didn't understand how he could have misread what was going on between them so completely. He'd thought she was just tired.

Of course she was. She was a junior doctor, it went with the job, there was no avoiding that. But there'd been more to it. He just didn't see it until it was already too late.

That final morning, she'd arrived home as dawn was creeping through the curtains. He woke up disoriented and there she was, sitting on the edge of the bed with her head in her hands. The digital display gave the time in alien green numbers as 7:05 am. He rubbed his eyes, reached for her and put a hand on her back. She let out a breath so long, so bone weary, he wondered if she'd fallen asleep before she could climb into bed but then she straightened up, ran her fingers through her hair and turned towards him. The thin antiseptic hospital smell hung around her. He squeezed the knotted muscles in her shoulders. She winced and batted his hand away. 'Sorry,' she said. 'I'm tired. It's been a long night.'

'Want to talk about it?'

She was silent for a long time, the soupy half-light in the bedroom turning sharp and sour and colder. 'No. No, I don't.' She dragged her words out with grim determination, like entrails from a body. 'What's the point? You don't know what it's like.'

'So tell me.'

He knew their working lives had taken different directions. She was ambitious and he wasn't. He'd kept up the pretence of biding time until he decided what to do, but he was perfectly content working in Davey's music shop. Wanted nothing more. He had thought they would complement each other. In any case, love shouldn't depend on having compatible careers.

They'd been a couple since secondary school. Back then she had a sureness about her and being around her had made George feel more confident, like he had a natural place in the world. Every time he made her laugh it was like winning a prize. She'd excelled at every subject she approached, easily qualifying to take medicine at uni and was now well into her training. But her easy confidence had become something harder and more driven under the weight of her studies and punishing hours. He'd lost the knack of making her laugh but still believed they had a future, if they both wanted it enough.

Sitting on the bed, Zoe was silent, staring into space, frowning at whatever she saw there.

'It's okay. You can talk to me.' He lifted his hand to touch her but pulled back, scared of annoying her.

'You can't understand unless you've been through it.' Her angry sigh smelled of vending machine coffee. 'I'd be wasting my breath.'

'You don't mean that.' He shivered and pulled the duvet around his shoulders. 'Come to bed.'

She didn't move. When she started speaking again, her voice was hard and cold. 'The stuff that happens to people, George. You don't know. It changes your perspective, even if you don't want it to.'

'What are you—'

'And all of it,' she interrupted, 'all this death and disease, all this tragedy, it's completely random. Nothing happens for a reason. There's no plan. No meaning.' Her words were like stones dropping down a bottomless well.

'You're tired. That's all.'

'No!' she rubbed a hand over her face then looked at him with pity. 'I'm not just tired. I'm tired of this. Tired of us. Of holding on to something that's nothing more than a habit. Life's too short to play make believe. I can't do it anymore.'

He was dumbstruck. He got up and went to the bathroom, looked in the mirror to check he was still the same person and hadn't woken up in someone else's life. When he went back to the bedroom she was curled on top of the covers, still fully dressed, sleeping. Or, if she wasn't asleep, she wanted him to believe she was, which was worse. He gathered his clothes from the pile beside the bed, dressed in the living room, went out and walked the streets until it was time to go to work. All day he felt numb, recoiling from the slap of her words. He thought over the past months and re-ran their

80

arguments, giving himself better lines this time. He knew it was futile but he wanted to rework his responses so that they were more persuasive and would have healed the rift between them. It didn't work. His answers were still full of silences and irrelevant waffle, with the word *but* repeating like a Laurie Anderson loop track.

When he got home she was gone. So was enough of her stuff to show she wasn't coming back. There was no note. He supposed it wasn't necessary. She'd said what she had to say. There wasn't anything to add.

At first it was agony. He felt like that Greek guy tied to a rock who keeps getting his guts torn out by some big angry thing with wings, over and over with no hope of it ever stopping. But after a while he got used to it.

Arriving back on Junction Street, he saw that the Deep Sea was cordoned off with yellow tape, a police car sitting outside. Shit. What had happened? He stood staring at the shop, possible scenarios taking shape in his mind. Maybe it had been robbed. Or a fight. Oh Christ, what if that girl had been attacked or something? He felt sick. He realised how much he'd wanted to see her. There had been plans going through his head about meeting her, hitting it off, somehow making her laugh. Now he might never get the chance. He should never have gone off with Davey. He should have gone straight back into the shop. Perhaps if he had, he could have stopped whatever had happened to her instead.

He stood on the corner wondering whether he should go over to the police car and ask them what had been going on: would they tell him, or would they try to arrest him again?

Then there she was, a tall thin figure coming round the corner with her head down and hands pushed into her pockets. She stopped and looked at the Deep Sea, then across the road at the lap-dancing bar and hesitated. It was definitely her. The girl from the chippy. He ran up to her, holding the flowers out in front.

'You're okay!' He was so relieved to see she was unharmed. She didn't seem nearly so pleased to see him. She just stared. He pushed his mask back off his face and saw her eyes flick up to the red mark on his forehead but she passed no comment. 'I went to get you these,' he said proffering the tattered bunch of flowers, 'to say thanks. For the chips and everything. And when I got back, the place was all, y'know? And . . . I was worried about you.'

She kept her hands in her pockets and ignored the flowers. 'You were worried? About me?' She sounded cautious, as if dealing with a lunatic, as if the very idea that anyone would be concerned about her was highly suspicious. He felt a surge of irritation. Why was everyone so determined not to give a toss? When, exactly, had that become a normal way to behave?

'I know,' he said sarcastically. 'Unbelievable that anyone would ever care about anyone else. But there you have it.'

'But you don't even know me.'

'True.' He took a deep breath and plunged on, the words falling over each other in the rush to get out. 'But that can be fixed. I think you're lovely, and kind, and it's just possible that I might like you. So there.' He held out the bunch of flowers again. She looked at them as if they might give her a disease if she touched them.

For a split second he thought she was about to smile but she frowned and shook her head. 'You're drunk. And hairy,' she said. 'Go away.' She turned and walked across the road to Fantasy Island and disappeared inside.

He watched her go, the flowers hanging limp by his side. Why was she going in there? She certainly wasn't a dancer. Not that she was unattractive, but not cartoon curvy like the neon figures on the club's frontage. Then again, what the hell did he know? His experience of these places was pretty limited. One time, he'd got dragged along to a club on the other side of the city; another stag night, couldn't remember whose. It had been much as he'd expected, hugely embarrassing and uncomfortable. He'd hated it, felt obscenely over-dressed next

82

to these near-naked women. He felt the crowd he was with were about to commit a horrible crime, something deeply shameful and he wouldn't stop them so was guilty by implication. It took all sorts though. There were plenty of these clubs around the city, all doing enough business to stay open.

He guiltily tried to picture her semi-naked, twirling round a pole, but even in his imagination she glared at him with a look that made his balls shrivel. He wondered briefly if she was gay but dismissed the idea. How likely was it that a gay woman would enjoy being part of an audience of sweaty men with semis?

So what was she doing? If not one of the workers, and not a client, what was she up to? Whatever it was, George couldn't help feeling curious.

NINE

light up my heart, baby

The bouncer was enormous. Couldn't be far off seven foot. His body was a high wall with a face like a brick balanced on top. He had no neck to speak of and his head was shaved in a way that made it look like it had corners. He raised his eyebrows and looked Beth up and down. He didn't have to ask the question, he just angled his head to one side.

'I'm looking for a friend,' she said, startling herself. Was she? Did she really think of Amber as a friend?

The bouncer shrugged indifferently and moved to the side.

The stairwell was narrow and smelled of damp. Beth climbed to a heavy black door which opened onto a short hall. Music and voices leaked through the gap between a pair of swing doors at the far end. Just like any other pub, she told herself. She pushed the door open and stepped through.

Inside the club, it took a minute for her eyes to adjust to the low lighting. She stayed close to the door while shapes emerged from the gloom. A downbeat bossa nova was playing as partly-clothed women floated between the groups of men. Most of the clientele wore suits, giving them a solidity in comparison to the shifting curves of the women. Beth thought of mist curling around stone ruins.

She scanned the room for Amber. Behind the bar, a girl in a leopard-print bikini top stifled a yawn as she filled an ice bucket and ground a bottle of champagne into it with a practised twist. Beth asked her where she could find Amber.

The girl glanced towards a curtained doorway at the back of the room. Walking towards it, Beth tried to look as if this was something she did every day. She was doing fine until she noticed the two familiar-looking men in one of the booths.

The young one appeared hypnotised by a woman in a sparkly g-string who was stroking the side of his face and leaning in close towards him. The older man was adjusting his watch but looked up quickly when he felt Beth's eyes on him and met her gaze. A frown drew a single straight line between his brows as he looked her up and down.

She knew she didn't fit. She was wearing too many clothes and they were too scruffy. She shivered and looked away, moving faster now, eager to escape those cold eyes. There was no doubt these two were the pair in the picture the police had shown her, the ones they warned her to stay away from. She reached for the curtain to the staff area. The sooner she found Amber and passed on the warning, the sooner she could get out of there. Her hand hovered for a second, just short of touching the red velvet. The material and the way it hung reminded her of a crematorium, of the small curtain that drew aside as the coffin trundled towards it; slow-motion bull fighting for dead people. Lifting the curtain now, going through it voluntarily felt like a bad move. What if it led straight into the furnace?

A narrow corridor with curled lino and blood coloured walls stretched before her. There were doors on either side. Someone was leaning against the one at the end, putting their shoulder to it and twisting the handle. As the figure stood back, Beth recognised her. Amber had changed clothes and was wearing her hair up in a severe looking twist. She seemed preoccupied and jumped when she saw Beth walking towards her.

'Oh. You. Hi! Everything okay?' Her voice was a few notes higher than normal and she was glancing up and down the corridor.

'You tell me,' Beth replied. It was obvious something was up.

Amber raised a finger for silence. 'Wait,' she said. She tiptoed back to the curtain into the club and pulled it aside enough to peer through. Then she let it fall and doubled back.

'So?' Beth couldn't keep the impatience out of her voice. She was beginning to think that she was owed an explanation, or at least a little recognition.

'Okay, okay. Come with me.' Amber walked past her to the other end of the corridor and despite her misgivings, Beth followed. They went through another door, up a flight of narrow stairs and emerged on the roof of the building.

The night was wide open above their heads. Beth looked up at the sky. The clouds had cleared and the stars were visible, their light muted by the glow from the city but still there. She felt a tug on her coat. Amber was pulling her over to the low wall bordering the edge of the roof on the side facing Junction Street. From here, the illuminated world below was miniaturised, more like some intricate clockwork toy than the real world. Amber, however, was pointing not at the street but at a patchy section of slates on the eaves below the wall.

'That's what killed him.'

'I don't get it.'

'It's like this,' Amber filled in the story of her earlier dealings with John and the piece of slate that had fallen and narrowly missed the guy in the monkey suit. At this part Beth interrupted.

'A monkey suit?'

'Yeah. Twat.' Amber shrugged and rolled her eyes. 'Probably some stag do or something. Anyway, he was fine, but look. There's another bit missing. I think it came loose and John wasn't so lucky.'

Beth remembered John's surprised expression and stiff walk as he'd entered the shop before keeling over. Could he have been struck on the head on the other side of the street and still made it that far? She knew shock could numb pain. But there were far more likely possibilities. Like having his head staved-in by one of those guys sitting in the bar. 'You can't be sure about that,' she said, wondering if Amber felt responsible. 'It wasn't your fault, you know,' she added. 'You were in the shop with me the whole time.'

Amber pulled a handful of tissue from her pocket. For a confused second Beth thought she was going to burst into tears but Amber looked at her sideways and said, 'Course it wasn't my fault. Don't be daft.'

Beth watched as she unravelled the tissue to reveal a dark shard of stone. It was deep blue-grey with an oily translucent gleam and one edge chipped to razor sharpness, like a prehistoric tool. Amber reached an arm through the lower railing and held it against the closest roof slates. It was a perfect match.

Beth looked down to the street below. Apart from the Deep Sea covered in yellow tape and a police car still parked outside, it looked like business as usual. People eating and laughing, cars and taxis stop-starting through the lights. She wondered why the police hadn't been over to the club yet since they obviously knew John's identity, having shown her his photograph. And probably she should tell someone about the loose slates in case anyone else got hurt, although the rest of the roof looked stable enough, for now at least. She found herself looking for the guy in the monkey costume. Not that she cared if he was still there but he was becoming strangely familiar. She spotted him sitting on a low wall outside an empty office block on the corner, his monkey face lying limp on the stone next to him. He was plucking at the bunch of flowers he'd tried to give her, dropping pink petals in a pile between his feet. She felt a faint pang of remorse but pushed it away. Even if she hadn't had other things on her mind, she probably wouldn't have accepted the flowers although, under the mask, his human face was not unpleasant. There was that weird mark on his forehead but he had friendly eyes and a soft-looking mouth. She watched as he brushed a few stray petals out of the fur on his chest then raised his head and looked across the street to the club. Was he waiting for her to come out again? She moved away from the edge of the roof in case he looked up. Good looking or not, she needed a monkey stalker like she needed a hole in the head.

She turned round and saw that she was alone on the rooftop.

'Er . . . hello?' she called. Could Amber have done a runner again, and left her standing here like an idiot, staring into space?

'Over here!' Amber's voice was coming from the rear of the building which overlooked a narrow lane cluttered with outsized wheelie bins and abandoned skips. Beth looked over the edge of the roof. Amber was standing on a fire escape that was attached to the wall below and seemed to be counting windows. Then she muttered something and used the sleeve of her jacket to rub at the glass of the nearest window before bending down to peer inside.

'What are you doing?' Beth asked.

'I don't suppose you've a torch on you?'

Beth was about to say No but then remembered the tiny light on her key fob. She dug it out of her pocket. It was red plastic in the shape of a heart with a button on one side which activated a surprisingly bright bulb. Danny had bought it on impulse when they'd stopped at a garage for petrol on the way to a gig. Before they had all climbed back into the van, Danny had pulled her back from the group, given her a mock-serious look and pressed a hand to his chest. A bright glow had burst from between his fingers and shone through his shirt. 'You light up my heart, baby,' he'd laughed and pulled the plastic key fob from his pocket and handed it to her. It was no big thing, just a joke really. She didn't even know if the battery was still working. She pointed it at Amber and pressed the button.

Amber blinked and raised a hand to shield her eyes. 'Jesus! Yeah, that'll do. Chuck it over.' She cupped her hands to catch.

Beth took her finger off the button but didn't throw the

light. 'You still haven't explained why you left me like that.' She swallowed down the hard knot that was blocking her throat. 'In the shop, I mean.'

'There isn't time right now. Can you just give me the light?' Amber opened and closed her outstretched hand in a give-me gesture.

'Does this have anything to do with those guys in the bar?'

'You know them?' asked Amber, dropping her hand to her side and giving Beth a sharp look, which answered her question.

'No,' said Beth. 'But the police do. Warned me about them in fact. I only came back here to tell you. I was worried about you.'

'But you don't even know me.'

Beth felt her face colour as she recognised, almost word for word, the exchange she'd had with the monkey guy. She'd been on the other side of that one and realised now, it was a far safer place to be. This way round she felt exposed and stupid. 'I guess that's true.' She hesitated then pushed her hands into her pockets and turned away. 'I'll see you around then.'

'Hey! Don't be like that. Come on, come down here and I'll tell you everything.'

'You're insane,' said Beth when Amber had finished talking. They were sitting together on the fire escape and Amber had just outlined her plan to step in on John's deal and get her hands on Murdoch's money.

'And?' said Amber. 'Look, I owe you for covering for me so I'm willing to cut you in. Especially if you help me find the stuff because if I don't find it soon, the whole thing falls through anyway.'

Beth held her hands up to ward off Amber's insanity as if it might be catching. There was no way she wanted to get mixed up in anything involving the pair she'd seen in the club. And the quantities of money and coke Amber had mentioned made her dizzy. She wasn't fazed by the drugs but the scale of it was a whole other ball game. This wasn't recreational, this was serious shit.

'Are you honestly telling me you don't want any more from life than shovelling chips on minimum wage?' Amber demanded sharply.

Beth thought about it but the question didn't make sense. There was no point in *wanting* things from life. From what she'd seen so far, life was a process of taking away. That much money would take care of her rent situation but that was just a detail. It wouldn't change anything else and it wasn't worth the risk. 'It'd take more than money to solve my problems,' she muttered.

'Yeah? So join the club.' Amber's voice was getting louder and she was jabbing a finger at Beth. 'But it'd be somewhere to start, don't you think? Make a few changes?'

'So what are you going to change then? And why do you need that much money?'

Amber was silent for a moment, staring into the distance. 'I've not told anyone this,' she said without looking at Beth, 'but what the hell.' Her voice was flat, resigned, and she fell back into a long silence after speaking.

'What?' Beth prompted.

When Amber turned back, her features were immobile and she looked years older. There was a weariness that Beth hadn't seen before. 'I'm pregnant.'

Beth looked at her, the word *pregnant* suddenly draped around Amber's shoulders like a coat that was all wrong for her, something heavy and woollen that smelled of stale milk. The effect was so disconcerting, she thought at first she'd misheard. But what other word sounds like pregnant? She was so surprised, she didn't think before asking, 'Do you know who's the . . .' then broke off and looked at her feet.

'It's okay. Natural enough question, but as a matter of fact, yes, I do know who the father is. He's dead.'

It took a moment for the implication to hit home. 'Not John?'

Amber nodded.

Beth swallowed. 'Wow.'

They stood in silence looking out over the rooftops. Beyond the back lane that lay beneath the fire escape, Beth saw a landscape of stone and glass with lights that snapped off in some windows and burned bright in others, a shifting patchwork of light and dark with no pattern she could make sense of.

Surely, if John was little more than a client, they wouldn't have skipped the precautions. 'Did you not—'

'Course we did. But nothing's fool proof. Couple of months back, one split. Happens sometimes. Didn't think anything would come of it.'

Beth looked at her closely, still trying to fit the word *pregnant* into her image of Amber, but it was like an outsized piece from an entirely different jigsaw. 'Decided what you're doing yet?'

'Until tonight, having a kid would have been about the stupidest thing I could do, for loads of reasons. Not fair on the kid either. But now . . . perhaps it's fate, y'know? I could use that money to get away, really far away, find a nice place, start again. Give the kid a proper chance in life. Like I never had.' She looked hard at Beth. 'Like you didn't either.'

'You don't know me,' said Beth, sounding defensive even to herself. Amber didn't know anything about her. Nobody knew anything about her, and they had no business making assumptions.

Amber shrugged. 'So tell me I'm wrong.'

Beth wondered how the conversation had suddenly turned to her. 'And if you can't get the money?' she asked, changing it back again.

Amber looked down. 'I honestly don't know,' she said.

It still wasn't any of her business, Beth told herself. Despite the fact that so far tonight she'd seen someone die, lied by omission to the police and was now on a fire escape listening to all this, it didn't mean she was actually involved. Did it? She groaned, rubbed a hand over her face and looked up to

91

the stars. Too many choices. She'd been fine, staying on the edges of life, sticking to her routines, avoiding attachments. Now this. One false step and she was dragged right back into the muck and blood of it all whether she liked it or not.

'What do you need me to do?'

'Just give me that light. That's all.'

Beth held out the key fob and Amber snatched it out of her hand, leaned in towards the window and pressed the button, cupping her other hand around the light. Beth rubbed the dirty glass with the cuff of her jacket and peered into the gloom. Powerful though it was for its size, the little light didn't penetrate far but as she squinted, she thought she could make out shapes. Pale outlines emerged from the darkness, like bones rising to the surface of deep water. They looked almost human in form. She took her hands down and stepped back, breathing hard. She told herself not to be stupid. There was nothing to be scared of in there. Nothing moving. They were probably mannequins or something. She looked again. To the left, a jagged line resembling the edge of a huge wing curved back into the darkness.

'Can't see a fucking thing,' muttered Amber, pulling back and attempting again to shove the window up, making the frame shake as the lower pane bumped against something.

Beth could see the window was snibbed from the inside. It looked like the original fitting so not exactly Fort Knox. 'You want in there?' she asked.

'Well, duh,' said Amber, throwing her hands up.

'Why didn't you say?' Beth pulled a plastic bank card from her inside pocket, slipped it between the split frames of the window, jiggled the snib across and slid the window up.

'Where did you learn that?' asked Amber, looking at Beth with something like admiration.

Beth shrugged. 'Misspent youth.'

She looked down at the lane below. No one was watching as she followed Amber in through the open window. The first thing she heard as she got to her feet was the brittle crunch of breaking glass and a muttered 'Shit' from Amber, then the room was full of light. They were not alone.

Stacked around the walls of the small box room were four door-sized black panels with angel silhouettes in moulded glass tubes mounted on them. These were not church angels. There were no flowing robes and no harps to be seen. These angels had breasts and hips jutting in provocative poses below their wings. Two had their arms raised, frozen in mid-gyration. One looked over her shoulder, hands on hips. Another bent over, offering up her rear. All around them, wings fashioned from the same bent glass tubing flared and arched.

'Looks like your boss was planning to give the club a face lift,' said Beth.

'I had no idea,' said Amber in a quiet voice as she gazed at the winged figures.

The sound of crunching glass, Beth now realised, had come from the shattered foot of one of the angels. Amber must have stumbled against it in the dark when she was looking for the light switch. Fragments of glass lay in a circle below the jagged end of the angel's ankle. Something was protruding from the hollow tube of the leg. It looked like a piece of white plastic. She walked over, crouched down and tugged at it. The plastic was transparent but filled with some kind of white powder. A neat package the length and width of her index finger slid out into her hand, followed by another, linked to the first.

Amber was squatting down next to her now. 'Bingo,' she said and grinned.

Beth continued to pull more from the broken figure, one package after another. Crouched there together, intent on the angel's feet, Beth imagined they looked as though they were performing surgery. The glass tube itself was opaque so they couldn't make out the contents but eventually the string ended. Half a dozen packages of white powder, all joined together like a string of butcher's sausages. She handed them to Amber.

Amber folded them into a solid bundle which she weighed thoughtfully in one hand. 'There must be more,' she said, casting an assessing glance at the other angels. 'They could all be carrying.'

They both jumped as the sound of male voices broke the silence, loud and close as unexpected thunder. It was followed by an insistent knock on the door. They froze and watched the handle of the door turn. Of course, Beth remembered with relief, it was still locked since they'd come in through the window. The voices moved away and they could hear knocking on other doors.

'Shit,' said Amber. 'That'll be Murdoch and his pet weasel looking for me. I've been away far too long. They'll be getting twitchy. Tell you what, you keep them busy while I deal with this lot.' She moved to unlock the door.

'What do you mean, *keep them busy*? What am I supposed to do?' Beth protested.

'Just improvise. Don't worry. You'll think of something. I'll only be five minutes.'

Before Beth could reply, Amber had shoved her out into the corridor, closed the door and was locking it behind her.

She was about to demand to be let back in when she noticed the curtain at the end of the corridor was still swinging. They must only that moment have gone back through to the other side. Perhaps she could still get out of this. Too late. The curtain pulled back again and two men stepped through. As they walked towards her, she could see the older man – Murdoch it must be – matching her face to the mental picture he'd taken of her earlier when she'd passed his table. Once he'd seen you, a little piece of you would always belong to him. His looking was a camera that stole a bit of your soul.

'I wonder if you could help me,' he said. His voice was soft and melodic but she could hear a razor sharp edge. 'I'm looking for someone. Female. Blonde. Very attractive. Wearing a white shirt and black jacket? Perhaps you've seen her?'

Beth's instincts were telling her to run, to put as much

distance between herself and this man as was humanly possible but behind him the younger, dangerous-looking one was blocking the only escape route. For now at least, the only thing to do was to play along.

'You must be Mr Murdoch,' Beth said, keeping her tone light. 'If you'll just wait in here.' She swung open one of the doors on the opposite side of the corridor and glanced in, praying it wasn't a broom cupboard or a toilet. Mercifully it was a well-furnished office with a large desk and a long leather couch. She held the door wide and gestured for the men to enter. 'My . . . associate will be with us presently.'

TEN

because it gets unravelled

Amber pushed the door of the small room closed and locked it. Leaving Beth to handle Murdoch and his sidekick was a risky decision but what other option was there? Fran must have run out of ideas. This was the only way to buy more time. She hadn't expected the girl to show up at the club at all but she'd proved herself useful so far, so maybe she would again. All she needed was five minutes.

She looked around at the group of angels. They seemed to be waiting for her. She wondered if John had really been meaning to use them as new signs for the club, replacing the tropical island theme, or if their only function had been as disposable containers, like those piggy banks you had to smash to get the money out. If they *were* for the club, were the wings some kind of twisted compliment to her? She remembered he'd had a bit of a thing about her wings, always running his hands up her back and out over her shoulders, following the lines. Whatever he'd intended, she'd never know and what did it matter now anyway? She studied the smooth glass limbs, trying to figure out how best to get at what they might contain.

They were wearing high heels and nothing else, or close enough to nothing to avoid any interference with the outlines of their bodies. The details were mostly suggestion. Anyone seeing the angels as intended, from a distance at night, would unconsciously supply the rest of the story from the curve beneath a breast, the swing of a hip. She supposed there was a knack to that, choosing which lines to include and which to leave out. The wings too were basic but implied speed and strength, reaching above their heads, the tips swooping down to knee level. These girls were no Cupids or Tinkerbells. Further down, the spikes of their high heels continued to the base of the mounting board, where they were blacked-off with some kind of matt paint and finished in metal caps with bits of wire sticking out. She stooped to the feet of the closest figure and twisted one of the metal caps but it didn't budge. She tried the other with the same result. She pulled. Nothing. She knew the suggestion of a smirk on the angel's face was just her imagination, but it got to her all the same. She straightened up and put her mouth close to the empty face. 'Don't make me hurt you,' she whispered.

She didn't want to have to break them all. The noise would attract attention. Glancing around at the silent figures, the feeling that they were watching her grew stronger. The sooner she got this done and got out of here the better. She looked around for something heavy. There were a few boxes and bits of discarded packaging scattered about. She rummaged through them and uncovered a small black sports bag with a zip. It was empty. The very thing, she thought, and stuffed the plastic packages from the first angel into the main compartment. There was nothing she could use as a tool though. Looked like she'd have to improvise.

She took off her jacket, wrapped it round the glass foot of the next angel, steadied the black mounting panel with one hand and stamped down hard. The glass broke with a muffled crunch. She removed the jacket and a small bag like the others poked out from the broken end of the leg. She pulled on it and was rewarded with another string of narcotic sausages. She repeated the procedure on the angel's other leg with the same outcome. She worked her way around the rest and had moved on to the fourth and final angel when a wave of dizziness made her topple sideways and land on her backside. She sat there, breathing hard and blinking to clear her vision.

A sudden pain swept around her rib cage and bony fingers seemed to circle her heart. She curled forwards, her arms wrapped around her middle, squeezed her eyes closed and swallowed bile. Her scalp was swarming with cold pinpricks and a thick fuzz like static on an old television set was closing in from the edges of her vision. She tried to fight it but it was no use. Her consciousness was dissolving and she was falling back into a dead faint.

The garden smells of summer, warm earth and a thunder storm not far away. She walks up a crazy paving path with moss growing over the cement joins. Some of the misshapen stones move under her feet. At the end of the path is her father's shed where he keeps his birds. Canaries and finches mostly, cages stacked on top of one another, filling the space with darting movement and high trilling song. The door is open. Through it, she can see her father standing beside a metal dustbin training a garden hose into it. The water makes a ringing echo as the dustbin fills up. He looks up but doesn't see her even though she is standing right in front of him on the path. His face is rigid and blank, his movements robotic as he walks out of the shed and turns off the outside tap, disconnects the hose and coils it up, wrapping it round and round between hand and elbow. There's a metallic tang to the air and everything is hard-edged and too near as the thunder draws closer. She wants to look away but can't. The volume of bird song rises as he lifts a cage down and holds it in front of his face. His eyes click back and forth, watching the yellow bird hop from perch to perch, before he sinks the cage under water and holds it there. Her breath stops in her throat. She tries to move her legs, to raise her arms but the air is too thick. She tries to shout but the sound emerges from her mouth sealed in bubbles that drift upwards towards the surface of the sky. The cage comes up again, silent, dripping, something matted at the bottom. He puts the cage to the other side of the shed then lifts another. The birdsong is louder now, and the movement inside the cages quickening. A single lemon yellow feather twirls out between the bars, escaping only to land on the wooden floor. One cage after another. He is methodical and resolute. Finally all the cages are on the other side. And all the time he weeps without making a sound, only blinking occasionally, his face striped with tears that flow thick and slow as oil. The first fat drops of rain burst from the steel coloured clouds and make black holes in the crazy paving. She stares as one of them expands, the circle blooming into a well of darkness towards which she is irresistibly drawn.

Amber opened her eyes, looked up at the empty faces and outspread wings surrounding her and closed them again. It took an effort of will to slot herself back into reality after one of her weird fainting spells. These episodes were coming more often now. That was the second in a week. She hated them. Like dreams but worse. More real. It was as if some electrical storm in her brain was rerunning memories, like old movies with the soundtrack out of sync, or the film a little over-exposed. The settings changed from the house and garden to the school gym hall to the hospital, of course, with its endless white rooms and the smell of failing bodies. These early memories were the most vivid. Her father only appeared in the first twelve years. After that there was just her mum. There weren't many scenes with happy endings but that was a fair reflection of the source material.

She hauled herself up from the floor and back to the present, trying not to notice how similar the sound of broken glass sliding under her boot was to wings scraping desperately against metal bars.

There was nothing for it but to pick herself up and carry on. She looked at her watch. She'd only been out for a minute at most. This was the same as the other times she'd passed out. Time seemed to shrink inside her head so what seemed like hours could play out in seconds. She rubbed her thumb over the thin skin on the inside of her wrist, just below the watch strap, turning the flesh white and emphasising the three words etched there in arterial blue. She was glad she'd let Mac talk her into it in the end.

Over the weeks she'd spent in Phoenix Tattoo with Mac, they'd developed a way of being together that suited them both. They could pass hours in silence quite comfortably but when they felt like it, the chat was relaxed, as if they'd known each other for ages.

One Tuesday afternoon, when her wings were nearly complete, Mac said, 'I've been thinking about a motto for you.'

She didn't respond at first. What would she want a motto for? The wings themselves were enough of a statement. She looked at the copies of tattoos pairing images with lettering ranged around the walls of the shop. There was a whole section of hearts and flowers wreathed in banners with *Mum* snaking over them. Not a chance; she'd sooner have one of the *Death or Glory* flags that adorned a collection of grinning skulls on the opposite wall. There were some in different languages. She didn't know Latin or Chinese and wondered why anyone would want to have words they couldn't read inked on their bodies. Nevertheless, she was curious as to what Mac had come up with.

He seemed to sense her hesitation. 'Nothing over the top. Just small cursive script. Three words, maybe in a column here.' He placed a hand between her shoulder blades, just above where the wings met in the middle. 'No one would be able to read it unless you let them.'

'Spit it out.'

Mac cleared his throat and spoke slowly and deliberately. 'Alis Grave Nil,' he said. 'It's Latin.'

'What's that mean? Is it proper Latin?'

'Nothing is heavy to those who have wings.'

'For all I know it could say *Nothing without gravy*. I heard about this guy once, got some Chinese characters tattooed on his arm, thought it meant strength, courage and truth. Turned out it actually said fat, ugly and stupid. And he only found out because all the staff in this Chinese restaurant he was in were pissing themselves laughing at him. He'd been walking around with that on him for years.'

Mac snorted with amusement. 'Deeply unprofessional of course, but it happens. The guy must've been a major pain in the arse.'

'Not to mention fat, ugly and stupid.'

'None of which apply to you, so you've nothing to worry about. Anyway, I thought you trusted me?'

'I do. But I wasn't really thinking in words.' All the same. She turned the phrase around in her mind.

'Up to yourself,' said Mac. 'I was just wondering what these wings meant to you and that's what I came up with. I may be well off the mark. Folk have tattoos for all kinds of reasons. Some add a motto as a reminder of what inspired it. Y'know, one of those moments when you reckon you've got all your shit figured out. You can't hold it in your mind every day because it gets unravelled so they make a permanent note.'

'But why Latin?'

'It's economical. Packs a lot of meaning into a few words.'

They lapsed back into silence broken only by the hypnotic buzz and drone of the needle on her back. She was going to miss that sound and sensation when it was done. Maybe the motto wasn't such a bad idea. The English translation did fit with her thinking; about the power of flight, about leaving behind what had weighed her down for so long, about finally being free.

'Could it go somewhere else. Somewhere I can see it?'

'Course. Anywhere you like.'

'What about here?' She held out her left arm, wrist turned up, a network of blue veins visible through the skin.

'You have a knack for picking the most painful areas to work on but sure. No reason why not.'

101

'I'll think about it.' She was silent for a while then added quietly, 'And thanks.'

Mac had given her shoulder a gentle squeeze in acknowledgement and carried on working.

Her head was clearing now. She stood up, wiped her hands on her jeans and took a deep breath. Nearly there. It was so close she could taste it: the salt wind blowing in over the Dead Sea; the mimosa and pine-laden air of Southern France, the petrol fumes and hot dog stands in New York, the rich black coffee she would be drinking in Sao Paulo. Soon, if her luck held.

Everything she had dreamed of was there in front of her, vivid with promise, but it had no more substance than a mirage unless she made it real. Time was running out, moving away from her at speed. No matter how good Beth was at stalling them, Murdoch was bound to be losing patience by now.

She kind of regretted involving Beth, but not really. That girl needed something to shake her up. She'd said that it would take more than money to solve her problems and fair enough, maybe it would. But surely she could do something with her cut to allow her to think about her life, to figure out what it was she wanted. To engage, to connect, to fucking actually live a little. Beth's problem was she didn't know what she had.

The sports bag was lying at Amber's feet. She picked it up and packed in the last parcels from the fourth angel. It was half full and a good weight now. She didn't know enough about the business to know exactly what it was worth, but it was certainly a lot. John and Murdoch would have worked out all the details in advance, she hoped, and all she'd have to do was hand the stuff over, accept the money and look like she knew what she was doing. She'd better get her arse back to John's office and hope that Beth had managed to keep them happy. Glancing around the room at the four angels, who now seemed to be hovering above the floor, their ruined legs dangling over a mess of broken glass, she realised a single leg was still intact. The first angel now appeared to be pirouetting on one high heel. Fucking fuck. She didn't want to be taking any longer. But if Murdoch was already suspicious, then he'd be likely to notice any shortfall.

She put the bag down and was taking her jacket back off again when there was a small pop and the light went out. The bulb had blown. She waited for her eyes to adjust to the dark. She could see the ghostly figures around her. They looked a lot closer than they had with the light on. If she was the sort of person who was easily freaked out, she thought, she'd be scared shitless right now. Just as well she wasn't that sort of person. She felt her way down the angel's leg, muffled the ankle with her jacket and snapped it quickly and cleanly. She removed her prize and packed it into the sports bag.

The mutilated angels seemed to glow, palely reflecting what little light leaked through the window from the streetlights below. She felt a certain affinity with them. She was hiding secrets as well. To look at her, no one would know about the life growing inside the dark space of her body, cells dividing and multiplying. It was as if the angels were giving her their blessing. They understood that she too had to keep flying and could never, never land. With a short nod to their hovering forms, she whispered, 'Thank you,' went to the door, threw the lock back and walked out.

ELEVEN

that's just something we tell ourselves

Beth showed the two men into the office and gestured to them to make themselves comfortable. The younger man flung himself down on the couch and sprawled out, putting his shoes up on the upholstery. Murdoch walked around the desk and folded his lean body into the swivel chair as if it was his own. He was obviously accustomed to assuming authority. She noticed he was carrying a black leather briefcase which he placed carefully on the floor close to where he sat. He rotated the chair from side to side a little, his eyes remaining fixed on her.

'Interesting,' he said. He leant forward and put his elbows on the desk, pressing his fingertips together. His hands looked small and delicate and his fingernails were perfectly manicured. 'Somehow, you know my name but I don't know yours.'

'Helen,' said Beth. It was the first name that popped into her head. 'I'm Helen.'

'So, tell me, Helen.' The pause before the name was just long enough to imply tolerance of an obvious but inconsequential lie. 'How do you fit into this little operation?'

'Me?' she squeaked. This evening was full of questions and with no right answers. Most of her day-to-day exchanges were so routine and familiar that she didn't need to think about them. The only person she really talked to was Helen and that was different. Helen didn't ask questions. But tonight she'd somehow allowed herself to be drawn into more two-way conversations than she'd had in years: Amber, DS Page, the monkey guy and now this. It wasn't so much the talking – she sometimes talked to Helen for hours at a time – it was the questions. Why were people so keen on asking her questions?

Murdoch looked around then raised his eyebrows, suggesting he didn't see any other likely candidates so, yes, he was asking her. Beth wished she was back at home with a drink in her hand, rolling the liquid warmth around her mouth and feeling her gums tingle, swallowing and letting the glow wash down through her body to the base of her spine, loosening her roots.

'Catering.' It came to her suddenly. 'I'm in catering.' She quickly scanned the room for a drinks cabinet and was relieved to see a glass-fronted unit and small fridge in the corner. 'What can I get you?' She walked over and tugged open the door of the fridge as if she'd done it a million times before. Inside there were beers, a couple of bottles of white wine and soft drinks. The unit above held glasses and bottles of spirits behind smoked glass. She busied herself poking through the fridge and tried to ignore Murdoch's stare boring into her back. She didn't dare turn round and look at him again, certain he'd read the fear on her face.

His silence seemed to last for minutes but eventually he replied, 'Vodka, straight, ice. Please. If you would be so kind.'

'No problem.' She turned to Ryan on the couch. He was staring at the tattoos on the backs of his hands, rubbing them and frowning as if he'd just noticed them there and was having trouble deciphering them.

He glanced up at her, a look of wounded concentration still crumpling his low brow. 'Beer,' he grunted and went back to decoding his knuckles.

The silence while she fetched the drinks was oppressive. Even over the limited course of their short conversation so far, Beth could tell that Murdoch communicated more in his silences than he did with words. His precisely positioned pauses and hesitations conveyed his authority. An extended silence in his presence was uncomfortable in the extreme. She'd have to think of a way to fill in the blank space until Amber arrived.

Strange how silences could have different qualities, different textures. The silence in this room was jagged and cold as a broken bottle of vodka, whereas the silence in Helen's hospital room was like soft cotton, consoling and forgiving as a familiar pillow. From that second silence she had no difficulty drawing things to talk about. When she'd exhausted her own news, which rarely took long, she would gaze on Helen's peaceful face and allow herself to imagine what it would've been like growing up with her as a mother. Of course, there would have been a father as well; this was an ideal childhood after all. She did wonder briefly where Helen's real-life husband or partner, if she had one, might be. Someone must have fathered the absent daughter. But she didn't wonder about them for long. Neither she nor Helen needed them when she could construct a new, better, shared history for them both. She didn't have to reach very far to take hold of these new memories. They seemed to circle in the warm air currents above Helen's bed, like small brightly-coloured birds. As Beth sat on the edge of the chair close to Helen's bedside, stories would come threading down through the air, into her mind and out through her mouth, as if she was simply giving voice to something that was already there; a past being recalled and reclaimed more than invented. She'd relax then and listen to the oddly intimate sound of her own voice, speaking freely and naturally, even laughing occasionally. At these times she was both storyteller and audience.

Do you remember that time we visited that old castle? I think I was about seven. What was the place called? Something to do with cheese but I can't remember which one. The cafe and gift shop were full of the stink of it and I complained so much we had to go and eat our sandwiches outside. The entrance fee to the castle itself was a bit steep and Dad said the inside was probably full of boring old plates and flags, so we walked around outside, making stuff up about who might have lived there. Then we found that old well in the woods nearby. It was massive and looked like something out of a fairy tale. Dad held me round the waist and let me lean down and shout for the echo and we dropped stones in and counted the seconds until we heard the splash in the water and it was so far away. We dropped pennies and made wishes and you said not to tell anyone what I'd wished for or it wouldn't come true. I wanted to tell you my wish so badly. I remember thinking mine was the best wish anyone had ever made but, it's funny, now I can't remember what it was. I never did tell anyone so perhaps it's already come true. Or maybe it's still going to come true in the future. Maybe one day, something totally amazing will happen and I won't even know it's my wish. Mind you, if it turns out I wished for a talking unicorn or something like that, I'll probably notice.

Now, in the room with Murdoch and Ryan, she couldn't even put together complete sentences. The ice cubes cracked as she poured Murdoch's vodka over them. She replaced the bottle on the shelf. The temptation was there to pour herself a generous double, but no, best not to lose focus right now. She delivered the drinks. Ryan grunted and waved away the glass, grabbing the bottle by the neck and half emptying it in one go. Murdoch sipped his vodka in silence and watched her. In an attempt at invisibility, she reverted to the reliable facelessness of the service industry. She opened a packet of salted nuts from the assortment of bar snacks piled up near the fridge, filled two small bowls and placed one on the desk and the other on the coffee table by the couch. Taking a handful herself, she chewed slowly in what she hoped was a nonchalant fashion. There was no moisture in her mouth. This made swallowing difficult but at least she couldn't say anything stupid while her mouth was welded shut.

What was keeping Amber? What if she'd thought better

of her plan and legged it out of the club, leaving her with this pair? Murdoch drummed his fingers on the desk and looked at the ceiling. He was obviously not one for small talk and Ryan didn't seem to talk at all. Beth opened another bag and offered it around. 'Twiglet?' she said, trying on a smile that hung on her face like tinsel on a dead Christmas tree.

Murdoch glowered at her and waved the packet away as if it contained something offensive. Ryan, apparently having lost interest in his knuckles, stuck his hand in the bag while peering down her top as she leaned towards him. He crammed a fist-full into his face in one go and chewed with his mouth open, watching her all the while. She looked away but could hear him swilling beer around his mouth and sucking twiglet bits from between his teeth before burping. 'Nother beer,' he said, and she jumped to it, glad of something to do. He swung his legs down from the couch when she brought it. 'Sit,' he commanded.

She looked at the space on the couch next to Ryan and then over at Murdoch. He was watching them with detached curiosity, the same way someone might watch a fly that's fallen into a half-full glass.

'I said, Sit,' Ryan repeated, louder. 'You deaf?'

Beth opened her mouth but nothing came out.

Just then the door opened and Amber came in. 'So sorry to keep you waiting,' she said. She was carrying a black sports bag. Beth could have kissed her.

'At last,' said Murdoch. 'Everything in order?'

'Of course,' said Amber. She put the bag on the desk and opened it, showing a stack of neatly packed fingers of white powder. Murdoch lifted the bag and dangled it from two fingers by the handle, closed his eyes and bounced it gently up and down. He's weighing it, Beth realised. His mind was a machine and the mechanism included a finely calibrated set of scales. He put the bag back down on the desk and nodded. Amber made to close the zip again but he shot out a hand and stopped her.

'Ryan?' he said. Ryan lumbered up from the couch, brushing twiglet crumbs from his jacket. He took a swig from his beer and surveyed the contents of the bag, selected one parcel at random and opened it. He licked his little finger, slid it into the powder, extracted it again, put the white-frosted tip into his mouth and rubbed it around his gums. After an agonising few seconds he looked at Murdoch and said, 'Yeah. All good.'

Murdoch inclined his head. Ryan sealed up the parcel again, his large fingers surprisingly agile, and replaced it in the sports bag.

'Your turn now,' said Amber. She zipped the bag shut and held on to it. Beth had to admit she was pretty convincing.

Murdoch picked up his own briefcase, placed it on the desk, snapped the lock open and lifted the lid. It was full of money, bundles of notes, used twenties and fifties wrapped in white paper bands. Beth's mouth dropped open. She had never seen this much cash and the effect on her was disturbing. Her pulse was up and her eyes felt like they were popping out of her head. She wasn't excited by money, never had been, so why this physical reaction? Probably just conditioning. She was reacting like a cartoon character because she was in a cartoon situation. That was all.

Amber closed the briefcase, drew it towards her and handed the sports bag over to Murdoch. Beth closed her mouth.

'Don't you want to count it?' Murdoch asked.

'I trust you,' said Amber.

Murdoch looked sceptical, as if wondering whether he'd just been insulted. Beth suspected that trust didn't play a large part in his life. Then he smiled. 'How charming,' he said. 'Well. It's been a pleasure doing business with you ladies. If you'll excuse me, I really must be getting along.' He had the sports bag in his hand and was walking towards the door. With his hand on the door handle, he turned back to them. 'Ryan will thank you properly. He has a particular flair for hospitality.' Murdoch smiled again, nodded to Ryan and left the room, closing the door behind him.

Something was going wrong here and whatever it was, it had put a great big smile on Ryan's ugly face. He rose from the couch and started to advance on Amber, who was gripping the briefcase tightly and backing away from him.

'Come on,' he said. 'Don't be stupid. You didn't really think we'd let a pair of chancing slappers like you keep it, did you?'

Amber was backed up against the desk as Ryan closed in on her. Beth saw Amber's leg whip out but he was ready for it, caught her by the ankle and twisted her foot to the left. She reacted fast and threw herself into a mid-air spin that probably saved her from a broken ankle. When she landed, the briefcase was knocked out of her hand. It skidded across the floor and stopped right at Beth's feet. Amber was struggling back up, her look wild. Before Beth could even think about picking the case up, her head snapped back and light exploded between her eyes. There was something wet over her mouth. She licked her lips and tasted blood. Ryan smiled. There was a dull throb in the middle of her face and she blinked at him. She saw his arm go up and then her face was resting on the carpet. She watched red seep into the weave and realised it was coming from her own nose. He'd not only hit her, but hit her twice. The bastard. She tried to get up but her vision swam and she sank back down. She could only watch.

Amber was walking towards Ryan, slow and sinuous, her hips swaying. She was talking to him in a low voice. Beth couldn't make out the words. Then she shook her hair down and pressed herself up against him, her buttons came undone and her shirt fell open. She put her hand to the front of Ryan's tight jeans and moved her fingers back and forth over the visible bulge. His eyes clouded over and he moaned as Amber unzipped his fly and got down on her knees. Beth did not want to see this but couldn't look away as Amber's head tipped back then plunged forwards and began moving back and forth in a steady rhythm. Ryan stood swaying, his eyes closed. Amber upped the pace. Without breaking the rhythm, she grabbed hold of the bunched-up top of his jeans and boxers. There was a wet slapping sound as she drew her head back then yanked the whole lot down around his ankles, snatched up the briefcase and stood back. Ryan's eyes flew open. He tried to take a step towards her but stumbled, shackled as he was by the tangle of cloth round his ankles. Amber was holding the handle of the briefcase in both hands and swinging it in a wide arc. 'Fucking bi—' Ryan's shout was cut short when the metal corner of the case connected with the side of his head and he crumpled into a heap in front of the door.

Amber hauled Beth to her feet. 'You coming or what?' She threw open the window and climbed out. Over by the door Ryan groaned and shifted.

Beth watched Amber disappear through the window and then followed, lifting one leg over the sill and climbing half way out. She looked down. Bad idea. The ground see-sawed beneath her, both closer and further away than it had been when viewed from inside. She looked up and saw Amber swing over to the fire escape, one hand gripping the drainpipe, the other holding the briefcase. She hooked a leg around the metal staircase and levered herself across. She made it look so easy. Beth knew her own body didn't possess that kind of strength. Her muscles felt puny and limp, barely holding her bones together and she was shaking all over. She didn't know if she could make it.

From the fire escape, Amber gestured impatiently for her to hurry. Beth reached up, gripped the stone above the window and pulled herself the rest of the way out to stand on the ledge. All she needed to do was get a good hold on the drain pipe, use the brackets for toe holds, climb a couple of metres then she'd be able to stretch over to the fire escape. If she could do that, she thought, the rest would follow, though not as gracefully as Amber had managed it.

Maybe her hands were still a little greasy from the chippy,

maybe she misjudged the point at which to transfer her body weight, perhaps her foot slipped at just the wrong moment. Whatever the reason, things didn't work out the way she'd planned. Gravity tugged at her legs while she grappled wildly for something to hold onto, and then she was just hanging, her feet dangling into space. She looked down. Between the toes of her boots she saw tarmac. She saw the individual stones sunk into the tar, the way they shone in the reflected streetlight.

She'd heard that if you fall or jump from high enough then you're dead before you hit the ground; the human brain can't process the experience and simply switches itself off. Bullshit, she thought. That's just something we tell ourselves so we don't have to imagine the alternative, which is that the falling mind knows exactly what's going on. Time slows down so a split second journey lasts long enough to feel your clothes parachute uselessly around you, to listen to the air whistle past your ears and to watch the ground inch steadily closer, coming into sharper focus. To feel your bones shatter on impact, one at a time. To experience the warm flush as each of your internal organs bursts and your body splits open like a dropped shopping bag. To see and feel all of this in fine detail. Nobody wanted to think about that.

She was dangling from the edge of the platform at the top of the fire escape. The metal dug into her finger bones and the muscles under her arms groaned in protest. She tried to pull herself up but didn't have the strength, tried to swing her legs round to latch onto something but they just cycled in mid-air. This wasn't supposed to happen.

But then maybe it was. Maybe this was exactly where she was supposed to be. Maybe this was an opportunity.

She could let go.

She could simply uncurl her fingers and let herself drop into darkness and that would be that. Whatever happened on the way down, falling from this height couldn't be survived. Maybe this was fate presenting her with the chance to put right what went wrong two years ago when she'd been flung clear of the wreckage. Tying up loose ends. Neat, in a way. The metal dug deeper and she felt her grip weaken. Only then did a single small word solidify in her mind. No. Just No. The weaker her hold on the fire escape became, the larger this small word grew and with it the conviction that given the choice, she'd prefer to stay alive.

She looked up and saw Amber's face peering down at her, her head on one side, half-smiling. 'Do you need a hand there?' Then Amber's hands reached down and closed around her wrists and hauled her upwards. As soon as she could, she got a knee onto the platform and then she was rolling across it. She lay on her back and looked up. It was the same sky, a gaping bottomless pit of darkness, but defined and measured by points of light.

'Thanks.'

'Later. Get up, let's go.' Amber snatched up the briefcase and started down the fire escape. Beth scrambled after her. They circled fast down the metal staircase, their footsteps ringing like a demented xylophone, until it ended with a short ladder that stopped about eight feet from the ground. Amber climbed down and jumped off, landed like a gymnast, bending her knees and bouncing back upright. Beth landed like a sack of potatoes, knees buckled and hands slapping the tarmac. She got to her feet and heard a noise above her. Ryan was leaning out of the window, shouting something she couldn't make out, but it didn't sound friendly.

Amber grabbed her hand and they ran.

TWELVE

the averagely useful lives of non-shark people

George stood wondering what to do next. A gust of wind knifed up the street making him glad of the thick fur of his costume. He looked at the frontage of Fantasy Island with its incongruous tropical scene and noticed that the yellow neon hair of one of the women was no longer lit, leaving her looking as if half her head was missing.

He started walking, telling himself to go home and get some sleep and forget about the girl from the chip shop. He had no idea why she'd gone into the club and still didn't know what had happened in the shop to involve the police, but it must have been serious for the place to be taped up like that. There were still people straggling home through Junction Street on unsteady feet. A small cluster formed outside the chip shop. The window of the police car rolled down, words George couldn't hear were exchanged, and the group dispersed.

He wondered about going over to the car himself and making enquiries but he didn't want to talk to more police right now; they were prone to jump to conclusions about monkeys. He turned on his heel and walked back in the opposite direction. Where the hell was he going? Why didn't he just go home? There was a heaviness in his limbs as if someone had turned gravity up a notch. Although he wasn't drunk, the alcohol he'd put away in the course of the night was catching up with him. He sat down on the low wall outside an anonymous office block on the corner. Built as part of a doomed urban regeneration project, the building had been standing empty for a couple of years; faded *Space To Let* signs taped inside the windows curled at the edges. Some joker had penned an *i* on the glass, between the last two words of one notice.

George didn't want to go home. It wasn't home any more than these empty offices were thriving businesses. It was just a place he ate and slept. It was lonely. He was lonely. He hadn't fully admitted this to himself before and felt a sharp twist of self-pity. He hung his head and looked at the tatty carnations he still held. He wasn't any good at being on his own. He'd gone from living with his folks to sharing a flat with some mates, to living with Zoe. Nothing had prepared him for solitude or the way it got harder to handle, not easier, the longer it went on. He'd never imagined his life working out this way. He felt cut loose, floating off into the sky, clutching his empty memories of Zoe, like a gigantic bunch of balloons, carrying him over the rooftops, further and further away.

He'd always assumed that he and Zoe would start a family at some point. This had seemed so obvious and natural to him, like breathing out after breathing in, that maybe he'd taken her agreement for granted. Zoe's reaction, when they'd finally talked about having kids, had come as a shock.

'You're so predictable, George. You want to reproduce the family you grew up in. Another little suburban nuclear unit, two point four children living in a little hutch with one of those whirly things for the washing in the garden. And a shed. With curtains,' she'd said.

He hadn't even mentioned sheds and got the feeling he'd wandered into the middle of an argument she'd started without him. He wondered what he'd missed. 'Okay. No shed. But what's wrong with wanting a family and a home?'

'I'm going to be a doctor, George. I'm not just playing at

all this training. I do actually mean it.' She was raising her voice and her grey eyes had turned stormy.

'I know you do and I'm really proud of you.' He squeezed her hand and smiled, trying to appease her. 'You'll be an amazing doctor. But, it's still only a job. It doesn't have to be everything, does it?' he asked, his voice trailing off towards the end as he saw something flash behind her eyes at the words *only a job*.

'I don't think you get it,' she said, and he thought he could smell burning, an acrid thread of electrical discharge forking through her words. 'I am not about to spend even five minutes of my life stuck in suburbia with a fucking pinny on, baking fucking fairy cakes.'

Even years after that argument, George hadn't been able to think of a good answer to the fucking fairy cakes. But he had developed a never before suspected fondness for them, periodically satisfied round at his sister's house, although he had to fight his niece and nephew, all two point four of them, for a fair share. The kids thing, he saw now, was only one of the cracks in their relationship. Another had been her trainee doctor mates. Increasingly, instead of spending her precious off-duty hours with him, she went away hill walking or skiing with them. He wasn't offended that they never asked him along, in fact he was secretly relieved. Being in their company was like being trapped in a relentlessly jolly Gap advertisement; all ruddy faces and chunky woollies.

He remembered Zoe being all excited one time because one of her group was featured in some Sunday supplement's *Most Eligible* list. She'd pushed the article under his nose as if it was irrefutable proof of something long disputed. The article gave the ages, accomplishments, likes and dislikes of a hundred single, professional and, he thought, probably borderline psychopathic individuals. Zoe's friend was a twenty-four year old snow-boarding champion who had survived a usually-fatal childhood kidney condition and gone on to set up a charity which raised funds for further research

116

into the illness, while training to be a doctor, and running the first profitable urban organic farm in the Borders. He had California surfer blonde hair and teeth so terrifyingly white they'd be a road hazard if he smiled while driving at night. Top of his *dislikes and turn offs* was *lack of self-esteem and ambition*. George had a mental image of a shark berating a prawn for its lack of teeth.

Zoe had looked at him expectantly.

'Quite a guy,' he'd said. The world probably needed people like Shark Boy. But too many were plainly a very bad idea. He felt defensive on behalf of the smaller scale, the averagely useful lives of non-shark people. Where was the place for prawns?

'There's no need to be sarcastic. Honestly, George. Don't you want to achieve anything?'

'Sure I do. But don't you ever wonder who's going to clear the tables? Who's going to drive the buses, deliver the post, do all that ordinary stuff while everyone's getting their teeth whitened and winning ice sculpture competitions? Don't you think if more folk concentrated on achieving a basic level of decency towards each other instead of trying to win at everything, we'd all be better off?'

Zoe had snatched her magazine back as if she feared George might contaminate it with his mediocrity.

'I understand what you and your friends do is more important than what I do. You fix people's bodies, put them back together again. I just muck around with music. But have you ever thought that maybe we're both doing the same kind of thing?' This was a theory he'd nursed for some time but hadn't tried out on Zoe because he was still trying to understand it himself. He'd seen people find a connection in music that could transform and heal. Davey was a perfect example. If he hadn't returned to his love of music, he'd probably still be in the Veterans' Hospital, tearing his bed sheets into useless bandages. George wanted Zoe to see that their goals were the same. Only their approaches were different.

'Don't be ridiculous,' she'd sneered. 'A rare live recording of Van Morrison isn't going to stop someone bleeding to death when they've got a great fucking hole in them, is it? Even Mozart is not going to mend bones. No, George. Music doesn't do that. I do that.'

So much for the theory. She'd stormed off, magazine in hand and he'd put a CD on and let the music wash away the headache that had been threatening his temples. It had worked quicker than any aspirin.

Sitting outside the empty office block, he watched the rest of the people-traffic trailing past, shouting and whistling, taxis pulling into the kerb, a hand on an arse, giggles and shrieks. Perhaps Davey was right and everything did boil down to sex and food. The pizza shop along the road was doing a great trade with the chippy being closed. People ate while they walked, balancing flaccid triangles over their palms and trailing long strings of melted cheese from their mouths. It looked disgusting but his stomach still grumbled reflexively. There was definitely something to be said for the simple pleasures.

Why was he still waiting? What would he say to the girl when she reappeared? There had been something about her expression as she went into the lap-dancing club; something going on behind those shuttered eyes that seemed to want to tell him something. He felt tired but doubted he would sleep if he went home now. So why not wait?

He may as well give up on the carnations though. He looked at them. As a gift, they had crossed the line from slightly pathetic to downright insulting. He fingered the limp pink petals and started absently tugging at them. The drooping blooms didn't need much encouragement and came apart in his hands, petals drifting down to land in a pile on the pavement between his feet.

'She loves you *not*!' The owner of the loud, drunken voice sat down heavily on the wall next to him. George ignored him. With any luck he'd take the hint and go away.

'All right there, George?' the voice said.

He looked up. The guy seemed familiar but George couldn't place him straight away. 'Hey,' he said, noncommittally, hoping for some clues.

'What happened to you then?' asked the guy.

George didn't know where to start. The answer could go on for years or could be very short indeed. While George mulled this over, the guy started talking again, answering his own question.

'We ended up in this music club with dry ice and lasers and all that, pitch bloody dark it was and so loud my brain was actually vibrating in my skull, y'know? Anyway, it was doing my head in so I goes outside for a smoke and the bastards wouldn't let me back in again. Said I was staggering. I goes, Course I'm staggering, my fucking ear drums are bleeding. But they weren't having it. Wouldn't even let me go in and tell the rest of them. Course, they can't hear their mobiles in there so that's me. Out on my arse. Ears are still ringing. So, what you been up to then?'

George knew who he was now. He was the neon guy. Friend of Davey's. He put what was left of the flowers down on the wall on his other side and brushed some stray petals off his chest. 'Just took Davey home. Otherwise not much. I'll probably head off soon—'

'See them,' interrupted Davey's friend. George wondered whether the guy really had gone temporarily deaf or just liked the sound of his own voice. He was gesturing towards Fantasy Island. 'We got a contract for one of those places. Really big contract too. Same kind of idea as that, y'know, girls, but different. Angels it was. Angels with big tits. I'm not kidding. Magic. Spent ages on it. I like doing stuff that's a bit different. Mostly it's just lettering, must have done a million *Open* signs. You know those ones? They all look the same. Red letters with a squashed blue circle, like a ring round a planet, yeah? Anyway. So, we did all this work but then they pulled the plug. Said they didn't want us to finish the job. The boss went mental. But they paid for the work we'd done, materials and everything, even came and collected the signs. But they weren't finished, y'know? Just empty glass shapes. No real use to anyone. Dunno what they said to the boss but he quietened right down when they came round, not a peep out of him. Couple of really dodgy looking blokes just loaded them into a van and that was that. Back to planet *Open* for me.'

George noticed the neon girl with the dud hair seemed to be in more trouble now; one of her legs was flickering on and off. He shrugged. 'As long as you got paid, eh?'

'No questions asked,' said Davey's friend, standing up. He was tapping the side of his nose in a gesture of secrecy but missed and poked himself in the eye. 'Ow. Shit. Right, I'm off.' He blinked a couple of times then reached down and shook George's hand, bouncing it up and down enthusiastically. 'Good to see you mate. Take it easy, eh?' And he was away, staggering along the pavement, waving to a group of girls crossing the road, shouting 'Hallo, Ladies!' then putting his hands in his pockets and whistling tunelessly while they ignored him.

Something was happening on the other side of the road. A woman with long blonde hair, carrying a briefcase in one hand and buttoning up her blouse with the other, was running out from the alley at the side of the club. With her was the girl from the chip shop, also running but limping too. They kept glancing over their shoulders, like they were being chased. They dodged through the cars and taxis, pausing on the traffic island to let a bus go past.

George stood up and hurried towards them. Realising he didn't know the chip shop girl's name he called out, 'Hi! Um, excuse me?' The blonde girl turned and looked at him, flicked her eyes over him like a slap and turned away again, intent on judging the speed and distance of an approaching taxi. 'Are you okay?' he shouted, trying to direct his voice towards the other girl.

She looked over and her eyes widened. 'You again?'

George squinted at her. There was something on her face, around her nose and on her chin. Was that blood? 'Can I—' he began but was cut off by the blonde.

'Come on, Beth. NOW!' she grabbed the girl's hand and pulled her across the road. There was a covered lane a few shops down from the chippy which must lead to the back of the building. They ran into it and disappeared from view.

At least he knew her name now. 'Beth,' he said to himself. He liked it. He gave himself a shake. This was no time to be mooning around. She was obviously in some kind of trouble. He wondered if he should follow them and was looking into the darkness of the cobbled lane when an old chip van came chugging out in a cloud of petrol fumes. It turned onto the main street. It was only when the van passed in front of his face that he realised Beth was driving and the blonde girl was in the passenger seat. The van backfired and bunny-hopped into the stream of traffic. As they passed Fantasy Island, two men burst out of the entrance. They looked furious about something and the younger one was doing up his trousers. The other one pointed and shouted as the chip van laboured past, then both men started running towards a row of parked cars.

George saw immediately that these men were chasing the women in the van and felt sure that it would not go well for them if they were caught. Without stopping to figure out the how or the why of it, he was running, knowing only that somehow he had to help them.

He sprinted across the road and started dancing around in between the men and the cars. This worked for about ten seconds until, impatiently, the older man reached into the inside pocket of his suit and pulled out something dark and metallic. It jerked in his hand and there was a noise that George felt in his body rather than heard, and then his left foot was burning hot. He staggered sideways and looked down. There was blood running from under the fur covering his shoe. He looked up again. The man had put the gun away and was getting into a car. The younger one shoved George out of his way like a sack of rubbish and got in the passenger side.

George stumbled again then fell over and lay curled on his side on the pavement. Bastard had shot him in the foot. He supposed he should be grateful it hadn't been the head or some other part of him that he was really attached to. He couldn't feel his foot. Maybe he was in shock or maybe it was a more ominous sign. As he lay there waiting for the pain to arrive, he wondered if he had done any good. Had he helped at all? He'd slowed those guys up for maybe a few extra seconds. He hoped they were important seconds.

A Ferrari pulled away from the kerb and roared into the street. George's hopes deflated. There was no way anyone was going to outrun a car like that in a clapped out old chip van. He blinked and when he opened his eyes he saw a blue saloon car swing sideways on the street with a squeal of tyres, right in front of the Ferrari, blocking its path. From his viewpoint on the pavement, George was reminded of being about ten, lying on the floor watching Starsky and Hutch with his face too close to the telly, his senses full of flashing paintwork, spinning tyres and revving engines. The Ferrari skidded to a stop and immediately began backing up but a police car was blocking its exit in that direction. Finally, the police car that had been parked outside the chip shop pulled across the street and completed the box around the Ferrari. It was trapped, its engine still growling impotently.

A man and a woman in dark clothes – he guessed they must be detectives – jumped out of the saloon car and approached the Ferrari. Uniformed police moved in from the rear. The sports car gave one last roar before falling silent. The doors swung open and the two occupants climbed out, their hands raised. They were promptly seized and spun round by police, pushed against the car, spread eagled and searched, which yielded up the gun from the older man's inside pocket.

One of the detectives leaned into the Ferrari and pulled out a black sports bag. He laid it on the bonnet of the car, opened it then closed it again quickly. The two men put up no resistance as they were handcuffed and pushed into the back of the waiting police car.

He heard a familiar voice behind him. 'Apology not accepted then, I take it?'

He twisted his head and saw it was the same burly policeman who had almost arrested him trying to buy the flowers back at the twenty-four hour garage. 'I was just trying to help.'

'What are you like? You some kind of vigilante super-hero now? The Hairy Avenger or something?'

'It seemed like the right thing to do,' said George weakly.

'Uh huh,' the policeman gave George a sceptical look. 'You should put that in your statement.'

'My foot.' The feeling was returning to his foot now and it was not a good feeling. In fact, it was a very bad feeling and was growing worse by the second. He thought he might be about to pass out.

The policeman knelt down and examined the mess on the pavement around George's foot. 'Nasty,' he said and straightened up again. 'Right. We better get you an ambulance. But don't think you're getting out of giving a statement.'

Two paramedics carried George on a stretcher towards the back of the ambulance. As they passed the two detectives, George overheard snatches of their conversation.

'I'll radio Traffic to bring in the pair in that chip van, shall I?' said the woman.

'No,' replied her male colleague. 'Not yet. Plenty of time for that. They won't be hard to trace.'

'Yes, but shouldn't we just—'

'Thank you for your suggestions, Constable Chan,' the male voice cut her off. 'But I'm in charge here. Now shut up while I do my job.'

'Of course, sir. Sorry, sir.'

As the ambulance rocked from side to side on the way to the hospital, like a small boat on choppy water, George ran through the events of the night. Things certainly hadn't gone as planned but, apart from the foot situation, he was surprised to find he felt better than he had done in ages.

He looked at the deflated rubber monkey face in his lap, the empty eye sockets collapsing in and the mouth dented into a lopsided grin. Perhaps all he'd ever needed to do was take the mask off. Perhaps it really was that simple. He felt it all draining away from him and smiled just before passing out.

THIRTEEN

some doomed romantic bullshit

The magnified echoes of their footsteps clattered around them as they ran through the covered roadway towards the back of the tenement block. Beth winced as a loose cobble shifted under her feet, throwing her weight onto the ankle she'd twisted jumping from the fire escape.

They emerged into a narrow, pot-holed lane that ran along the back of the building. Wrought iron railings, lumpy with decades of reapplied tarry paint, divided the road from a grassy area: a long-suffering triangle of green, strung up with washing lines. The back doors of the shops were locked and chained for the night and deep shadows leaned against the walls.

Beth skidded to a halt, narrowly avoiding running into Amber. She bent over, her hands on her knees, coughed and spat. The short run had left her breathless but Amber seemed completely unaffected.

'Where does this come out?' Amber asked, taking a few steps to the right, along the lane.

'It doesn't,' replied Beth. 'There's only lock-ups that way.'

Amber turned and started jogging in the other direction. 'This way then. Come on. Let's go.'

'You can't. This is just a service lane. Doesn't go anywhere. Only one way in and out.'

'You are fucking kidding me.' Amber spun round and glared at her. 'Why the fuck didn't you say so?'

'You didn't ask. And you were in front. I thought you knew

where you were going.' Beth realised she hadn't questioned the fact that Amber would lead and she would follow, even when she didn't know where she was going.

Amber threw her hands up and gave her an incredulous look but then sighed and shrugged, appearing to accept the situation as beyond her control. She glanced back towards Junction Street. 'Away from here was all I had planned. I thought we could cut through. Shit.'

'So what now?'

'Wouldn't be too clever going back that way. They're probably not far behind us.' Amber hefted the briefcase by her side and stared off into the drying green like she was hoping to find a noticeboard with instructions on what to do next. 'Don't suppose you've got a getaway car stashed in one of those lock-ups, have you?' She laughed weakly, in a way that showed she knew it was a dumb idea but they were out of other options.

'Well . . . not exactly,' Beth replied.

'What? Have you? Christ, don't fuck around!' Amber came towards her and Beth thought she meant to grab her by the lapels and shake her. 'Anything with wheels that'll get us out of here would do.'

Beth gestured for Amber to follow and led her up the lane to a small bay by the back door of the Deep Sea. A thin yellow light seeped out through the rear window and played over the sagging flanks of the ancient chip van. Beth put a finger to her lips and moved cautiously. The light meant there were still people inside the shop, although they were more likely to be in the front than through the back.

Despite its long years of service, Beth had to admit that as a getaway vehicle the van didn't have much going for it. It wasn't built for speed, and it stuck out like a sore thumb. What it did have in its favour was the fact that the keys were always there.

Beth popped open the left wing-mirror, retrieved the keys and climbed into the cab, then pulled up the black plastic golf-tee lock on the passenger door for Amber. The interior was musty: part old dish rag and part compost heap. Everything from the seat covers to the steering wheel was impregnated with decades of grease that no amount of cleaning could ever shift. Possibly it was the only thing holding the van together. Beth liked the smell, with its echoes of her gran's kitchen, but Amber wrinkled her nose. Beth turned the key and pumped the accelerator pedal, prodding the engine into life. It farted and grumbled as if woken up from an uneasy sleep after eating too much of something difficult to digest. Before the noise attracted attention, she eased the hand-brake off and coaxed the van along the lane, through the passageway and out onto Junction Street.

They joined the flow of traffic, coughing out dirty clouds of exhaust fumes. Beth looked to her right as they passed the entrance to Fantasy Island just in time to see Murdoch and Ryan burst from between the neon palm trees. Murdoch was blazing, his eyes scouring the pavements, dissecting the groups of people who drifted past. Ryan was tugging at his fly with one hand while wiping blood from his forehead with the other. The effort of coordinating these two tasks appeared to be too much for him and he staggered into Murdoch, knocking him sideways. The movement jolted the beam of his searchlight in the direction of the van. His eyes locked first on Beth's face, then Amber sitting in the passenger seat. He pointed and shouted something to Ryan. Beth gulped as the two men ran towards a sleek sports car parked by the kerb.

'Shit,' said Amber, having seen them as well. 'How fast does this thing go?'

'With a tail wind, on a good day, about fifty,' Beth said. She didn't have the heart to tell Amber that even that was a wildly optimistic estimate.

Amber slumped in the passenger seat. 'We're fucked,' she said.

Beth thought Amber was probably right. Then she spotted two figures sitting in an anonymous-looking blue saloon car parked a little further up the street. Something odd about that. Why would they be just sitting there? As she drew closer her suspicions were confirmed by the yellow gleam of the streetlight reflecting off DS Page's bald head. She never expected to feel so pleased to see the detective again. She pulled up alongside his car and rolled down her window, making fast circles in the air with her finger to encourage Page to do the same. He did not look best pleased. His window slid down with an electronic growl. Either he didn't like following instructions from her or he was annoyed at being so easy to spot. Whichever, she didn't have time to spare his pride.

'Those two guys you warned me about?' Beth got in before he could open his mouth.

'Yes?'

'They'll be coming along here in about twenty seconds with a bag full of coke. Just so's you know.'

Page's mouth fell open and his eyebrows shot up so fast and so far, Beth thought for a second they might disappear right over the smooth summit of his head, never to be seen again.

'How do you? Now hang on a—' he blustered but Beth was already rolling her window up and standing on the accelerator.

There was a loud bang. Could there be a worse moment for the engine to decide enough was enough? But to her amazement the van kept chugging along. It must have been a particularly loud backfire, she decided. In the rear view mirror she could see that Page had swung into action and swerved his car right out across the street, blocking Murdoch's path. She hoped someone had radioed for help; she wouldn't like to be the one standing between Murdoch and something he wanted. But dealing with that kind of risk was what the police were for, she reasoned, so they could get on with it. She turned the van onto one of the forks at the southern end of the street.

Amber put her feet up on the dashboard and started laughing.

'What?' Beth didn't see what was so funny.

'You! I thought you were all Little Miss Goody-fucking-two-shoes. But you're hard-core!'

Beth kept her eyes on the road. Maybe she looked composed, like none of this was fazing her, but her hands shook as she steered. Perhaps Amber was mistaking it for the vibration from the engine. Her nerves were jangling like cheap wind chimes in a hurricane but despite that, as Beth's adrenaline levels fell, the sides of her mouth started to curl in response to Amber's infectious laugh. Eventually she allowed herself the smile. 'Thanks,' she said. 'I'll take that as a compliment.'

Amber got a hold of herself and stopped giggling after a minute or two.

'Where are we going exactly?' asked Beth. She'd been taking random turns in any direction, putting as much distance between themselves and the scene they'd left behind as possible.

'My house first. We'll worry about the rest later. Just head south out of town and I'll show you the way.'

For a while they drove in silence. The buildings shrank in height as they moved further out of town and passed parks and open spaces, stone gradually being broken up by green. Amber lifted the briefcase onto her lap and opened it, letting out a low whistle. 'Must be at least three hundred grand here, I reckon,' she said. 'Now that is definitely the best paid blow job I've ever done.' She laughed, picking out a bundle of notes and running her thumb over the end, making a flicking sound. 'Mind you, it was an exceptionally good blow job, though I say it myself.'

Beth shook her head. The scene in John's office played in her mind, not that she wanted to watch it again. It was incredible, the way Ryan had let Amber do that, apparently without a single thought that it might not be too clever, given the circumstances. 'I still can't believe you got away with that,' she said.

'What? Penguining that guy?'

'Penguining?'

'Yeah.' Amber put her arms down straight by her sides, hands flexed outwards like little wings and rocked stiffly side to side in her seat. 'You know? Handy move sometimes.'

'Right,' said Beth, filing away that bit of information with a shudder, trying not to imagine the possible situations where immobilising a man in that way would be useful. 'How come he just let it happen though?'

Amber gave a derisive snort. 'Easy. Guy like that? Not enough brains to go around in the first place, so all you need to do is get whatever he's got down to his cock, and the head's automatically empty. Like flicking a switch. You never noticed that?'

'I guess.' There was an element of truth to it, Beth supposed. The way some guys would go completely vacant when they were turned on. She'd never thought of it that way before, or considered it as a purely male weakness.

Before Danny, during most of her teenage sexual encounters, she'd generally been so drunk she couldn't see straight, never mind think straight. She'd had no idea what she was doing or why she was doing it, but something kept making her want to do it again. It made no sense but sex wasn't reasonable or rational on any level. Surely it was like that for everyone, man or woman?

After she joined the band, she'd had less time and inclination so had been accidentally celibate for a while. Until Danny happened.

The first time was in the middle of the afternoon one nondescript weekday when Al and Craig had both been out, and her and Danny were mooching around the flat, eating toast, playing old John Martyn albums on vinyl. There had always been a level of mutual attraction between them but with it went an unspoken agreement that in the interests of not complicating things for the band, they'd just not go there. Still, she sometimes looked at him and wondered. And sometimes she caught him looking back at her, his gaze lingering.

That afternoon, she'd still been wearing the t-shirt and boxers she'd slept in. She hadn't showered yet and her hair was pulled into a tangled ponytail; not exactly sexually irresistible. They were listening to *Solid Air* when Danny came and lay next to her, where she was stretched out on the couch, and started running a finger up and down her leg. He let it travel a little higher with each stroke then inwards, trailing over the sensitive skin on her inner thigh. They both watched while he was doing this, as if his hand was some third party beyond their control. Then he stared into her face. She knew he was looking for clues, for an answer to the question raised. She didn't have a coherent answer but she knew she didn't want him to stop. Her body was responding to his of its own accord.

His hand went higher, under the t-shirt and closed over her breast. She felt her nipple stiffen under his fingers. Thinking about it now, that would have been her light-switch moment. She sniggered to herself, picturing her boob as one of those old fashioned dome light fittings with the flip switches. On off, on off.

'What?' said Amber.

'Nothing. S'okay. Just ignore me. Left here?'

After that, consideration for others had gone out of the window. Suddenly they couldn't take another breath apart. If she could have looked into her own eyes at that moment, would she have seen the transfer of control from brain to body? That same clouding over and loss of function she'd seen on Ryan's face? Probably, although she really hoped she hadn't looked that gormless.

Danny's mouth was on hers and they were pulling at each other's clothes like they were both drowning. She'd given herself up to it, dimly aware of the record jumping, jangling guitars and mandolins falling all over each other, the couch bumping across the floor. Then nothing but a delirious vertigo rising through her veins, taking her higher.

Afterwards they'd lain in a tangle of sweaty limbs and got their breath back, sneaking shy glances at each other. She wiped a hand over her face and pushed back the strands of hair that had come loose. He gulped water from a pint glass, turned and met her eye.

'Oh dear,' he'd grinned.

'Oh my,' she'd replied and they'd laughed.

That had been the beginning and they'd never really moved on from it. The sex was always good. The friendship was easy. Sometimes they slept together, sometimes they didn't, retiring instead to their own rooms for the night. They didn't talk about *us*, what they were to each other, what it all meant. And that was what they both wanted. It didn't have to mean anything other than what it was. There was no rush. She hadn't known then that they would be robbed of the time to figure it out at leisure. Had they been in love or were they simply, in Craig's charming terminology, *fuck buddies*? It hadn't mattered when Danny was alive so it really shouldn't matter when he wasn't. It certainly shouldn't matter more. But somehow it did.

She'd been with no one since. The idea terrified her. It wasn't that she thought no one else could ever measure up, and not that she'd be betraying his memory or some doomed romantic bullshit like that. It was the worry of what would happen if it was good. Bad sex would be fine but the good stuff . . . that was dangerous.

'Left here,' said Amber.

Beth steered the van into a quiet suburban street. This couldn't be where Amber lived. She wound through a pebble-dashed estate with careful gardens and mid-range family cars in driveways. Cars that probably got washed on Sundays. In the anaemic orange light cast by the street lamps, the houses looked boxy and unreal to Beth, as if they had driven into a child's drawing of home.

'You live here?' she asked, disbelieving.

'Why would I not?' Amber demanded.

Beth shrugged. 'No reason. It just seems a little . . . not very you.'

Amber pointed to a semi-detached, two-storey house with a red door. Beth parked outside and turned the ignition off. The engine shuddered to a grateful halt and silence swept through the van. It made her ears tingle, like resurfacing from swimming underwater.

'I just need to get a few things,' said Amber. 'Won't be long.' She opened the door and started to get out of the van.

'But I'm bursting,' protested Beth, squirming in her seat. 'My bladder feels like a football.'

Amber looked reluctant. 'Come on then. Just be quiet. Don't want to wake the neighbours.'

They got out of the van and Beth closed the door as quietly as possible. Amber lived in suburbia and worried about what her neighbours thought? If anything, this was even harder to square with her view of Amber than learning she was going to be a mother. That still hadn't sunk in. She realised she hadn't considered Amber's condition since they talked. Was it on Amber's mind the whole time or did she forget about it sometimes too? She hadn't exactly been behaving like your average suburban mother-to-be. Beth thought back through the fairground ride of sex, drugs and violence that they'd been on since they'd talked on the fire escape. Amber's kid had already been in more dodgy situations than most folk saw in a lifetime. Hopefully by the time it came into the world, all that would be left far behind.

Amber opened the gate gently and as they walked up the path, Beth could see that the garden had at one time been neatly laid out. Symmetrical paving slabs were dotted around between shrubs and gravel. Now it was well on its way to reverting to nature, weeds pushing up in clumps between the hexagonal stones, like gate crashers at a church party. Her grandad used to say the definition of a weed was simply *a flower growing in the wrong place*. The plants didn't know any different; it was only our way of looking at them that put them in the wrong and made outlaws of them. The rear end of a car leaned to one side on a flat tyre in the shadows at the side of the house.

On the doorstep a garden gnome grinned, his rosy cheeks like hard little apples above his pointy white beard. He stood with his legs apart, hands on hips. His expression suggested he was welcoming back an errant favourite. Amber reached out, pulled his head off and shook it violently. A key fell out into her hand. She opened the door then replaced the key inside the gnome's head and put his head back on his shoulders. He was still smiling but Beth thought she caught an angry glint in his eye as she followed Amber into the house.

FOURTEEN

this might not be about you

Amber went into the house and flicked the hall light on. Ash grey carpet and magnolia wood-chip walls, paper globe light shade and a doormat that said *Welcome*. Some joke.

Beth gazed wide-eyed around the hall. 'This is your house?'

'No. It belongs to my parents.'

'You live with your parents?' Beth's mouth was hanging open. She shouldn't do that, thought Amber. It makes her look thick.

'They don't live here anymore.' She hadn't had anyone else in the house since she'd moved back, hadn't wanted to, and didn't much like it now she did. People had a tendency not to mind their own fucking business. 'Do you want to play Twenty Questions or do you want to use the bog?'

'Sorry, I—'

'Top of the stairs, on your left.'

'Thanks.'

Amber walked down the hall as Beth climbed the stairs. Familiar with every creak of the boards, without turning around she knew Beth was pausing, looking at the photographs. She'd be putting together a life for her, constructing a past from those fragments. But what hung on the walls was the version of her that her parents had wanted to display, the fantasy girl they wished they'd had. The one who grew up clean and blameless. The reality of her wasn't something they'd liked to broadcast.

Since she'd been back, she'd paid no attention to the house except as somewhere to eat, wash and sleep, moving between kitchen, bathroom and bedroom, seeing only the functions each room provided, nothing more. Now, someone else looking at the place as a home with a family history was not what she needed. It scared the old ghosts into flight like a flock of dirty pigeons. *Rats with wings*, John used to call the pigeons that nested around Junction Street. Filthy bags of feathers, all mutant feet and always shitting. He'd had to pay a fortune to get the mess cleaned off the roof of the club, or it would've caved in eventually under the weight. A little bit ironic that, as it turned out.

She'd flown the nest the first time as soon as she could, at sixteen, scraping together a month's rent on a box room. She'd no qualifications so took the first job she could find, stacking shelves at night in a supermarket. It was from that job she'd saved the money for her tattoo. Her wings were supposed to carry her away from everything her life had been up to that point, but in reality they hadn't taken her far. Much of the next decade was a blur of interchangeable squats and rooms in shared flats in different cities, a shifting cast of friends and lovers, scraping along from day to day, signing on, some casual work. She'd done the odd stint dancing at various clubs when she needed the money. There was always work available, but she never stayed for long. Nothing mattered beyond the next weekend and she'd been happy to live that way, until circumstances left her with no choice but to return to the family home. The decision to move back had been purely practical. She needed somewhere quiet and cheap to stay while she saved.

She arrived one night with no more than a single suitcase. Everything was the same, as if she'd only gone out to the shops and come back half an hour later. She told her mother why she was there and what her plans were. The news was never going to go down well.

'Please. Don't do this to me,' her mother begged in a quiet, shocked voice. She was sitting at the kitchen table, drunk and tearful as usual.

'I'm not doing anything to you.'

'Yes you are. You're doing this to punish me.' Her tone changed to indignant and accusing.

Amber had almost forgotten how her mother's emotions worked like a pinball machine, firing her from one over-reaction to another, lights and bells going off so fast it was exhausting and pointless trying to keep up. 'Have you ever considered that this might not be about you? Even once?'

'But I could look after you, if you'd just let me.' Bang. Back to submissive pleading.

'Don't make me laugh. When have you ever done that? All I need is somewhere to stay.'

Her expression had turned bitter, her face red and twisting. 'You come swanning back here after all this time and think you can move in, just like that. On your own terms. Who do you think you are exactly? Bloody royalty?'

Amber said nothing. She shouldn't have allowed herself to be drawn into an argument she could never win. Her mother's tantrums had always churned and boiled impressively, but they never lasted very long. It was best simply to wait them out. She watched, waiting to see what angle she would try to attack from next.

Her mother glared, defiant in her martyrdom, tears spilling down her cheeks. 'You are an evil bitch!' She threw down the frayed remains of a tissue and pulled another from the box. 'You've always been a bitch. I knew as soon as you were born, as soon as you opened your eyes, there was something wrong with you. After all the sacrifices I made for you. Everything your father and I did, we did for you.'

'Oh, please. Spare me the clichés.' She'd heard all this too many times before. The only thing it made her feel was tired. She yawned, without bothering to conceal it.

Her mother scowled at her. 'I don't know where you came from. You're no child of mine.'

Amber sighed and raised her hands in surrender. 'Okay, Mum. Can we talk about this in the morning?'

The answer was a sulky shrug and a dismissive wave towards the staircase.

She'd gone up to bed. Her room was just the same. It had obviously been cleaned regularly. Even the bed sheets were fresh. It made no sense but she was beyond caring and crawled under the duvet and closed her eyes. She heard her mother banging about downstairs, blowing her nose, the kitchen cupboards being rifled, a glass smashing and eventually the slam of the front door and the sound of her car driving off.

The fact that she hadn't come back in the morning was no big deal. It wasn't the first time she'd disappeared. She had vanished periodically when Amber was a kid, leaving her to fend for herself, which meant eating whatever she could reach that didn't need cooking, and staying out of her father's way as much as possible. She'd be gone for two or three days then show up, hair dirty, smelling of drink and self-pity. Then there'd be a stage of casseroles and concern, sometimes lasting months, until the next time. And there always was a next time. But her mother's most recent disappearance had been the last. She hadn't come home since.

Amber had stayed on, living rent free, hassle free and guilt free, as only an evil bitch could. She hadn't planned it that way but it worked out better than she'd hoped. She'd taken the job at the club and started saving.

She already knew that the *look don't touch* rule of the lap-dancing industry was a bullshit lie, put about to make the idea look safe for the public. The truth was a different story. It had never bothered her the way it did some of the other girls. She had a knack of distancing herself from her physical body so that she used it as a tool. It wasn't *her* they had their hands on, their fingers inside, it was only the thing she lived in. The handling affected her no more than someone going through her coat pockets. So the rest of it didn't come as a big leap. There was money to be made

138

there. She'd never crossed that line before but then she'd never needed to.

It had only ever been a means of speeding things up. After all, she had a time limit. And it wasn't just a round-the-world ticket she wanted; she had enough for that within a few months. What she wanted was to be able to keep going, to do what she liked, to go wherever she wanted. And she didn't want to have to come back again. Ever. That took serious money.

She walked down the hall and paused at the door of her father's study. Beyond this point was dangerous territory. Like the warnings on old maps, *Here Be Monsters*. She thought about her father.

When she'd been small, he was the person she was threatened with. The Bogie Man. *You wait till your father gets home.* And it was effective. He'd been a silent, uncompromising man, with sandy blonde hair, weather-worn skin and hands like shovels. A single well-timed blow, delivered with a kind of scornful disgust, could knock her right off her feet and into the nearest wall. At the time, she didn't think it was anything unusual. Everyone she knew got hit by their parents sometimes. *This is hurting me more that it's hurting you*, was what they'd say. In her father's case, she thought it did hurt him more, much more, but it was still a selfish act, something that satisfied his own need to punish and control.

He had a grim Presbyterian air about him and, if he hadn't been an atheist, he would have been a natural minister of the Old Church. As it was, all he believed in was his own moral code which although clear to him, he never bothered explaining to anyone else. Occasionally, he would shrug off this role and insist upon some doomed day trip, the three of them piled into the car, off to see some ruin, or on a forced march into the countryside with unsuitable footwear, egg sandwiches and a flask of tea; as if play-acting happy families would mean they were one too. One trip in particular had featured recently in the short films her subconscious hauled from memory.

She must have been about seven. It had been getting dark and they were lost. They were in the countryside and they didn't belong there. The pretext was some ruined castle that smelled of cheese. They hadn't even gone inside but had wandered around the grounds instead. The woods were overgrown and darkness was starting to clog in the ivy that bound the trees. They came to a clearing with a dilapidated well. She peered over. There was a smell of decay and a darkness so absolute it make the skin on her face shrink away from the bones. But before she could retreat, she felt herself hoisted up and tipped over. The blackness yawned open to receive her. Eager. Hungry. She tried to scream but couldn't get the breath. Someone was holding her by the ankles so that she was suspended inside the mouth of the well. 'What do you see?' Her father's voice came from back in some other world. There were plants growing from the sides, things so dark they looked black, pointed leaves reaching out to pull her in. 'What do you see?' She couldn't speak. She felt her bladder release and hot shame ran up her chest and back, around her neck and ears, soaking her hair and dripping from the ends of her pigtails. She started to cry. The sound fell and echoed in a downwards spiral. Then she was pulled out, straight up into a day that was now impossibly bright. Placed back on her feet, she squinted in the sudden light and saw her mother hanging back, doing nothing more than wringing her hands. This picture burned itself into her understanding. There would be no help from her, not while he was around. And then his hands were squeezing her shoulders, telling her to stop her whining for christsake, he had hold of her. Did she think he'd let her go? Well did she?

On their way back to the car, he found an owl pellet as big as his thumb. He pulled apart the cottony lump, showed her the tiny bones of the owl's last meal. They looked like doll's bones, delicate and perfect. Barbie bones. 'There's two

140

types of creature in this world,' he told her, 'predators and prey. You need to decide which you're going to be.'

She hadn't been in his study for years and, as far as she knew, neither had anyone else, but this would be her last time in the house, ever. That wasn't a reason in itself. She could walk away without a backward glance but she had made the challenge to herself and couldn't back down now. She turned the handle.

It was a small room dominated by an ugly, too-large desk which itself was pinned down by the crouched form of a gunmetal angle-poise lamp. A wing-backed armchair was pushed into the corner. Framed pictures of birds hung on the walls, pencil drawings and paintings, prints and photographs, a gallery of claws, beaks and intent black eyes. No reason at all to feel they were watching her. Shelves were filled with books about birds, wild and caged; neither had escaped his scrutiny. She walked over to the window. There, at the end of the garden, almost hidden in the darkness, was the shed that had once contained his show birds. Those birds had received whatever tenderness the man had in him to offer. They had his love.

In amongst the pictures of birds was a black and white newspaper clipping that showed a blonde girl with bobbed hair and a sailor collar, sitting next to a caged canary. Robbed of his brilliant colour in the monochrome print, he glared out from between the bars. She'd only wanted away from the photographer. He'd been a creepy bastard who'd pinched her cheeks and fingered her hair. The caption read *Only a Bird in a Gilded Cage*. She remembered the day that photograph was taken.

The hall had been filled up to the ceiling with a hurricane of birdsong. Her shoes crunched over seed-scattered boards. Rows and rows of cages, stacked like supermarket shelves the whole length of the hall.

The British Section: Bramble Finch, Yellow Bunting, Redpoll. The names recited like a litany in a murmur of male voices. The Foreign Section: Fire Finches, Green Avadavats, Dhyal Birds. They fluttered and called in mysterious dialects, eyes focused on some faraway freedom they'd never reach. They tilted their heads, waiting for a reply, straining to hear the answering song that never came.

She'd got lost in a forest of unfamiliar overcoats. A cockatiel screeched and wobbled the black knot of its tongue at her. The noise of the birds got louder as it rose from the cages and became a single, living thing, wheeling and pressing against the arched ceiling. She ran between the rows of cages, wheat-tasting dust catching in her throat, her heart throwing itself blindly against her ribcage, her breath coming in tight gasps, searching the crowd for her father's blonde hair.

It was coming for her. She could feel its eyes on her as it plummeted downwards, invisible talons outstretched. She would be snatched up. There was nowhere to hide and no one to help. She ran faster, then tripped and fell, skinning her knees on the floorboards. It had her now. She squeezed her eyes shut and put her hands over her ears to block out the triumphant scream of the predator as it closed on her. She felt its talons tug at the shoulders of her coat and opened her eyes. There was a man crouching in front of her.

He pulled her back up to standing. She noticed a camera slung around his neck. There was a sour smell about him. He smiled, showing yellow-grey teeth, then looked behind her and said, 'May I borrow your daughter?' and she realised her father was right behind her. The man said, 'It's for the paper, y'know? Bit of human interest.' They all moved to the back of the hall where, in a side-room full of smuggled silence, a black cage held a small yellow bird. It hopped from perch to perch in a way that scared her. Hop turn, hop turn, keeping a relentless rhythm. The photographer picked her up and sat her on the table next to the cage. His hands patted her bare

legs, rearranged the material of her skirt. 'Watch the birdy!'
he said.

Afterwards, in a corner where the dust clung to her face
like a second skin, she'd eaten two stale biscuits and drank
a cup of orange squash.

They didn't have to die. He could've given them to someone
else, or even released them, but that wasn't enough for him.
He said he did it for her. Liar. He did it for himself. He did
it because he believed severity was a virtue. That harshness
was always right.

She should never have come in here. There'd been a reason
she'd kept out. Something about sleeping ghosts. This room
had been the backdrop to more than one of her fainting
flashbacks. It was the only way the memory could get in.
She'd never have consciously allowed it. For years she'd kept
it firmly in its place and refused to even look at it. But now
it was closer to the surface and here she was, standing in this
room, as good as asking for it.

She was twelve. She'd woken to the sound of her mother
screaming that night. In itself that wasn't so unusual but there
was something about the particular pitch of that scream, like
the note of a kettle when it reaches boiling point. She'd
followed the noise downstairs and along the hall to this room.
Her mother stopped screaming and rushed towards her, fell
to her knees and clung to her. Amber patted her back and
watched her father's body rotate.

The rope creaked and his body turned. His face was dark
purple and his tongue poked out, black and swollen as a
parrot's. On the floor beneath his feet, naked and curled like
claws, lay a scattered pile of books. He must have climbed
up on them then kicked them away.

Her mother had taken it hard and Amber had never
understood why. The walls were thin and she'd heard enough
over the years to make her wonder how it could be anything
other than a relief that he'd gone. She certainly didn't miss

him. She'd been surprised more than anything. She didn't think he'd ever grant them freedom like that and half-suspected a trap. She despised her mother for her fake grief, the weakness that made her perform for him even when he wasn't there to see. Perhaps in some ways they'd been made for each other after all. Bullies and victims need each other to play their parts.

She realised her hands were clenched into fists, her nails digging into her palms. She forced them open and watched the red crescent moons fade away.

She ran a finger over the spines of the bird books: *Care of Caged Birds*, *Common Bird Diseases*, *Bird Fancier* and there at the end of the lower shelf, on its side, big enough to use as a bookend, was the *Book of British Birds*. She'd replaced it after Mac had finished her wings – the wings she had claimed for herself.

The toilet flushed upstairs, starting a familiar percussion in the pipes. She'd almost forgotten Beth was in the house. There were things she needed to do instead of wasting time and energy staring into dark corners, disturbing shadows from the past. As she turned towards the door, a lump in her jacket bumped against her side. The piece of slate was still in her pocket. She took it out and laid it on the desk. Just another piece of excess baggage she had no use for. She left the room and closed the door. Nothing would weigh her down now, she promised herself.

She went upstairs to her room. Beth emerged from the bathroom and hovered uncertainly in the doorway.

'I'm going to change and pack a case,' Amber said, quickly stripping off her clothes and underwear and dumping them in a pile. She looked up and saw Beth's face had flushed bright scarlet. 'You okay? You look a bit weird.'

'No. Yes. I'm fine. I just, eh. Nothing.' Beth's eyes dipped to Amber's body then flicked away again, her gaze flapping around the room looking for something to settle on.

Amber laughed. 'Oh come on! I think you've probably seen something along these lines before. No?' She turned her back and opened her cupboard to find something to wear. 'Why don't you go downstairs and make us a cup of tea while I get ready. Yeah?'

'Sure.' Beth sounded relieved.

'Two sugars.'

'Right.'

Amber shook her head and sighed as she heard Beth bump into the door on the way out then stumble down the stairs. That girl definitely needed to get out more.

FIFTEEN

even with the walls scorched black

'Ah, shit,' Beth swore under her breath as she examined her face in the bathroom mirror. Her nose was swollen and caked with blood and some had dried like a scab on her chin. She filled the sink with warm water and gingerly washed it off. Purple shadows were spreading under her skin. There would be at least one black eye, maybe two. She pinched the bridge of her nose and gently wiggled it side to side checking for breaks. It seemed to be okay. She wasn't going to win any beauty contests but she'd live.

She ran her hands through her hair and gave her reflection a hard look. What the holy fuck did she think she was doing here? She'd risked her life for a woman she hardly knew. Judging from the evidence, a woman she didn't know at all.

In the photographs she'd seen ranged up the staircase walls, Amber had looked like butter wouldn't melt. There had been baby photos at the bottom, then a toddler in a party dress, clutching a balloon. As the stairs climbed higher, Amber grew older, progressing through school snaps with outsize teeth and squint fringes, but always with a confident smile for the camera, the smile of a girl with absolutely nothing to worry about. Beth felt like she'd been conned. How could Amber say she'd not had a chance in life? What the hell was all that then? Compared to her own childhood it looked cereal-box perfect.

*

Beth's grandparents' house had been a lower villa in a 1930s council block of four – a hulking grey pebble-dashed building quartered up between four families with a shared drying green at the back. The furniture was too big for the four small rooms and there was always, *always* something boiling on the hob. She resented the way the damp vegetable smell clung to her clothes and hair, marking her out as different from her schoolmates even by the way she smelled. Marooned a generation behind everyone else's family, she wished for her life to be different.

Like her gran used to say, *Be careful what you wish for.*

She'd been twelve when they had died in a fire she survived because she'd been staying at a friend's house that night. The report said it had started in the kitchen. Probably the chip pan. Happened all the time.

After that there wasn't much to choose between the residential homes and the occasional foster family placements. That was when she'd learned how to open windows from the outside – breaking back into the burnt-out shell of her grandparents' house. No matter where they placed her, she still preferred her old room, even with the walls scorched black and the floorboards charred where the carpet used to be. Bits of it clung in melted blue clumps around the edges of the room like the shoreline of a country to which she could never return. Her few clothes and possessions had gone but her old radio still worked, despite its warped casing. She would lie on the floor listening into the small hours.

Hiding at the far end of all the static, like a secret placed there especially for her, she found a station that played old jazz tunes that she recognised from her grandad's now-melted vinyl collection. The DJ burbled away in a language she didn't understand but it was better that way. She didn't want anyone else's thoughts in her head, only the music. Those crackly old songs didn't fix anything but they made her feel less crushed by the burden of guilt she'd taken as her due. If she'd stayed home that night . . . If she hadn't been so eager to get away before teatime . . . If only . . .

She'd gone back to the old house as often as she could until one time she'd arrived to find a building site, the house gone, and that had been that. From then on, she learned to step around feelings that were too big or too painful by tiptoeing through her own mind like it was a burnt out building, with floorboards liable to give way if she didn't tread carefully.

The floorboards in the hall creaked as someone walked by. It was time for some answers.

Amber's bedroom walls were the pale lilac of sugared almonds. The atmosphere was sweet and stale. Kids' books and cuddly toys lined the shelves, all covered in a film of dust. On the wall next to the bed, dance and gymnastics certificates were pinned up with medals and ribbons hanging from their edges and cartoon children leaping across them as if trying to escape. The only areas that looked used were the crumpled bed and the dressing table which was strewn with make-up and an overflowing ashtray.

Amber had her back to her and was taking her clothes off. She ditched them on the floor without any fuss. 'Found the bog then? You feeling better now?' She tugged her bra off and dropped it on the floor.

All the questions, all the righteous indignation Beth had felt, was instantly forgotten, the accusations dissolving before they reached her mouth. Amber had wings.

The tattoo covered her skin from the nape of her neck down to the base of her spine and spanned it from shoulder to shoulder in a spectrum of shades from pale sunrise gold to blackest ebony. The wings seemed to ripple, the feathers settling as Amber straightened up. Beth blinked hard. The impression of movement was so vivid, the correspondence between Amber's well-toned musculature and the individual feathers so precise, that they seemed a natural extension of her body. Their power was unquestionable. Beth reached a hand out to touch them but snatched it back, quickly realising the gesture would be about as advisable as patting an eagle.

Amber was not like her, not like anyone she had ever known, and could not be judged by the same criteria. Beth had no idea what had happened to change the ordinary girl in those photographs into this fantastical creature, but the transformation was total and complete. She was something else.

She turned towards Beth and laughed at her dumbstruck expression. Beth seized gratefully on the suggestion of making a cup of tea and went downstairs.

The kitchen formed an L-shape with the dining room at the back of the house. Beth found the kettle, filled it and put it on to boil.

Rummaging in the cupboards she came across a stack of cookery books. The one on the top looked like a ring binder. Its cover was lilac satin, matching the decor of Amber's bedroom and the edges were worn and grubby. She tugged it out and set it down on the worktop, ran a hand over the cover and brushed the dust off.

SIXTEEN

count down with me from ten

George was moving. Bumping along on the horizontal, without even trying. *Riding along on the crest of a wave and the sun is in the* . . . A low white ceiling peeled away to reveal the night sky. It was filled with bright specks that spun and wheeled overhead like a cloud of midges. Were they stars? Stars should definitely not be moving like that, swarming around the sky like they were alive. He closed his eyes as a wave of dizziness threatened to overwhelm him. The trolley he was lying on tilted and he felt something slip out of his hand. 'My head,' he tried to say but it came out as nothing more than a mumble, 'dropped my head.' Then the officious *whoomph* of automatic doors and everything was incredibly loud and frantic, faces leaning over him, shouting words he didn't understand. People shining lights in his eyes.

'He said something about his head.'

'Could be a concussion.'

'Or a blood clot.'

'Check for a fracture.'

'No. Outside. Dropped it,' George mumbled. His lips felt thick and rubbery and the light was hurting his eyes. There were altogether too many surfaces in this place, all of them either giving out or reflecting a bullying white light.

'He's altered.'

'Better do a tox screen and blood alcohol.'

'IV anti-biotics and prep him for theatre.'

'Get him to X-ray. Better know what we're dealing with first.'

'What's with the hairy pyjamas?'

'God knows.'

'Well it's not the weirdest I've seen.'

'Nothing surprises me anymore.'

'There was that clown with the torch up his arse.'

'Ah yes. Who could forget Chuckles?'

'Well, get them off.'

George tried to object as scissors sliced through the fabric of his costume. Cold metal slid up his arms and legs as his second skin was stripped away. He'd have to pay for that now. Cold air drenched his exposed skin. He lay shivering on the trolley, new-born, peeled and raw, pink and helpless as a freshly shelled prawn.

'ARE YOU EXPERIENCING ANY PAIN?'

George stared in horror at the shouting mouth. He couldn't tear his eyes away from the enormous white teeth glinting behind the lips that had formed the words and megaphoned them into his face. The mouth seemed to have a life of its own, a purpose it was going to fulfil, regardless of what face it called home, whatever head and body carried that face around. The mouth had its own agenda. George had the distinct impression that it would carry on, even disembodied. It was unstoppable. He closed his eyes and wished it away.

He couldn't feel his foot anymore, only a dull metallic ache in his ankle. He was being wheeled through corridors, zapped with x-rays and stuck with needles. The distances between the places where each task was performed seemed inordinately vast. Surely they could arrange for everything to be within, say, a half mile radius? Was that beyond the planning powers of modern medicine? Between each procedure he was wheeled at speed down never-ending corridors and banged through swing-doors feet first. This made him flinch involuntarily, even though he knew the trolley would take the blow, not his feet. He'd never been good at judging the relative distances between things. He hated walking across road bridges because he couldn't shake the feeling that the next high-sided lorry was going to smash right into it. He'd try to walk all slow and controlled then end up running for his life to the other side. When he was in a car or on a bus, low bridges would make him duck. It came to him then, as he crashed through yet another set of double doors that perhaps this lack of spatial judgement was what complicated his personal relationships. He always thought people were closer or further away than they actually were.

He was in a small dark room now with two doctors. An x-ray film of his foot was slapped up on a wall-mounted light box for examination. George squinted at the blurry black and white image but couldn't make head nor tail of what he was looking at. The foot, if that's what it was, didn't even look human. Great long toes like something prehistoric, and so many little bones. Were there supposed to be that many or was his foot all smashed to bits? He tried to count the toes, he could at least check they were all there, but he kept getting lost at *this little piggy had roast beef for tea* and had to start again. What had they given him? He felt perfectly lucid inside his own head but communication with the outside world was beyond him. It was like trying to operate exceptionally delicate machinery while wearing boxing gloves. He didn't know how to work his own face anymore. He decided to give up and listened to the doctors instead. They seemed to know what they were doing. They were standing close together pointing to an area on the x-ray.

'That's damn lucky.'

'Bullet passed right through between the first and second metatarsal. Must have been a small calibre handgun. Doesn't look like there's any serious damage.'

'What's the chances of that?'

'Got to be a million to one.'

'Jammy bastard.'

'We'll still need to debride that wound at least.'

'Yeah. Could still be nasty if there's anything left floating about in there. Let's just do a general then we can have a proper look and clean it out.'

'Better safe than sorry.'

'True, true.'

Another room. Bright lights overhead. More needles.

'This shouldn't take too long. Just relax. When you wake up it'll all be over. If you'll count down with me from ten.'

George counted: nine, eight, seven, seven, seven, eleven, something . . . nothing.

He was swimming underwater, his body supported in glowing blue eddies – an infinite progression of blues, from the palest duck-egg to a deep thrumming indigo, moved around him. He watched them twisting together, forming patterns and releasing, only to come around and join again to form new ones. He tried to name a few of the different shades he could see: azure, corn flower, turquoise, cobalt, cyan, sky. He ran out of names to describe the blues long before he ran out of blues to name. Naming was overrated anyway. Who needed labels? He drifted along happily, letting the colours permeate his mind in all their subtle, indefinable variety. There was music coming from somewhere, or was it just a property of the light? Or perhaps the other way around? Music. Light. Same difference. All wavelengths. Lengths of waves, bending, looping and harmonising around him and an enormous feeling of contentment as he spun and drifted along on the tide. He was singing a song to himself. Or was he the song? Again, the difference, if there was one, didn't seem to be important. Then he noticed the music was receding, getting fainter and further away, and the brilliance of the blues was starting to fade, some of the paler ones already virtually transparent. The temperature of the water had matched his own body temperature but now it felt chill. And he was no longer supported but falling, or being blown sideways, or rising up, it was hard to tell which, but whatever direction it was, his movement had changed from joyous and free-floating to a frightening acceleration.

Then he was out of the sea altogether and hovering above a huddle of people dressed in pastel greens and blues. They wore strange caps on their heads and bags over their feet. A couple of them had small white masks tied over their mouths and noses. They were gathered around a table, or bench, passing elaborate silver cutlery to each other. Perhaps they were having a meal. But there were no chairs around the table. At one end there was a bank of electronic machinery that beeped and hummed. One of the green-suited people was twiddling the buttons and looking at the dials. 'Uh oh,' a voice said, 'I think we might have a problem here.' The machinery started emitting a continuous *beeeep* that made George's ears ring. So he decided to tune it out. He was pleased to realise that this was as easily achieved as muting a television set. He wished he could return to the sea but changing the channel didn't appear to be within his power. The air here was thin and white, like a picture taken on top of a mountain. It was an aggressive light. One that wanted to take over. The little blue and green people were now very excited about something. He could see their mouths opening to shout as they rushed around fetching things. He turned the sound back on and heard voices overlapping. 'Adrenaline in . . . Shit, didn't he have a medical alert card on him? . . . BP still low.' There was a body on the table, a pale, lost looking thing with a bloody foot. Nobody moved. The whole scene had simply stopped, like someone had hit the pause button. George dropped down and hovered an inch above the body on the table. That was his own face, wasn't it? His face, his eyelids, his mouth, that mark still on his forehead. He felt a wave of tenderness towards his poor battered body – tenderness and remorse. He hadn't been taking very good care of it lately. He wanted to apologise and promise to be more careful in future but before he could say anything, the scene around him started moving again. 'Secure the airway,' somebody shouted.

With a sudden lurch, he was pulled straight down through the body on the table, which offered no resistance, and further down into the darkness beyond. Down he sank, beyond light and outside of time.

The next thing he knew, he was on an island. Of course, he couldn't be sure it was truly an island but it felt that way. Isolated, tenuous. He was lying on a soft sandy hillside held together with coarse grass listening to the languid calls of sea birds overhead. The sky was a certain, solid blue, no clouds, and there was a warm breeze blowing. He raised himself to his elbows and looked about. Below the shallow plateau on which he lay, the landscape gentled down through rugged dunes to a curving shoreline that disappeared back around the higher ground behind him. What was this place? Was he alone? He lay back and gazed up, turning these questions over with no sense of urgency. As he stared upwards, he became aware of something behind, or underneath the surface of the sky that seemed to shimmer and shift; streaks of gold through the blue. After a while he began to discern patterns and could make out individual figures swooping and gliding. Birds? No, not birds, bigger than that and with a definite human aspect. Three of these shapes now detached themselves from the larger mass and descended towards where he lay. They had the forms of women but lowered themselves slowly on wide, graceful wings that glowed and pulsated as they beat the air. He felt the force of the downdraft rifling through his hair as they alighted close to him. Were they angels? Had he died and this was some kind of heaven? Surely if it was he wouldn't feel so unsure of himself. He didn't have any fixed ideas about the afterlife but if one existed then the removal of doubt must surely be part of the package.

'Am I dead?' he said out loud, but the three figures didn't seem to be paying any attention to him. They were talking and laughing amongst themselves. He couldn't tell whether they were ignoring him or simply hadn't heard. He tried to sit up but found he couldn't even raise his head. His body felt slack, his muscles loosened. He couldn't achieve the tension necessary to move his limbs.

The three women – they looked more like women now they were on the ground – moved closer to him. They appeared to be solidifying, their bodies dark blue marbled with gold, their wings folded into a flickering heat haze at their backs. Their heads were smooth and hairless, their facial features indistinct, shifting. They seemed to have, if not identical, then strikingly similar faces: large dark eyes, full lips, high cheekbones. Or rather it seemed as though they had only one face between them and were sharing it, so none of them could have a whole face at any one time. 'Who are you?' he thought more than said.

They laughed and took turns at answering.

'Maiden, Mother, Crone.'

'Virgin, Madonna, Whore.'

'Hubble, Bubble, Trouble.'

'The Good, the Bad, the Speak For Yourself Mate.'

'The Mother.'

'The Daughter.'

'The Holy Fuck.'

Their laughter was like pealing bells as they rocked and shoved each other playfully. When they composed themselves they sat and stared at him.

'What is it?'

'It's a man.'

'Really? Are you sure? They look bigger on television.'

'Why is it so hairy? Are you sure it's not a monkey?'

'Definitely not a monkey.'

'Maybe we should give it a typewriter. See what happens.'

'What? And if it writes *Hamlet* then it's a monkey?'

'Or Shakespeare.'

'Poor thing.'

156

'But what is it *for*?'

'What do you suppose it *wants*?'

The three women frowned at him, puzzling over the questions. He wanted to talk, wanted to justify himself, prove his worth. What had he done while he was alive to warrant an afterlife where he was naked, paralysed and mocked by sarcastic angels? It wasn't fair. He wasn't a bad man. He'd never killed or beaten or raped or intentionally done anyone any harm. He tried his best to be kind. He knew he didn't always get it right but he tried, for pity's sake, he tried. Wasn't that the point? He struggled again to raise himself up but still couldn't move.

Since there seemed to be no way out of the prison of his inert flesh, George considered the second question. What did he want?

What he wanted most was an uncomplicated life. And someone to share it with so that it meant something. Otherwise, why bother? He wanted to meet an uncomplicated woman and for them to love each other. To have uncomplicated sex which might at some point result in uncomplicated children and they'd all be together in a straightforward, understandable, no bullshit sort of way. Was that really too much to ask? It wasn't that he didn't enjoy complexity in certain things. He'd just rather not have to make room for it everywhere, all the time. If that was okay. He'd even happily give up on the fucking fairy cakes if that was what it took.

He wanted to stop feeling like he should be apologising for things other men had done to other women at other times and in other places. He wasn't there. He didn't do it.

He wanted everyone to stop fighting for control, for power, for the moral high ground. He wanted to step in and shush everyone and say, 'Look. People. This plainly isn't getting us anywhere. Let's all just shut up and sit down and see if we can come up with something that works for everyone. Are we not grown up enough to do that? Do we not all want the same things in the end anyway?'

He wanted to get off this fucking island!

'Is it thinking?'

'You know, I think it might be.'

'Well, that's new.'

'Just goes to show. You *can* teach a new monkey old tricks.'

'Not a monkey.'

'Whatever.'

'We better send him back then. He's not finished.'

'Can't we keep him?'

'A man is not just for Christmas. Well, some are, but not this one and it's not Christmas anyway. No, no, back he goes.'

The figures rose to their feet and joined hands, unfurled their wings and began to rise into the air. A fierce wind lashed against George's skin, lifted him bodily off the ground and spun him up into the sky, like a scrap of paper in a whirlwind. He struggled to take a breath and the wind suddenly dropped, and he was falling back down, accelerating towards the ground. He squeezed his eyes shut, sure he'd be smashed on impact.

Instead, he landed with a violent jerk and opened his eyes. White lights and a vague chemical toilet smell. He was back in hospital.

'THOUGHT WE'D LOST YOU THERE!'

It was the mouth. George steadied his breathing and told himself this was reality. Certain rules would be observed. No one was going to start growing wings. The mouth was not going to eat him. Everything was going to be okay. He could handle this.

SEVENTEEN

have a little play at being frightened

The lilac folder looked like it might contain family recipes, snippets cut from magazines or torn off packets. A relic from Amber's family history, it obviously hadn't been touched for years. How a family ate reflected how they lived and Beth wondered what the contents would reveal about Amber's past life, about who she really was.

So much of what she remembered about her own childhood was dominated by food; her grandparents' grim reliance on mince and potatoes as an almost daily staple. The way everything was boiled into submission until it gave up all taste and texture. Mealtimes had come to symbolise everything she saw as wrong with her grey, lumpy, monotonous life.

After the fire, eating became a purely mechanical thing; food was fuel to keep her going which she barely tasted as she shovelled it in. In the care homes and with foster families, she was given a greater variety but by then she had lost interest. Food gave her no pleasure. Even now, she didn't cook for herself but ate from tins and packets and didn't give it much thought.

She knew the rest of the world had a more complex relationship with food. Over the years working in the chippy, she'd noticed a lot depended on the time of day. There was a change usually about ten o'clock at night but it varied depending on the amount people had to drink. Dinner-time customers generally took an interest and watched closely as she cooked and wrapped their food. Later at night, folk didn't much care what they were eating as long as their mouths were full. They wanted it fast and salty, wanted that weight in their bellies to anchor them. Anything to make their hunger go away.

She put the unopened folder down on the worktop and continued her search for tea bags and sugar, finding them in the last place she looked. She lifted a mug from the draining board and selected another from the cupboard. She chose an outsized one with *I'm the Biggest Mug in the World* printed on the side in fat brown letters. It came away from the shelf with a grudging crack, like a seal being broken.

She could hear Amber moving about in her room upstairs and wondered if she should take the tea up or just wait for her to come down. She looked out of the kitchen window but couldn't see much beyond her own reflection on the black glass. It was still pitch out there. The clock on the kitchen wall gave the time as a little past three thirty in the morning. It felt like it should be much later considering everything that had happened but there was the evidence. There was still a long way to go before daylight.

The fridge hummed and grumbled as she replaced the milk. She was about to put the folder back where she had found it too, not wanting to pry, but something made her hesitate. She felt over-caffeinated although she'd not yet had a sip of her tea. Something had changed. It was as if, in the last few hours, her vision had sharpened by several degrees. Her deliberately unfocussed mental picture of the world had suffered an outbreak of vivid detail. It was an uncomfortable feeling. Was it possible to be too awake? What if it was permanent? She fought down a rising sense of panic. It reminded her of the time her grandad had given her an encyclopaedia, thick as a brick, with colour illustrations. She hadn't known where to start. Every entry was interesting and important, each one demanded her attention. She'd had to limit herself to a maximum of two pages a day and put the book out of reach at night to stop herself being overwhelmed. Everything in that book, every object, place, time, person, had a story, sometimes more than one, and they all somehow fitted into and changed one other. She'd handled it by focusing only on what was in front of her and blocking everything else out. That skill had proved so useful, it became a habit, her way of dealing with everything life threw at her, good and bad.

Now, all around her, details were vivid again. Colours were brighter, edges sharper. She'd been able to control and manage the specifics of her own inner world but the details of the external world were unpredictable and dangerous. People, places, histories, all calling for her attention.

When she picked up the folder, curiosity tingled in her fingertips. She was itching to know more about the family who had once lived in this house. She opened it and started flipping through the pages.

The plastic of the inner pockets cast a bluish underwater tint over their contents. This wasn't what she had expected. Where she'd hoped to find recipes, she found letters and appointment cards. NHS logos, white letters reversed on a blue background, swam around under the plastic like shoals of fish. Prescription forms showed unpronounceable drug names unfurling like long dark strings of seaweed. The word *Radiography* caught her eye like snagging coral on the sea bed, *Oncology* a sunken hulk.

She picked up the folder and carried it in one hand, tea in the other, to the table and sat down. It seemed ridiculously light for the weight of the things it held. Someone here had been very sick. Was this what had happened to Amber's parents? Was this the reason they didn't live here anymore? That they weren't living at all?

And then there were the photographs. It was the photographs that took away the option of closing the folder, putting it back and leaving well alone. She was so absorbed that she didn't hear Amber come downstairs and into the kitchen. She didn't register her presence until her suitcase hit the floor with a loud smack.

Beth jumped in her seat and guiltily flapped the folder closed, her face burning. Amber's expression was a volatile mix of resignation and anger; impossible to predict how she was going to react. She swung the briefcase of money onto the table, dumped a handbag on top, picked her tea up off the worktop and sat down at the table opposite Beth. She wrapped her hands around the mug, raised it to her lips, took a sip and closed her eyes.

'It was with the rest of the cook books,' said Beth, flustered. 'I thought there might be recipes. I'm sorry. I didn't mean to pry.'

Amber opened her eyes and looked at the closed folder on the table. 'Yes you did,' she said gently, giving Beth a small smile to soften the accusation. She reached over and began flipping through the pages herself. 'Kind of hard to put down, isn't it?' She stopped at a photograph.

A young girl, thin and pale, her face pinched, sat propped up on a bank of pillows. A soft toy was wedged beside her in the bed but she wasn't touching it, seemed to be doing her best not to. It was a fluffy owl with dark glassy eyes and speckled plumage. Despite being a cuddly toy, it managed to look threatening, and somehow more real than the girl next to it. Beth concentrated on the girl. Mousy hair hanging in strings around her face, irritation clear in her eyes. She obviously had not wanted her picture taken. She bore a strong family resemblance to Amber. An appointment card on the next page gave the patient name as *Alice Neale*.

'Your sister?' Beth asked. The girl looked so like Amber she could almost be a twin. Beth felt a twist in her stomach. What if that was true? Losing a sister would be bad enough but the breaking of a bond that went back even before birth would be something else again. She cursed her new-found curiosity. She should drop this now, apologise again and put the folder back.

Amber didn't reply. She seemed lost in the story herself as she turned another page. Another photograph.

The same girl, asleep, surrounded by machines and hooked up to various drips. A nurse checking the fluids in a drip bag looked toward the camera with an expression of annoyance. More letters, some *Get Well Soon* cards. The breath caught in Beth's throat as Amber turned the next page to reveal an image of a pitifully bony naked back. A puckered red wound ran from the nape of the girl's neck to half way down her torso.

Amber's lip curled in apparent disgust. 'Sick bitch,' she muttered and turned another page.

Beth blinked, gulped and broke into a coughing fit as she choked back her shock. How could Amber refer to the girl that way, in that tone? Then the thought struck her. Who was taking these photographs? What kind of a sadist were they? The very existence of this voyeuristic record pointed to a kind of sickness behind the camera, possibly more alarming that the one in front of it.

More paperwork. More photographs. The girl again, even thinner, more gaunt, haunted, sitting in a huge chair that looked as if it might eat her alive, tubes running into her stick-like arms. A bald child in a pale blue gown, gradually turning into a ghost of herself. A close-up of her face. She had no eyelashes, no eyebrows, the bones of her face stood out, terrifyingly fragile. Her eyes were huge and hopeless.

Beth reached a hand out and put it over Amber's to stop her turning any more pages. How far had the photographer gone with this? She wasn't sure she could take any more. But at the same time, she wanted to know how this story ended, despite her suspicion it was not going to be happily ever after. Amber brushed her hand away and carried on.

In the next photo, the girl was still gaunt but there was more flesh on the bones of her face, her skin was less grey and she was smiling. Her hair was an impossibly thick and shiny blonde bob – a very obvious wig. But there was no doubt that this photograph showed an improvement, possibly the beginnings of a journey back to health. Beth let out a long breath.

The final photo confirmed it. The girl stood, dressed in a red jumpsuit, looking like a miniature cosmonaut with her improbable helmet of hair. Beth was disappointed to see Amber had come to the end of the folder but thankful the ending had not been as she'd feared. In this final photograph, unlike all the others, the girl was not in a hospital, but in what must be her own bedroom. Beth looked closer. She had seen that room before. Very recently.

'You?'

The word hung in the air, floating above the sound of the clock ticking and the two of them breathing. Amber gave a heavy sigh. She turned sideways in her chair, bent over and dug her fingers into the roots of her hair. There was a tearing sound like Velcro being pulled apart, or a plaster being torn from a wound. When she straightened up again, the hair stayed in her hands, golden strands spilling through her fingers like shining sand. Her head was completely bald.

'You're . . .' said Beth, stupidly. She couldn't take it in. If the girl in the photographs was Amber, then who was Alice? And if they were the same person, and she'd got better, why was she still bald? Beth stared at Amber's head. It was shocking in its hairlessness, its bony white perfection. 'You're . . .' she said again, her spinning thoughts getting in the way of sensible speech.

Amber's eyes were hard and defiant, glaring at Beth as if daring her to finish her sentence. 'Yeah. Total slap-head,' she said, finishing it for her, her voice rough. 'Like it? It's not a look that goes down too well at the club, I have to say.'

'I was going to say beautiful.' Beth said quietly. It was true. Amber was remarkable looking with hair but without, she

164

had a beauty that took the breath away. Alien and more than a little terrifying, but also magnificent.

'Yeah. Right.' Amber snorted and looked away. She ran a hand over the top of her head. 'You haven't seen the rest.' She put two fingers to the side of her eye, dragged the eyelid taut, pinched her lashes between thumb and forefinger and peeled them away. She did the same with the other eye, dropping the curled strips of lashes onto the table. She blinked and rubbed her eyelids. The few pale hairs that remained only underlined their own scarcity. She reached into her handbag, produced a pack of wipes and drew one across her face, taking eye-makeup and almost all of an eyebrow with it. Two further wipes later, an unrecognisable girl sat across the table. Beth found it hard to look at her but impossible to look away. Amber's face looked smaller and more childlike, the alien beauty more stark than before. 'Meet Alice,' she said.

'Why didn't you tell me?' Beth felt a sudden, irrational burst of anger. Did Amber think she'd be unsympathetic? Or was she just not worth telling? She knew this anger was selfish. She had no right to know anything about her. But it was hard to shake off.

'Why? Like a bit of death porn, do you?'

Amber's tone, disconcertingly paired with her changed appearance, was angry and confrontational, but Beth got the impression the anger wasn't directed at her. She just happened to be the only person around. Perhaps she wasn't handling this situation very well but, if there was a right thing to say, she didn't know what it was. She understood the tone of Amber's words but the meaning was beyond her. It was like she was speaking a foreign language. Death porn? 'What?' she said. 'What's that supposed to mean?'

Amber shrugged impatiently. 'Some people seem to get off on it, that's all.'

'But I—' Beth protested but Amber cut her off.

'It's not pity. It's worse than that. It's like they enjoy it.' Amber was glaring off to the side at a patch on the carpet

165

and spitting the words out as if she'd been keeping them in too long and they'd turned septic. 'I'm like a scary movie. Turn the lights out and have a little play at being frightened, then after a while the lights go back on and you can leave. Chuck away the rest of your popcorn and go back out into the night feeling better about yourself and your life. About the fact that you actually have one ahead of you, even if it is a bit shitty sometimes. It's entertainment.'

Beth opened her mouth again to speak, to tell Amber that whatever she was accusing her of, she was not guilty, but Amber beat her to it before she could even start.

'Like the guys at the club. All excited to be close to something raw and naked like they don't get in their normal lives. But a big part of why they're turned on in the first place, is because they can walk away, whenever they like. It's all about control.'

'Look,' Beth broke in, 'I don't know what this has to do with . . .' she tailed off, at a loss. In the silence that followed, the kitchen tap dripped water into the sink, drops that hit the stainless steel and burst into nothing.

Eventually, Amber looked up at Beth. 'Sorry. I'm sorry,' she apologised. 'I just . . . I had years of it when I was a kid. The way people looked at me. The way they talked to me. Everything.'

'But I don't understand.' Beth turned the folder around, still open at the last photograph; the happy ending. 'You got better, right?'

'Yeah. I did.' Ambers voice was flat and colourless.

'Then how come . . .' Beth looked at Amber's head.

'The hair never came back. They said it would but it didn't. The other stuff did though.'

Beth decided the time for being squeamish had long past. 'The cancer?'

'Whatever,' Amber waved a dismissive hand. 'Did you know, there are over a hundred different diseases with that name? What I had, what I *have*, is something they haven't seen before. But it's basically cells growing where they shouldn't be. Like weeds in a garden. So they call it cancer and treat it like cancer. Whether it actually *is* cancer is anybody's guess. It's just a word. What you call it doesn't make any fucking difference to anything.'

'Shouldn't you be in hospital?'

'No!' Amber shouted, as if Beth had threatened to drag her off there immediately. 'No way I'm going through that shit again. Had everything the first time around. See for yourself.' She jabbed at the bundles of hospital notes. 'The Full Bhuna. Fucking deadly. Way worse than anything the cancer ever did to me. But, yeah, I went in, couple of years back now, when I first realised something was up again, had all the tests. And they wanted to start all that bollocks again. They didn't even think it'd work. I could tell. They just didn't want to admit they couldn't do fuck all about it.'

'How bad is it? I mean, did they say . . . Are you . . .?' Saying *cancer* was one thing and Amber was right, it was just a word. And so was *dying*. Just another word. But one that Beth couldn't quite manage to bring to her lips.

'Four years maximum, they said. But they don't really know. Could be less, unlikely to be more. I reckon they're just making it up as they go along. I'll take my chances.'

Beth sat and gaped.

'Close your mouth for fucksake. That look really isn't doing you any favours.'

Beth snapped her mouth shut so fast her teeth clicked together but she still didn't know what to say.

'Just don't pity me, alright? We're all dying, y'know. Happens all the time. Only difference is I know when it's coming. Some folk might think that was an advantage. And don't start calling me Alice. I was never sorry to leave her behind.'

Beth looked at the clock on the wall. The hands had moved on to four o'clock which was plainly ludicrous. Less than half an hour had passed since she came down here to make tea.

Like the lightness of the folder, the expanse of thirty minutes, less, seemed insultingly inadequate for its contents. Physical measurements were pure nonsense in this situation. Trying to apply weight, time, density, and velocity made both the numbers and the reality of the experience look distorted and ridiculous. The length of time it took to tell a story had no bearing on the extent of the repercussions it could generate. The domino effect could go on forever.

At that thought, a forgotten piece toppled. 'What about the baby?' A wall of new questions tumbled down. Would it be healthy? What would Amber do with the kid once it was born if she wasn't well enough to look after it? And what would happen to it when she wasn't around anymore? She must have a plan. This wasn't only about her.

'There's no baby,' said Amber flatly, staring into her empty mug.

'What?' The world lurched sideways again. It seemed that just when Beth thought she was getting her head around reality, it started to move away from her again, turning and sliding into something else entirely. Things had been so much steadier when she wasn't listening to anything but the contents of her own head. She looked at Amber. Her idea of who this woman was had been through so many revisions she was having trouble keeping up. Amber could have said just about anything to her right now, announced she was from another planet, used to be a man, was working for the CIA, anything, and Beth would accept it. She put down her tea, the brown lettering curled around the mug in a brown grin. *Biggest Mug in the World.* Seemed about right.

EIGHTEEN

made the whole thing up

Amber was not sorry. She'd done what she had to do. She'd invented a new person. Blameless and innocent. A person who mattered. It had been the most effective lie she could think of at the time.

Women like her were way down on the list that ranked people's value. She knew that. Everyone, whether they were aware of it or not, had this list in their heads of who counted and who didn't. How else could anyone watch the horror shows on the news and still go about their lives, worrying about the size of their own arse? If a whore got killed, people weren't that bothered. They should know the risks. That was the way it was, the way it had always been. To be fair, she had no idea if Beth thought like that but, fuck it, the baby lie had worked, hadn't it?

She watched Beth frowning into her empty mug. 'Want another?' she asked, but got no response. She switched the kettle back on. Beth didn't say a word. Just sat there sulking. Amber banged down two full mugs, splashing tea onto the yellowed pine. 'Oh come on. What did you expect? I couldn't tell you the truth. There wasn't time, apart from anything else.'

'You didn't have to lie though. Not like that.' Beth sounded like a sullen teenager. It really was about time she grew up.

'Would you have helped if it'd been only for me?' She waited and watched Beth's frown deepen. She counted to ten,

169

slowly. Still no response. 'I'll answer that for you then. No, you wouldn't. The baby was someone you could give a shit about.'

Beth looked hurt. 'You really think I'd care more about your baby than I would about you?'

'Wouldn't you?'

Beth hesitated.

Amber didn't blame her personally. It wasn't really her fault. Like everyone else, this shit was wired into the brain early on and it was hard to break away from the unwritten rules. Kept everybody in their places. 'See?' she said.

'I was still thinking!' Beth protested.

'The fact it takes you that long, pretty much proves my point. Don't you think?'

'No. I don't. All it proves is I'm a slow thinker.'

Amber decided to let it go. What did she want from the girl anyway? 'Look, for what it's worth, I'm sorry I lied to you. Okay?' Amber lied. She wasn't sorry and she'd do the same again. Just had. She wasn't sure she could stop if she wanted to. She was so used to dealing out fantasy versions of herself that she couldn't get her head round the idea of anyone preferring the truth. It struck her as weird. 'I reckoned you'd walk away no matter what I said, so I went with the first thing I could think of. Maybe that wasn't fair.' It really wasn't, but anyone with half a brain knew that fair was for fairy tales.

'Definitely not fair,' said Beth. She was blinking back tears like a kid who'd just been told there was no Santa.

Amber felt like slapping her, telling her to grow up and stop being so naïve. She was leaving herself wide open to all sorts of exploitation. People would take advantage. Nasty, ruthless, self-serving people; people like her. Beth looked like she was trying to stare right through the table. Or maybe she was just trying to avoid looking at her bald head.

Whatever. It was time to get her shit together. She flung open her suitcase and pulled out her makeup box. She'd better put her face back on before she left. She could do without the pitying stares of strangers on the plane. She opened the box and assessed her reflection in the mirror built into the lid. She looked like a potato with teeth.

'Fucking hell. Right. If you want the whole story, I'll tell you as much as I can while I'm doing this.' Getting her face back on would take about fifteen minutes. That should be enough time to cover the highlights.

Beth nodded. 'Yeah. That'd be good.'

This would be the first time Amber had talked honestly about herself. Her life. Different people knew different parts, but no one had all the pieces. She suddenly felt more exposed, more naked, than she ever had on stage. She doubted she'd be making a habit of this truth business.

She could almost remember how it had felt to be twelve years old – still a kid but changing, biology taking over. She'd been really into her gymnastics and dancing. Used them as an escape from all the crap that went on at home. When she focused on achieving a particular position or sequence of moves, she existed purely within her body. No thoughts or emotions cluttering up her mind; only the working of muscle and bone. It was a good feeling.

When puberty kicked in, she felt she'd been press-ganged into something she never signed up for. Periods and tits were no real use, and just got in the way of what she wanted to do. *Becoming a woman*, as her mother put it, was nothing more than a collection of unpleasant symptoms. So, when the tingling sensations in her hands began and back pain stopped her getting comfortable at night, she assumed they were more side-effects of being female and did her best to ignore them. This must be what being a woman was about, she reasoned. You didn't get to choose any more. Your body took over and you had to do whatever it told you. It was her gym teacher who noticed that her balance was off and started asking questions, even suggesting she see a doctor.

Because she was still legally a child, she wasn't consulted when medical decisions had to be made. It was her mother who got to do the thinking for her.

'I would advise treating this aggressively,' the doctor said. Her mother smiled and nodded as if she knew what he meant. 'We'll hit it with everything we've got. Surgery first, then chemo, then a good dose of radiotherapy to finish it off and we'll take it from there. We've got plenty of heavy duty weapons on our side and I say we use them all, Mrs Neale. We are fighting in the dark but at least we are fighting.' The pompous dickhead actually punched his fist in the air as he finished speaking.

Mum had loved it. She was so busy trying to flirt with the doctor, so wrapped up in her fantasy of herself as the brave but vulnerable mother of a desperately ill child that Amber hardly came into it. And that doctor. The hero who would save the day or be there in his shining white coat to comfort the poor bereaved mother if they lost the battle. Of course he wasn't interested in her mother but he enjoyed playing the part she'd written for him.

Amber had no choice but to accept her new role as the Plucky Fighter. It taught her something though. The best way to go elsewhere in her head was to put on a show. If she presented an interesting enough version of herself to look at, people would leave the real her alone. The gap between what was inside and what you showed other people could be light years across, but people would accept what they wanted to see.

After the operation came the chemo. That took away all her remaining energy but she no longer cared. She'd been so weak that she could hardly clear her throat to avoid choking on her own puke and was sleeping all the time without ever feeling rested. She felt toxic; all those chemicals turning her blood into a polluted river. She tried to picture them as a friendly army only attacking the bad cells but they made her feel so staggeringly shit it was hard to think well of them. At other times, she almost felt sorry for the cancer. It just wanted to live, to survive, in the only way it knew how. It didn't know it was killing her, because what would it do when she was dead? It would have to die too. It was writing its own death warrant. Cancer, when she thought about it that way, was a really fucking stupid disease.

The line between asleep and awake became blurred and then no longer mattered. Most of the time she didn't have the energy to open her eyes. Breathing the shallow pockets of hospital air was an effort.

One day, after a chemo session, she'd been left propped up in the chair, a couple of pillows tucked behind her and a blanket over her knees. The tubes and bottles had been disconnected and wheeled away. Pretty soon they would need the chair for someone else but she had been left for now. Maybe they thought she was deaf as well as ill, or asleep, or they didn't care whether she heard or not.

'I think we should consider harvesting some of Alice's eggs, just as a precautionary measure. There can be problems with fertility in later life. The risk is small, but it *is* there. It's a simple procedure. Then, when the time comes for Alice to start a family, if she has difficulties, she'll have options.'

'You can keep them frozen for that long?' Her mother's voice was full of admiration, as if the doctor would be personally freezing them with his super-human powers, instead of putting them in the freezer.

'Virtually indefinitely.' The doctor was happy to prolong the illusion of this being down to his own prowess.

There was a pause. 'What if she never wants them?' Amber was surprised to hear her mother ask any questions at all, let alone one that actually mattered.

'Then they would be destroyed. Of course.' The way his voice dipped made Amber doubt he was telling the truth.

'She's been through so much already.' Amber could almost hear her mother wringing her hands.

'It's keyhole surgery. We can do it under local anaesthetic.

She won't feel a thing.' The doctor was so smooth and authoritative. Amber knew her mother would consent to virtually anything on her behalf. So this would happen; her eggs would be put on ice. In her half-conscious mind she imagined rows of gently pulsating spheres, stacked in cold storage; silent planets, dreaming of creation.

The nasal whine of her mother's voice interrupted her thoughts. 'You've been so good to us. I don't know how I would have coped without your support.'

'I'm sure your husband . . .' The doctor trailed off, sensing this was getting too personal.

She blew her nose and sniffed. 'Talks more to his birds than to me.'

'Your husband keeps birds?' The doctor's indulgent tone had evaporated.

'Whole shed full of them. Why?'

'Birds can carry infections. Usually no risk to a healthy individual but it's possible they could pose a problem for Alice, with her compromised immune system.'

'I'll tell him. He'll have to do something. Get someone else to take them. Or sell them. He won't be pleased.'

'Better safe than sorry.'

'Of course. Of course. You're right. Of course you're right.' Her mother's words became a chant.

His birds, Amber remembered thinking. It'll kill him to get rid of his birds. It wasn't a choice between safe or sorry. They were the same thing.

After the chemo came the radiotherapy. Her first tattoos: small dots and crosses inked on her back to line her up the right way when she went for treatment. Weeks of it, going back and forth from home to the hospital. It was around this time she lost what was left of her hair. 'Don't worry. It'll grow back,' the doctor said.

They let her off school. At first some classmates visited. They brought her the latest gossip and some homework and

174

talked too much while surreptitiously checking the time. They stopped coming after the first few weeks. Although she missed the chat, it was a relief to not have to witness their discomfort anymore.

After her dad was gone, her mum relied even more on the doctor. Now she was a single mother, her grace-under-fire persona had reached a new peak. The story of Alice in Cancerland was going along nicely – until she ruined the poignant ending by failing to die.

Funny how that pissed people off. When she eventually returned to school, the other kids seemed to think she'd made the whole thing up. People weren't supposed to get better from cancer. She knew this was rubbish. More people recovered than not. Far more. But that wasn't the story people had in their heads. Cancer victims were supposed to stay victims. They certainly shouldn't be wolfing down school dinners and going to gymnastics. Over the course of her last years at school, she became socially untouchable. Nothing she could say or do changed the situation. She skived off most of the time, didn't show up for her exams and left as soon as she could.

She paused to rummage in her makeup box for a tube of eyelash glue. She'd decided not to go into the specifics about her father, saying only that he left, which was true, in a way. His method was his own business.

Her face was mostly back on. Just the falsies and lippy to go. She glanced at Beth. The girl was staring at her intently, as if testing every word that came out of her mouth for its truth. 'You bored with all this yet?'

'No. Not at all. I'm just wondering how it joins up to now,' said Beth. 'Tonight.'

Amber leaned forwards and squeezed a thin line of white glue onto the inner edges of the lashes she'd peeled off earlier. They'd take a minute to get tacky before she could put them on. Might as well bring things up to date.

*

There wasn't much point going into the missing decade since the only remarkable thing about it was its lack of direction. The story restarted about two years ago. She'd put the tiredness down to too many late nights until the tingling started again. It was vague at first, a faint fizzing in her fingertips but within weeks it was sparking across her shoulders, sending forks of electricity down her arms. Sometimes there'd be nothing for weeks, then it started up again. Eventually she went back to the hospital, if only to find out if her symptoms were just in her head. She'd been hoping they were. Not that she wanted to be a nutter, but at least that wasn't technically fatal.

They hadn't been too impressed with her tattoo. 'Had a bit of work done there? Well, your choice I suppose.' The doctor put the scans up on the wall and pointed to the white masses, two of them this time, elongated on either side of her upper spine, between her shoulder blades. Growing out from these shapes, fine white lines tangled around her vertebrae and radiated outwards, tracing across her shoulders and down her back like fine lace.

There were tests. She even went back for the results. The doctor who'd been her mother's favourite had moved on. Now she was a teaching case, a curiosity examined by an audience of doctors and students.

'We've never seen anything quite like this,' the most senior medic spoke to his juniors, not to her. He had a nest of wiry white hair he probably reckoned made him look brilliant but eccentric. 'The cell division isn't following any pattern we can predict. It seems to be completely random. We could do nothing and perhaps she'd be healthy for years. Or, the cells could start dividing at an accelerated rate again, push their way through the spinal column causing complete paralysis before we could do anything to prevent it. Or,' he seemed excited by the possibilities, 'they could work their way into the brain and kill her within days. We can't give any guarantees either way.' He turned towards her and paused for effect. 'You're a one off,' he said, as if congratulating her.

They talked amongst themselves, the students coming up with theories and Einstein shooting them down. Eventually she spoke over all of them. 'So, I've got pretty much the same chances as anyone else then?'

They all turned to look at her as if they'd forgotten she was in the room. 'Well, no.' Einstein seemed to have decided she was six years old. 'Not everyone has unidentified tumours growing between their shoulder blades. Even at the slowest predicted rate of growth, we think you're looking at no more than four years. Which is considerably below normal life expectancy for someone of your age. However, if we begin treatment straight away—'

'But stuff can always happen,' she interrupted. 'I mean, you could be run over by a bus, or attacked, or have an accident. Anything. You can't give anyone guarantees.'

'That's hardly the point.'

'I think it is. Look, I know you probably mean well, but I've been through all this before. And I can guarantee that if this thing doesn't kill me first, then the treatment will. I'm not a kid anymore. This time it's up to me. And I say no. Thanks but no thanks. I'll take my chances.'

She wasn't kidding herself she was going to be okay. Her symptoms wouldn't allow her to play make-believe to that extent. Her diagnosis clarified one thing though. If she had limited time left then she wanted to use it to see as much of the world as she could before it was too late. There was no way she was going to spend that time staring at a hospital wall, waiting for the inevitable. She didn't know why she hadn't gone travelling earlier, why she'd wasted so many years kicking around doing nothing much. It was only when she was shown the bars that she realised she was in a cage. She'd constructed it herself out of habit and laziness but she didn't have to stay in it. She could simply open the door.

Getting hold of the money was the big problem. She didn't

have any, neither did her family. She had no credit history, no rich friends, no bank would lend her as much as she'd need, she had no job and no qualifications. So, she'd packed a bag the same day and moved back to her mum's house and started living like a nun. Well, nun-like in the sense of working hard and not drinking and socialising, not so much in the dancing naked and screwing for money.

'But you get the general idea,' Amber said, reaching for her wig. She pulled it on and tugged at the edges to get it straight. It would take too long fix it on properly but she didn't want the fucking thing lifting off on its own so shoved a strip of super-tape under the hairline at the top and pressed down. 'So when the chance came along tonight for a short cut . . .' The sentence didn't need finishing. Beth was nodding. It looked like she understood.

'Where will you go?'

'Everywhere! As many places as I can manage. The list in my head keeps getting longer. Been twice round the alphabet already. I just need to get started.' She stood up and closed her makeup box. 'Speaking of which – time I got to the airport. Are you giving me a lift or should I call a taxi?'

'Of course I'll take you,' said Beth.

Amber grinned and gave Beth a hug. She wasn't the hugging type but she wasn't the spilling her life story type either, so this was all new territory. Beth looked startled but smiled back.

'Okay, I've just got to make one call,' said Amber. It was a pain not having a mobile but dumping that had been part of her economy drive. She walked into the sitting room, realising it was the last time she would be in there.

Dried flowers mouldered in bowls, china figurines stooped under the weight of the years, framed pictures stood on the mantelpiece. Always her mother wanted the pictures – evidence of a family life that had never really existed outside of her own head. Their wedding photograph, her in a cheap frilly dress, him in a dark suit that would have done for a funeral, his face pressed stiff even then. One taken a couple of years before he died, the two of them sitting on a picnic blanket looking older, her smiling as if her life depended on it, and it probably had. Him watching her. One of her mum and Amber together, her mum with her arm clamped around Amber's shoulders, wearing that brave, stoic expression she'd perfected, Amber wearing that terrible first wig, not looking at the camera.

She was halfway through punching the number into the phone when Beth walked across the room and grabbed the wig picture off the shelf. She was holding it with two hands and they were both shaking. The colour drained from her face, leaving her even paler than ever. 'What's up with you?' Amber asked, but Beth was leaving the room, still clutching the silver-framed photo. The front door banged shut.

She'd left. Just turned around and left. That girl was seriously weird sometimes. Looked like she'd be getting a taxi after all. 'Bye then!' she shouted to the empty hallway.

NINETEEN

a shower of sparks before the darkness

Beth wasn't leaving. Instead she walked around the side of
the house and up the narrow weed-strewn driveway. She
needed to get a look at that car she'd noticed abandoned
there when she arrived. She squeezed between the wall and
the dirty wing of the car. It looked as if it hadn't moved in
years. Dust clung to the windows.

She stood at the front of the car and stared. There was
a rushing noise in her ears. She couldn't tell whether it was
the sound of her own blood or the wind in the trees. She
put her hands over her ears, sank down to her knees on the
cracked stone slabs and closed her eyes. Opened them again.
The car was still there. The bonnet was buckled into a
twisted grimace, familiar as a recurring nightmare. 'Look,'
she heard a voice say. It had the second-hand, fading quality
of an echo. She'd heard it before. Same voice. Same word.
It came again, gliding in from memory, out of her own
mouth and back in through her ears. A Mobius strip of
memory and repetition. 'Look.'

It was the same car. No doubt about it. Those shattered
headlights, the sockets now rusty, were the same ones that
had caught her and Danny, Al and Craig in their cold white
light. That red car. This red car.

She forced down the churning nausea in her stomach and
looked down at the framed photograph she still held in her
hand. It was impossible to deny the truth that the image

presented – that the dark-haired woman with her arm around Amber was Helen. Helen was Amber's mother. Not hers. Her face was younger but Beth could see the faint beginnings of those familiar lines at the side of her mouth. The hair was shorter but it curled the same way. The only shred of doubt came from the eyes. Her eyes were wrong, as if they'd been photo-shopped from a picture of someone else. These eyes held no trace of the warmth, humour and kindness of the Helen she knew. Reality gave her another shove; she didn't know Helen and never had. *These* were the woman's real eyes and this was the truth.

She stood up, dazed and unsteady. The wind whipped through the trees in the back garden, shaking branches over the night sky, black shapes against darkness. The shoulder of her jacket scraped against the wall of the house as she tried to avoid touching the car on her way back to the front door.

In the hall, she could hear Amber's voice coming from the sitting room, slowly dictating the house address.

'You got that? Yeah, a seventeen will take you to the main road. You can walk from there. No, I'm fine. Really. Don't worry about it. It's yours for as long as you need it. Plenty room for the kids. Keys are in the gnome's head. Yeah. Ugly little fucker by the front door. You can't miss him. Okay. Take care. Bye, Fran.'

There was the sound of the phone being put down. Amber emerged from the sitting room and brushed past her. 'Well, someone may as well use it,' she shrugged and carried on back into the kitchen.

Beth followed, a scrum of questions fighting each other for first place behind her teeth. She already knew the answers but didn't want to accept them. Surely there must be some other explanation.

Amber got down on the floor and crammed her makeup box back into her suitcase. She looked up. 'So anyway. You're back. I thought you'd buggered off there. What's up?'

Beth held out the picture. 'Is this your mother?'

181

'Yeah. That's her, with me and Wiggy the Wig. Long time ago. Why?'

'And that car. The car at the side of the house? Did that belong to her?'

'Yeah. It's a wreck. I'd get rid of it, but it'd cost me money to get it taken it away. What of it?'

Beth swallowed hard. 'What was her name?'

'My mum? Helen. Hell's bells, hell's teeth, hell in a hand-cart. What's all this about?'

Beth sank into a chair at the table and put her head in her hands. She pressed her fingertips to her skull. It felt solid enough but the barrier between her imagination and reality was under threat. Cracks had developed and soon the whole thing might give way. But she had to be sure. There was still a tiny chance that this wasn't what it appeared to be. 'What happened to her?'

Amber wasn't looking at her. She was bouncing on her suitcase, reaching between her knees to press the lock into place. 'Did I not tell you?'

'No.'

'Christ, I thought I'd told you bloody everything. Well, short story really. She didn't like my choices when I came home. We had a huge fight. She stormed off. Never came back. End of.'

'She was driving that car when she left?'

Amber got to her feet and pulled her suitcase upright. 'Yes. Look, is all this leading somewhere? Because if it's all the same to you, I kind of need to be going.'

'Was she involved in an accident?'

'What's the point of all this?' Amber sounded exasperated. 'Yes! Okay? Yes, she was in a crash. A bad one, as it happens. But, you know what? I don't give a flying monkey's! Can we go now?' She picked up her suitcase in one hand and slung her handbag across her body before gripping the briefcase with the money in the other hand.

Beth was too stunned to do anything other than follow her.

182

Outside, Amber locked the door and put the keys back inside the gnome's head. Beth felt sorry for him, other people's stuff rattling around between his ears like that.

The chip van took a while to start but eventually she got it going. They trundled out of suburbia and back onto the main streets, skirting around the fringes of town in the direction of the airport. It was odd, Beth thought, that the police hadn't caught up with them by now. The chip van wasn't hard to spot. Perhaps they'd been forgotten in all the excitement of capturing Murdoch. As long as she got Amber to the airport, she didn't much care what happened afterwards. Right now, the past was occupying her mind so completely there wasn't much space left for wondering about the future.

'I really appreciate this,' said Amber. 'The lift, I mean.' She hesitated. 'You going to tell me what was going on with all that stuff about my mum?'

She didn't have a choice. She'd have to tell Amber everything. It would be wrong not to, especially after Amber had told her so much about herself. Despite the pregnancy lie, there was now a bond of truth between them that she had to honour. Maybe since Amber obviously didn't have a great relationship with her mother, she wouldn't want to kill her when the truth came out. But Helen was still her mother. And Beth was responsible for her being in a coma. Whatever the consequences, she'd better get it over with. 'You're not going to believe this,' she said. 'I don't think I believe it myself.'

She filled Amber in on her side of that Saturday night: the band, the van, Danny, the crash, waking up in hospital. The other survivor.

'Shit,' said Amber. 'That sucks. No wonder you're so miserable.'

Beth couldn't believe she was missing the point so completely. 'But the woman in the other car. It was Helen. Your mum. Did you get that part?'

'Yeah. I got it. Small world isn't it?'

183

Amber was acting as if Helen was some mutual acquaintance and they were discussing a story that was already third or fourth hand. Beth glanced over to the passenger seat and saw Amber had stuck a cigarette in the corner of her mouth and was searching her pockets for a lighter, as if none of this mattered. It made Beth angry on Helen's behalf. 'Are you not even bothered? Even if she wasn't perfect, she was still your mother.'

Amber shrugged, put a flame to her cigarette and drew, held her breath until she'd rolled down the window a couple of inches then released a stream of smoke through the gap into the night. 'Not all mothers are the same, you know. They're not all saints. Some of them are really shit at it.' She took another drag and brushed some stray ash from her jeans.

'Still,' said Beth quietly, 'at least you had one.' Amber ignored her and opened the window a little further. In the darkness at the edge of their headlights, clusters of houses slept on. Beth knew she'd have to tell Amber the rest. Despite the cold air slicing in from the open window, there didn't seem to be enough oxygen in the van. 'There's more,' she said. 'This is going to sound a bit nuts.'

Amber seemed to perk up at the idea. 'Go for it. Seriously. I'm not easily surprised.'

This was the hard stuff. Beth kept her eyes on the road, the black ribbon of tarmac unrolling underneath them, as she unwound the rest of the story about Helen: how she'd started to feel about her, how she was still visiting, had even been at the hospital the previous day. Saying it all out loud made it sound so much more deranged than it had felt. When she'd been in that little world with Helen it had all made perfect sense. Their relationship hadn't seemed wrong, it had felt right and natural. Now, laying it out cold, trying to explain how it happened that way, it looked very different. Amber must think she was a complete head case.

Amber let out a low whistle. 'Aw man. Now that is fucked up.'

'I know.'

'What happened to your own folks?'

She told Amber what her grandmother had told her: that her parents had been involved in a car crash, her father killed instantly, her mother in a coma for eight months. If she'd known she was pregnant before the accident, she'd never told anyone, never visited the family doctor. Her body, even in her coma, continued to do its job through the physical changes of pregnancy right up to going into labour at the right time, although the birth itself had been caesarean. Not only had Beth never known her parents, it was entirely possible that neither of them had ever known she existed.

Amber was silent but for the dry hiss of her cigarette. She flicked the butt out of the gap and rolled up the window.

Beth saw the red tip bounce and flare in the rear-view mirror, briefly sending up a shower of sparks before the darkness swallowed it up. 'You must think I'm insane,' she said.

'Totally barking,' said Amber. 'But also not. Considering all the shit you've had to deal with. If you were normal, then you'd be completely crazy.'

'Really?' Beth was absurdly touched. Not only was she excused her mistakes and madness but she was understood.

'Yeah. Really. Shame you picked my mum though. She was totally crap at the mothering stuff. Well, sometimes she cooked, that was okay, but most of the time she was worse than useless. She could never face up to reality. It's just like her to dodge getting prosecuted by going into a coma.' Amber sat up in her seat and looked around. 'You do realise we're going about no miles an hour, don't you?'

Beth took her foot off the accelerator and pushed it down again, all the way to the floor, but nothing happened. They continued to slow down. She checked the petrol gauge. The needle was to the left of the big red E for empty. Slowly they rolled to a complete stop. 'Out of petrol,' she said. 'We'll have to push. I think there's a twenty-four hour place about a mile from here.'

Amber glared at her, threw her door open and jumped out. 'You are definitely cursed. You know that? You're the unluckiest person I've ever met, including me. You're like a shit-magnet for all the crap in the universe, you are.'

'Yeah, thanks,' said Beth, getting out of the van and starting to push with one hand while leaning inside and steering with the other.

Amber marched towards the back of the van. 'Don't mention it!' she shouted. 'Fucking jinx!'

'You know,' Beth called back over her shoulder, 'you're not exactly lucky white heather yourself.'

'Oh, just shut your face and push,' said Amber, and the van started rolling forwards.

They covered the mile quickly. It was mostly level ground so it was only a question of putting their backs into it and maintaining an even pace. As they rolled into the petrol station, Beth hopped into the cab, steered up to one of the pumps and pulled the handbrake. Amber leaned against the side of the van as Beth filled it with petrol.

'What would she be getting prosecuted for?' Beth asked. She'd been wondering about this while they pushed the van but hadn't had the breath to start a conversation.

'Who?' Amber pulled her pack of cigarettes out of her pocket and was about to take one out, then seemed to realise where she was and put the pack away again. 'What?'

'Your mum. Helen. You said she was dodging prosecution. Prosecution for what?'

Amber counted on her fingers. 'Driving while under the influence. Dangerous driving. Causing death by—'

'Wait a minute,' Beth cut in. 'Are you saying you think Helen was responsible for the crash?'

Amber looked at her as if she suspected she had finally lost her last marble. 'You must know.'

Beth remembered there had been letters and a few calls from the police but she'd never returned the calls and had thrown anything official straight in the bin. It had all seemed so pointless. Everyone was dead. Passing bits of paper about wouldn't change that. Especially, talking about what the van was worth had seemed about the smallest and nastiest idea anyone could come up with. She'd wanted nothing to do with any of it.

There was a clunking noise and petrol splashed back onto her hand. She replaced the nozzle and dug in her pocket for money but Amber was already at the teller's window pushing notes under the glass and shouting, 'Keep the change!' When she came back she jumped straight into the van and gestured for Beth to hurry up. She got in and started it up and they were underway again. Beth watched the white line with a growing sense of unease.

'Mother dearest,' said Amber, matter-of-fact, 'was apparently pissed out of her tiny little mind and on the wrong side of the road. The insurance company settled the claim.'

'I never made a claim.' Nothing could have mattered less. History was coming apart before her eyes. What she'd thought was real, all the stories she'd been telling herself, were unravelling on the floor. Not one shred of it was true. All this time, she'd known absolutely nothing.

'Well somebody did,' said Amber. 'Who owned the van?'

'Cameron's name would have been on the papers, I guess.' Beth remembered the way Cameron had seemed hollow and shrunken when she'd seen him in the hospital. Perhaps he'd been looking for something to do, something to organise, had taken up the paperwork to keep himself from falling apart. That would be like him. Exactly the sort of thing he would do.

The white line in the middle of the road curved and pulled her forward. In her imagination, she was back in the cab of the van with the band, everything bathed in white light, Al shouting for the phone, Danny madly scrambling for the joint, steering with his knees, the strains of *Ride of the Valkyries*. Of course she had thought it was his fault. It was so obviously his fault. But now she slowed it all down. She saw those seconds with a hyper-awareness she hadn't had access to before. The van had wobbled slightly but stayed on the left side of the road. Danny still had one hand on the wheel. In the distance, headlights were coming closer and *they* were weaving erratically, not the van. The van was steady. There was the flash of a red wing and the oncoming car veered across the white line, directly into their path. In the millisecond before impact, she saw Helen's face, mascara in black stripes down both her cheeks, eyes first unfocussed, then flying wide open. Too late.

'Hello? Green light. That means you can go.' Amber's voice brought her back to the present where the van was waiting at a set of lights. She couldn't remember stopping for them. The van coughed and backfired as she put it into gear and pulled away. She didn't know whether to laugh or cry so she did neither. She looked for the signs and she drove.

After a while Amber said, 'This isn't the way to the airport.'

'No, it's not. There's someone I need to say goodbye to first.'

'But *you're* not going anywhere.'

'Exactly.' Amber was right. She was going nowhere and had been going there for a long time. And the whole journey had been for nothing. She felt a sudden fierce clarity, as if the top of her head had lifted right off and the air was getting in for the first time in years. It was time to stop playing make-believe. She needed to make an end to all the stories, all the lies. To say goodbye.

'Look, I don't have time for your weirdness right now. If you're not going to the airport, just let me out and I'll get a cab.' Amber slung her handbag over her shoulder and started reaching behind her seat for her suitcase.

'It's five in the morning on the outer ring road. There are no taxis. Anyway, you need to see her as well.'

'See who for Christ's sake?'

Beth made a sharp left at a red sign showing a single capital H. H for hospital. H for Helen.

Amber dropped the suitcase and threw herself back in her seat in obvious disgust. 'Oh you can just fuck right off.'

TWENTY

everything that happens around you is significant

George's left foot hurt. It felt as though some practical joker surgeon had relocated his heart there for a laugh while he was unconscious. It was beating relentlessly. He wondered how long he'd been sleeping. The Mouth had explained what had happened to him. He'd had a severe allergic reaction to the anaesthetic and his blood pressure had crashed while he was on the table. His vocal chords and tongue had swollen up which was why he felt like he had half a pound of cold pastrami in his mouth. And he'd broken out in red blotches all over his body. They weren't itchy anymore but his skin was tight and hot as if he'd been lying in the sun for too long. But despite all of that, he'd be fine, apparently.

Once he'd got to grips with reality after those bizarre dreams, he'd looked properly at the owner of The Mouth. He was a tanned young doctor with sun-bleached blonde hair and a smile that belonged in Hollywood where it wouldn't scare people so much. He looked vaguely familiar. As George probed his memory, the theme music from Jaws started up, the deep two-note bass-line circling ominously at the back of his mind. He decided to ignore it for now.

Cautiously, he opened one eye and looked around. He was in a small room with one other bed which was empty. The windows were dark. So it was still night. He couldn't have been out that long. Or, he considered, it could be the next night, or even the next. Or maybe weeks or years later. How would he know? He opened the other eye. It was very quiet. He listened for noises from the corridor but heard only the quiet sighing of empty air. What if there had been a disaster or a plague, and he was like that guy waking up in the *Day of the Triffids*? Or that Woody Allen film when he gets defrosted in the future and they give him a whisky and a cigar. That would definitely be preferable to the killer vegetable scenario. George lay back on the pillows and played with the idea that he could have done a Rip Van Winkle. George Van Winkle, at your service. It had a certain ring to it. It was a name a person could have monogrammed on stuff; expensive leather stuff, like attaché cases, whatever they were. He thought of the briefcase he'd seen Beth's friend carrying and wondered what was in it. Considering the way events had unfolded, he made a guess that it wasn't a packed lunch and a newspaper.

A newspaper. That was what he needed. Something with a date to prove what day it was. He sat up again, too quick for his feeble blood pressure and felt his head emptying like a bucket with a hole in the bottom. He lay back for a minute before trying again.

As he slowly achieved the vertical, the throbbing in his foot became worse. The curtains were open and night had turned the windows into black mirrors. He saw his reflection in the glass, sitting on the edge of the bed. His pale body was draped in one of those humiliating green hankies with string, specifically designed to make a person feel as vulnerable and helpless as possible. It was certainly doing its job on him. He felt cool air going down his back to the top of his bum where the gown gaped open. He pushed a lump of tangled hair out of his eyes and felt a tenderness on his forehead. The mark! Of course, if that was still there then he couldn't have slept half his life away. That was something.

*

'Hello?' he called. His voice didn't sound like his. It was thick and distorted. He sounded like Quasimodo. 'Esmeralda! The bells!' he tried. Yep, he decided, he was a shoe-in for the part. He had it all: the facial deformities, the limp, the voice. Bloody perfect. He glowered at his reflection then eased himself back into as comfortable a position as he could manage, sitting up in the bed with his foot propped up on a pillow.

The sound of a trolley rattled and bumped along the corridor outside his room, its attendant whistling the first bars of *Strangers In The Night* then pausing and starting at the beginning again. Either the bloke couldn't remember what came next, or he had a special liking for those opening bars. As the refrain faded into the distance, the silence returned, and he wondered if he had imagined the whistling attendant. Then he heard voices coming closer. The world had been turned back on; it had a sound track. Deafness was George's greatest fear. Blindness, he reckoned, there were ways around. But deafness would be a wall that utterly cut a person off from the rest of the world. Without sound, everything was just pictures, stuff to look at. And looking wasn't really living.

The voices had stopped in the corridor, not far from the doorway to his room. A man and a woman.

'He'll be fine,' said the man. George recognised the voice as belonging to the doctor with the Hollywood smile. 'Gave us a scare on the table. Had a bit of a reaction to the anaesthetic. But we brought him back, safe and sound.' His voice changed from self-congratulatory to concerned. 'You sure you want to see him?'

'I can't just ignore him.' The woman sounded exasperated.

'Well, if you're sure. Just take it easy on him. He's had a pretty rough time.'

'Don't worry. I'll be gentle.'

'Okay then.' A pause, another change of tone, back to bright and breezy. 'Are we still on for lunch? You've got my parents' address?'

192

'Looked it up on Google Earth. It's hard to miss. You never told me they lived in a castle.'

'Oh, hardly. Now, remember to bring flowers. Something nice. You want to make a good impression.'

'I'll pick up a bunch from the garage on my way over.'

There was a longish silence before the man spoke again. 'You *are* joking, aren't you?' He sounded worried.

The woman laughed without much humour. 'God, Max, you're such an arse sometimes. Of course I'm joking. I'll be there for twelve. See you then.'

There was an exaggerated *mwah* sound and one set of footsteps retreated into the distance. A woman in blue medical scrubs entered the room.

'George?' she said. 'What the fuck have you done?'

He hadn't seen her in a long time but there was no mistaking her. She looked older, her skin had lost its glow and the eyes that had once made him think of the wild North Sea now looked like stone. She had hardened. It made his heart ache to see her so changed. At least he knew that it was still in the right place, because now it hurt far worse than his foot.

'Hi, Zoe. It's good to see you too.'

Zoe stood at the side of the bed. She frowned at him. 'So it is you. Your voice sounds weird but it's definitely you. When I saw your name on the intake board as *Admitted with a gunshot wound*, I honestly didn't think it could be you. I assumed it must be some other idiot with the same name. No way my George would be involved in anything that could get him shot. I mean, he might not be the brightest bulb in the box but he's not that stupid. But it appears I was wrong. You are that stupid. I obviously underestimated you.' She stood looking down at him with her arms folded.

'Your George?' Zoe had used the same bad tempered, belittling tone he remembered so well but in the middle of her tirade, she'd definitely used the words *my George*. Did she still think about him that way? That he still belonged to her, that he was still hers?

Zoe gave an impatient shake of the head. 'I didn't mean . . . You know what I mean!'

George smiled. *Her* George, he thought, and felt a small, warm glow. It was tiny and fragile but alive, and capable of so much, if given the chance. Zoe was probably just tired. Despite her manner and her dulled appearance she could still be lovely. Somewhere underneath it all, the girl he fell in love with so many years ago might still be in there, struggling to get out.

'I meant *mine* as in somebody I used to know.'

'Oh. Right.' So much for that theory. The little light blinked out as quickly as it had appeared. George wondered, again, if they ever had truly known each other. He still felt like the same person he'd been in school; a bit tubbier and hairier but essentially the same. Maybe that was his failing. Maybe he was supposed to change. Zoe certainly had.

'So what happened then? How'd you get in this mess? Tell me you didn't do it yourself. That would be just like you, shooting yourself in the foot.'

'No. It wasn't me. I was trying to help someone out.'

'By getting shot?'

'That wasn't part of my original plan. It just turned out that way.'

'And did you?'

'Did I what?

'Help. Did nearly getting your foot blown off prove useful?'

'I don't know. Maybe. I hope so.'

'Who were you trying to help anyway? Not that psycho Davey? Did he get you mixed up in something dodgy? He was always a bit close to the edge, if you ask me. And you always thought you had to look out for him.'

'I think Davey had enough of guns in Iraq, to be honest, Zoe. You know he has problems. And I've never felt I had to look out for him. It's just what you do for your mates.'

Zoe looked slightly shamefaced but shook it off quickly. 'Well who then?' she demanded.

'You don't know her. I don't really know her myself.'

'So it was a *her*? Rescuing damsels in distress now are you?'

'Something like that.' George was beginning to find Zoe's endless capacity to be pissed off with him exhausting. He didn't understand why she was still bothering, now they weren't even together anymore. 'So how about you?' he asked before she could start on him again. 'Still saving lives?'

Zoe seemed to deflate, her anger leaking out like air from a punctured lilo. She sank down onto the side of the bed, being careful not to knock George's bandaged foot. 'I'm still here,' she said in a flat voice.

'You don't sound too happy about it.'

She sighed and rubbed her temples as if massaging away a headache she didn't have time for. George was reminded of their last night together. He wanted to know finally what it had all been about.

'That night,' he said. 'That night you came home from the hospital and dumped me. I've always wondered. What happened? You wouldn't talk about it at the time and it's always kind of bothered me.'

'Oh God, George, it's all ancient history. What's the point in raking over all that now?'

'I'd just like to know, that's all. You don't have to go into everything that was going wrong between us. I know all of that. What I don't know is why you chose that particular day to end things.'

Zoe stared at the wall above his head for a few seconds before she started talking. 'You know how some days everything seems to come together? Like everything that happens around you is significant, and it's all making a point? Like the world is trying to tell you something?'

He nodded.

'Some of my colleagues would call that delusional thinking,

a classic symptom of mania. Maybe it was. I was so tired that day. I was virtually hallucinating by the time I got home.' She shook her head and studied her hands as she talked, picking imaginary dirt from under her fingernails. 'Remember I was part of that floating registrar system back then, moving us around the different departments?'

George had never managed to keep track of the intricacies of Zoe's training. Whenever he tried, and got it wrong, she'd taken it as a personal slight so he'd stopped trying. 'Absolutely,' he said.

'Well, I'd started in Oncology that day and we had this patient. Beautiful young woman. Clever, confident. The sort of person who should have the whole world at her feet. But she was terminal. The diagnosis didn't leave any doubt. And she'd decided to refuse treatment. Personally, I didn't blame her. Professor Stein – he was the consultant at the time – knew full well the treatment would probably kill her before the cancer did. But he wanted to go ahead anyway, to see what happened. So did everyone else. Like she was a lab animal. And I didn't speak up, didn't defend her. I don't think it made any difference to her because she wasn't easily intimidated, but it did to me because I realised then that I was a coward. I didn't have the courage of my own convictions. I was too worried about getting on the wrong side of Stein, scared of what people would think.

'I didn't have much chance to dwell on it for the rest of the day. It was constant, one thing after another. I lost track of how many hours I'd been on. I was about to go home when I got paged to A&E. Major road accident. Three people died, two at the scene, another on the operating table. I had to tell the one survivor that her friends were all dead and I couldn't get this other woman out of my head. What she had said about no one having any guarantees. On the way home it kept going round in my mind. How short and fragile life was and how I should stop being a coward and say what I really felt, about everything. When you tried to talk to me that evening, *everything* started to mean us, the state we were in, how it wasn't working because we didn't want the same things. So, I spoke up.' Zoe spread her hands. 'End of story. That's what happened.'

George nodded. It kind of made sense. For Zoe. Now he understood how she'd been thinking that day. What smarted was that he didn't figure in her thoughts very much. She'd made the decision to break up with him on the basis of a shitty day at work which she hadn't even mentioned. 'We could have talked about it,' he said, realising as he spoke that it didn't matter anymore. It was time to let all this go. He wished he hadn't asked.

'There was no point, George. We wanted different things from life. It was cowardly of me to let it go on as long as I did. Not fair on either of us. You'd always have been hoping I'd change my mind about settling down and having a family and . . .' She looked up to the ceiling and drew a ragged breath. 'Okay. The truth is, the thing that really terrified me, was that right then, that night, I saw how easy it would be, to be like you. To just ignore all the difficult choices and drift along not trying to be anything. If I let myself do that, I might have ended up with that house in the suburbs, the shed with the curtains, the fairy cakes and everything. If I stayed with you, that could have happened and I might even have liked it. But I'd always have known I was hiding from real life. From what I should be doing.'

If she had talked to him back then, George knew that he would have tried to adapt to her view of real life. He'd loved her enough to change pretty much anything for her. If she'd only asked. 'And what is it you should be doing?'

She shrugged. 'You know, the stupid thing is, I'm not really sure any more. I thought it was this.' She waved a hand at the empty room. 'Getting on, being a better doctor.'

'What about Max?' George remembered the conversation he'd overheard in the hall and wondered if Zoe's new boyfriend shared her views. He hoped for her sake that he did. It suddenly came to him where he'd seen Max before. He was

197

Shark Boy, the over-achieving friend from the colour supplement. He sounded like an arse, but if that was what Zoe wanted, then it kind of explained why George had been dumped. He was just beginning to feel better about the whole thing when he realised that Zoe was crying.

She was bent over with her hands covering her face and her shoulders were shaking. George shuffled awkwardly down the bed and put his arms around her.

She leaned into him. 'God, I've missed you so much,' she moaned into his hospital gown. Her tears soaked through onto his chest.

George was at a complete loss. This wasn't the Zoe he knew. He held on to her and hoped that was all that was required.

After a minute she sat up, pulled a tissue from her trouser pocket and blew her nose. 'I didn't think I would. Miss you, that is. And at first I didn't. I was so busy with work, and I thought that was all I needed. But it was lonely, George. I was so lonely without you. I still am. There's this thing with Max and it's all very . . . appropriate but I think I was a better person with you.' She swiped at her eyes.

'Come on now. It's okay. You're fine. You're just a bit tired and emotional. That's all.' George rubbed her back and wondered how the hell the conversation had got them to this point. He wondered if it might have been better if he'd just pretended to be unconscious when she came into the room.

She took his hand and squeezed it. 'Perhaps it's fate, you turning up here tonight. Maybe I got it all wrong. I thought it was you and me that was the problem, but maybe it was just me. All the things I thought were important turned out not to be. Nothing meant anything without you, George.' She squeezed his hand tighter. He was beginning to lose sensation in two fingers. 'What do you think? Could we try again? Can you give me another chance?'

George nearly swallowed his tongue. She would never know how many times he'd pictured a scenario like this, where she came back and admitted she'd been wrong all along, threw herself at his feet and begged him to take her back. But now it was actually happening, it gave him no satisfaction at all.

He still loved her. In a way, he always would. She'd been his first love and nothing could change that. But starting again? Trying to pick up the frayed ends of their torn relationship? No. It would never work. He knew that now. They had to move forward. Zoe didn't really want him back. She was clearly unhappy and wanted something to make her feel better, but that something wasn't him.

He took a sip of water, felt it trickle down over his swollen vocal chords, tried to find the right words. But there weren't any. Instead, he stroked her hand, looked her in the eye and gently, as gently as he could, shook his head. He was turning her down. He felt dizzy.

Zoe nodded and set her mouth in a tight line, as if to seal in any more rash words that might be about to escape. She put his hand back on the sheets, patted it twice and stood up. Just then, the pager on her belt bleeped and she turned and hurried from the room without looking back.

George had read Zoe's watch while she was holding his hand. Five thirty. He closed his eyes and slipped gratefully into a dreamless sleep.

TWENTY-ONE

not a tree

Beth parked the van, jumped out and started walking towards the building. She wasn't sure whether Amber would follow but was banking on her being too impatient to wait in the van. She hadn't gone far when she heard the door slam and the stamp of angry footsteps behind her. It was still dark in the car park but as they approached the hospital, they entered the twilight zone of greenish light cast off from dozens of lit windows. Flat against the night sky, the side of the building looked like a bank of television screens. The majority played only white or pastel coloured static but movement could be seen in others: a doctor looking at his clipboard while talking to someone out of shot; a nurse bringing an extra pillow and leaning down towards a bed; a white-haired woman, her hospital gown flapping limply at her back, paced to and fro on the third floor.

They walked towards the main entrance through the ambulance bays outside Accident and Emergency. Newspapers and discarded plastic cups skimmed across the tarmac and a lone gull screeched overhead. A piece of litter wrapped itself around Beth's ankle. She shook her foot to dislodge it but it clung on. She bent and pulled at it. Was that hair? She held the object at arm's length between thumb and forefinger trying not to imagine all the stuff hospitals might throw away. It twirled slowly then hung still. A rubber face with empty imploring eyes and a lopsided grin returned her stare. She'd seen that face before.

'Will you stop fannying around?' Amber was walking ahead of her impatiently. 'If we're going to do this then let's hurry up and get it done and get the fuck away from here.'

Beth looked at the rubber face and couldn't decide whether to smile or frown. She couldn't bring herself to leave it blowing around with the rest of the rubbish so she shoved it in her pocket. It might not even belong to her monkey, but what were the chances of tripping over two monkeys in one night? She wondered what he might be doing at the hospital, and without his head. She hoped he hadn't managed to get himself into more trouble. He did seem to have a knack for it.

They had reached the main entrance. The automatic doors parted and the hospital breathed on them. Amber took a step back, her eyes widening. She had the look of a horse about to bolt.

Beth put a hand on her shoulder. 'Come on. It's okay. This won't take long.'

Amber shot her an angry look, shook off her hand and shoved past her into the lobby, muttering, 'Fucking hate fucking hospitals.'

Behind the large circular desk in the middle of the room, a receptionist was talking into her headset while stabbing at a keyboard with one hand, and wrestling with a card index system with the other. She didn't look up as Beth and Amber walked past. No one challenged them on the way to Helen's room. She wasn't kept under tight security. Over the years she'd become less of a patient and more of a fixture, a thing to clean around.

They stopped outside Helen's room. Beth reached for the handle. She was sure this was the right thing to do. She would say her goodbyes and Amber would say hers, and everything would be as it should be. Not happily ever after, but at least reality would be restored.

'You know what? I could just wait out here,' said Amber.

Beth turned towards her. 'She's your mother and you're never going to see her again. You need to make your peace.'

'Oh, give me a break,' Amber huffed. She leant against the wall and crossed her arms.

'You'll regret it if you don't.'

'No.' Amber shook her head. 'I won't.'

'You don't know that.' Beth was horrified. Who'd want to run the risk of being wrong about something like this? What if Amber found herself on the other side of the world, running out of time, and regretted never taking this opportunity? It was now or never.

'Yes. I do actually.' Amber pushed herself clear of the wall and turned towards Beth. 'Is this why you dragged me here? Some big emotional farewell scene? What do you take me for? A tart with a heart? Is that it?' Amber's voice had risen. An orderly carrying an armful of laundry stopped at the end of the corridor and stared at them.

'Get in.' Beth opened the door and yanked Amber into the room. They couldn't afford to draw attention to themselves. Not now.

Inside, everything was as it always was. The bedside lamp cast a muted light over the figure of the comatose woman. Her white sheets reflected and magnified the light, making the whole bed glow. For Beth, this room was a sanctuary, her refuge from the confusion of the world outside. She felt herself relax, the way she always did when she came to visit. But as she approached the bed, something felt different. Wrong.

Of course, she'd always known that Helen had another identity, that she was someone else in her own life but that possible person had seemed so distant and irrelevant that Beth had almost forgotten she existed. Now, with Amber in the room, this other identity was emerging, distorting the lines around Helen's mouth, the fit of her eyelids over her eyes. She was starting to look like someone else.

Outside in the corridor, a trolley rattled past, accompanied by the sound of someone whistling *Dream a Little Dream of*

Me, slightly off-key and mournful, then disappeared into silence again.

Amber walked around to the opposite side of the bed. They stood, one on either side, the unconscious woman lying between them. Beth pulled up a chair and sat down, but Amber remained standing, her head tipped back as if trying to avoid a bad smell.

'You can have her if you want, y'know,' Amber said. 'If it helps, then she's all yours.' She paused and gave a short, ironic laugh. 'She's a better mother to you in a coma than she ever was to me when conscious.'

Beth considered the offer for a few seconds. 'Thanks. But now I know the truth, it doesn't feel right somehow.'

'Why let the truth bother you? It's just another story. Why not pick one you like?'

Beth thought back to the first time she'd sat in this room with Helen, the choice she'd made to do exactly that. But she couldn't do it anymore. The longing for things to be different was still there but now it was time to accept the facts. 'I can't have her,' she said, 'because she belongs to you.'

'But I don't want her.' Amber raised her palms. 'I really don't.'

To her surprise, Beth felt no anger towards Helen, despite knowing that she was responsible for the pointless deaths of her friends and for the half-life she'd lived these last two years. It was time to let go. She felt herself disconnecting from the Helen she had invented, pieced together from imagined memories and frustrated wishes, like some Frankenstein's monster of motherhood. She had never been real.

'This is stupid,' Amber said. 'Standing here arguing over who has ownership of a dead woman.'

'She's not dead.'

'Yeah, but she may as well be. She's just lying there, breathing for no reason.'

Beth looked at Helen's face, checking for the tell-tale eye-roll but there was nothing. 'How do you know that?' she said.

'Maybe there's something going on in there. Maybe she's taking it all in, thinking, having feelings.'

'Who cares? If it's all locked up then she may as well be dead.'

'Do you really think that?' The thought hit Beth like cold water down her back. This conversation could be about Helen or it could be about her. Her life.

'Yeah. I do.' Amber leaned forward, her brows drawn together in concentration, as if feeling her way around a new thought. 'It's like, if a tree falls in the forest and there's no one there to see or hear it, then who gives a shit? Y'know?'

Beth watched her with amazement. Amber seemed quite pleased with her theory. How could she stand there at her mother's bedside and talk that way? As if Helen was some kind of a philosophical problem she'd just solved instead of her own flesh and blood. 'Your mother is not a tree!'

'You keep saying *your mother* like it means something. You can say it as many times as you like and I'm not going to feel any different,' Amber said irritably, as if explaining something for the umpteenth time to a stubborn child.

They glared at each other over the bed. Beth was about to speak again when a sharp intake of breath broke the silence. Their gaze held and their eyes widened in unison. They both looked down at Helen. Her mouth was open. They locked eyes again briefly, then looked back to the bed. Could Helen be coming back to consciousness? Perhaps their arguing had been enough to drag her back from wherever she had been for the past two years. Beth held her breath and waited for Helen to open her eyes. But Helen's face didn't look right. Her jaw hung slack and her head flopped to one side. The intermittent beep of the monitors changed to a continuous loud tone.

'Uh oh,' said Amber. 'That can't be good.' She grabbed Beth's wrist and pulled her towards the door. 'Looks like this is goodbye after all.'

Beth stumbled as Amber dragged her from the room. She

could hear running footsteps and an alarm bell started ringing. Amber hauled her around the corner before they could be seen and stopped.

It wasn't until they were heading back through reception, their pace slowed to a walk, that Beth could speak. She pulled her arm from Amber's grip. 'I don't believe this,' she hissed. 'You can't just leave.'

'Oh yeah?' said Amber, walking straight for the exit. 'Watch me.'

The automatic doors slid open and Amber walked through without breaking stride or looking back. Beth watched her go, then stood blinking in the bright lights as the doors closed again. The receptionist glanced up at her, then returned to her fight to the death with the filing system. Beth started wondering how different things might be now if she hadn't been working tonight . . . then stopped. Where would that get her? She'd wasted enough time thinking about how things *could* have been. She was here, now, and she had a promise to keep.

Beth drove towards the airport with Amber slumped in the passenger seat beside her. The silence was loaded.

Eventually Amber broke it. 'No more detours, okay?'

'Definitely not.' Beth now realised that the hospital visit had been a mistake. She'd been selfish, looking for closure when Amber plainly had no such need. And what had she achieved? Amber was furious with her and Helen was possibly dead.

Amber nodded. 'And I don't want to hear another word about Helen. She's been as good as dead to me for longer than I can remember, so I'm not about to start mourning her now. Okay, for some twisted, fucked-up reason, she meant something to you. I'm sorry for your loss and all that, but it's done now. Yeah?'

Beth swallowed. Amber had the right to handle this however she liked. It might seem cold-hearted and plain wrong to her but she wasn't exactly a model of emotional health either. What right did she have to criticise? 'If that's what you want,' she said quietly.

'That's what I want.' Amber stuck a boot up on the dashboard and lit a cigarette.

They lapsed back into silence. Beth wondered if they'd speak again before parting. They were almost at the airport.

Amber suddenly straightened in her seat, her eyes on the rear-view mirror. She twisted around to look through the back window. 'Houston, we have a problem,' she said.

'What?'

'Car behind us. Been there since we left the hospital.'

Beth was almost glad to have something else to talk about but Amber was clearly more than a little worried. 'Coincidence?' she ventured.

'No such thing as coincidence,' said Amber. 'What am I saying? That's bollocks. Fucking everything is a coincidence. But let's not get into that now. The point is, I think they're following us.'

'Not Murdoch? They wouldn't have let him go again. Would they?'

'Doubt it. Could be friends of his, I suppose. Or enemies. Could've been someone watching him in the club.'

'Oh great.'

'Or it's the police.'

'Not exactly the best news either.' Beth looked in the rear-view mirror. A dark, unmarked car was maintaining a steady distance behind them. She pressed down on the accelerator but the pedal was already flat to the floor. 'Can you think of any nice reasons anyone would be following us?' she asked.

'Well, I don't think they want to give us flowers,' said Amber.

Beth gave a sudden laugh, which surprised them both.

'What's funny?'

'Oh, nothing. Just coincidence.' She cleared her throat. 'What do we do then?'

'If it's the police, why don't they pull us over?' Amber mused, more to herself than Beth.

'I don't know! I don't have much experience with this sort of thing.'

Amber continued with her line of reasoning. 'If it's *not* the police, then why not get us at the hospital?' Then answered her own question. 'Worried about cameras maybe. Could be biding their time, waiting for a secluded spot.'

Beth looked around. It was still dark, early Sunday morning, so there was hardly any other traffic on the road. They were in open country. If something bad were to happen, there would be no witnesses.

Amber scrambled over the seat into the back of the van. She started pulling drawers out and sliding cupboard doors open. 'Don't suppose you've got a gun or anything stashed back here?'

'Don't be ridiculous.'

'You do have a lot of potatoes though.' Amber was sizing up three large sacks of potatoes that Gianni had left in the van to save storage space in the shop.

'What? You're going to *feed* them to death? Might be a bit time consuming, don't you think?'

'I could chuck them out the back,' said Amber. 'Might slow them down.'

It was the most ludicrous plan Beth had ever heard, but she didn't have any other ideas. 'You'd definitely have the element of surprise,' she said. 'No one expects potatoes.'

'Have you got oil as well? Y'know, cooking oil?'

'Yeah. Buckets of the stuff.'

'Excellent. Give me two minutes.' Amber started dragging the sacks of potatoes towards the back of the van.

Two minutes later, Beth turned onto the long, straight road running parallel with the airport runways. All she wanted now was to get Amber on a plane. It was something solid, one simple goal to aim for. The car behind them suddenly accelerated, closed the gap and drew alongside. Beth looked to her right and just had time to register that the square-headed giant at the wheel was definitely not the police, before he swerved into the side of the van, clipped the wing and bounced back off. He was trying to push them off the road. The van couldn't go any faster but its age and size were in their favour this time. As long as she held it steady, they couldn't be knocked off course by some flimsy modern car. It was like a poodle trying to take down an elephant. The driver of the other car seemed to realise this and fell back again, tucking in close behind them while he considered his next move.

By this time, Amber had three sacks of potatoes and two cans of cooking oil rigged up at the back of the van. 'One. Two. Three!' she yelled, and booted the back doors open.

A rush of air was sucked through the cab. Beth gripped the steering wheel and flicked her gaze rapidly between the road ahead and the chaos unfolding in the rear-view mirror. Amber was kicking over sacks and upending cans, letting it all pour out the back, potatoes mixing with the oil, greasy spuds ricocheting and bouncing off the tarmac. A large potato took out one of the car's headlights; another hit the windscreen dead-centre and smashed straight through it, leaving a fist-sized hole and crazing the remaining glass with white cracks. Beth saw the car swerve and slide. The driver lost control and skidded right off the road and hit a tree. The bonnet crumpled and the tree shook with the impact. She slowed down. She hadn't really believed the potato plan would work. She certainly hadn't imagined anyone getting hurt.

'What the fuck are you doing?' yelled Amber. 'Keep going!'

Beth ignored her and let the van slow further, keeping her eyes on the mirror. The car rocked on the spot, the driver's door swung open and a man got out. He was enormous, at least seven foot tall. He staggered then steadied himself, pulled something from his pocket and pointed it towards the van.

'Shit!' yelled Amber. 'Fucking move it!' She was dangling

out of the back, hanging on to one door and trying to pull the other closed.

Beth put her foot back to the floor and the van lurched forwards. There was a muffled thud, then she heard Amber yelling again but her voice sounded further away. In the mirror she saw Amber sprinting after her down the middle of the road. She must have fallen out when the van accelerated. Beth stood on the brakes and waited while she caught up and threw herself into the back, hauling the doors closed behind her.

Something whizzed close over the roof of the cab as they started moving again. There was an ear-splitting crack and the wing mirror on Beth's side exploded in glittering splinters. She hunched over the steering wheel and willed the van forwards. If she lived through this, she swore, she would never waste another day, never take another second for granted. Why did it take the threat of sudden death to make life seem so desirable? She promised herself, and every deity she'd ever heard of, that this time she really truly had learned her lesson. The van picked up speed. The car and driver behind them dwindled in the mirror.

Amber climbed back into the passenger seat. 'Fuck were you playing at?'

Beth unclenched her jaw. She'd been gritting her teeth so hard her face was aching and there was an audible pop when she opened her mouth. 'I just wanted to make sure no one was hurt. That's all.'

'You really are soft in the head, aren't you?' Amber flapped a grazed and dirty hand in front of Beth's face. 'Look at the state of my nails!' She dusted herself down and tutted as she peeled off her ruined fake nails and threw them out of the window.

At the airport, Beth pulled into a space in the short stay car park and killed the engine. Amber reached under the passenger seat and pulled out the briefcase, laid it on her lap and opened it.

209

'Put that away, will you? Someone will see.' Beth glanced around the car park nervously. 'What are you doing? You should put that inside your suitcase.'

'I'm getting your cut,' replied Amber, raking up as much money as she could hold in her fists. She handed Beth two large bundles of notes.

Beth had pretty much forgotten about the money and now it was in front of her she really wasn't that interested in it. She wasn't at all sure what she would do with it anyway, whereas Amber had plans coming out of her ears. The amount she was trying to force on Beth could pay for another month's travelling, hotel bills, flights, anything.

'I can't take—'

'Shut up. Yes you can. Take the money and for fuck's sake do something fun with it. Live a little, eh?'

Beth took the notes and stuffed them into her pockets. She'd never had that much cash in her life. How much was there? Ten grand? More? Less than your average merchant banker could drop down the toilet and not bother retrieving in case he got his fingers dirty. But to her it was a life changing amount. She could think about all of that later. Right now, this minute, she had to get Amber onto a plane.

'Ready,' said Amber from the back of the van. 'Got my travelling cash.' She stuffed a few rolls of money into her shoulder bag and crammed the briefcase inside her main suitcase. 'You can have this.' She held up her pink makeup box with a flourish. 'Can't fit them both in.' She caught Beth's sceptical expression and shrugged. 'Or you could drop it off at the house for Fran. Whatever.'

Inside the terminal building, while Amber scanned the ticket desks, Beth gazed around the vast echoing space and felt extremely small and incredibly conspicuous. She eyed a security guard leaning against a pillar. He scratched the curve of his belly hanging over his trousers and nodded into his walkie-talkie. 'Where are you going to start then?' she asked.

'Doesn't matter. Wherever the next flight I can get a seat

on is going. Watch my case.' Amber walked away towards the Delta Airlines desk. Beth stayed where she was, rested a hand on the suitcase and pretended to be studying the glowing green lines of letters and numbers on the Arrivals and Departures board.

If she had to travel, and Beth hadn't gone anywhere for years, she preferred train stations to airport terminals. Terminals, apart from the clearly unlucky choice of name, were too sterile. The feeling of the building as a machine that drew you in and processed your possessions and identity made her nervous even under ordinary circumstances.

She looked around and saw Amber walking back towards her with a ticket in her hand and a broad smile on her face.

'Start spreadin the noos!' she laughed, and held up the slip of paper with both hands like it was a golden ticket for Wonka's factory.

'New York then?'

Amber grinned, grabbed her suitcase and hauled it over to another desk where she checked it in. 'Ready to go. Flight leaves in an hour and half.' She linked her arm through Beth's and launched into a showbiz staircase walk, singing, 'Ah'm leavin today-ay,' none too quietly.

The security guard fixed his gaze on them and looked Amber slowly up and down, replaced his walkie-talkie on his belt and blatantly rearranged his balls without taking his eyes off her. Beth tugged her arm and shushed her, trying to bring her back down to earth. 'Will you stop that? Could you please try to be a little less conspicuous for once in your life, at least until you're out of here?'

'If you insist.' Amber said, and stopped high-kicking.

They walked in step, arm-in-arm, to the escalators and rode up to the security desk that barred the way to Departures. 'That's us, then,' said Amber.

Now that Beth had finally achieved her goal of getting Amber to this point, she didn't want her to leave. This was the last time she would see or speak to her and she could find nothing to say. A well of emptiness opened up in her chest and all the words she could have used to form a decent farewell were falling down it. All the people she had lost were down there too and soon Amber would be joining them. She had never in her life felt more like an orphan.

Amber put her arms round her and squeezed. 'Promise me something will you?'

'What?'

'Stop being such an arse.'

Beth pulled back and looked at her.

Amber was smiling. 'And you could do worse than get yourself laid. As soon as possible.'

Beth narrowed her eyes. 'You know, I'm not going to miss you at all.'

'No, really,' Amber laughed. 'I mean it. You need to lighten up. Have some fun. Be yourself.'

'Okay. I promise.' Beth made a silent, cautious resolution to try to find out what *being herself* might involve. Seeing as just about everybody so far tonight had turned out to be somebody else entirely, she wouldn't be surprised to find that she was too.

Amber hugged her tightly then pushed her away. 'Thanks for the lift,' she said, then turned and walked off.

Beth felt an urge to grab hold of the Amber-shaped gap by her side – an absence so emphatic it felt like a physical presence. Instead she fixed a smile on her face and waved as Amber passed through security and disappeared from her life.

TWENTY-TWO

let me do something nice for you

Amber waltzed through security, smiled at the jaded-looking staff as she cleared the metal detector and picked up her shoulder bag from the tray at the other side of the x-ray machine.

Before the departure gates, there was a shopping mall of chain stores, franchise cafés and duty free shops. The heels of her boots tapped out a fast rhythm across the polished floor. She'd really made it. She was finally free. She gave a little skip outside the chemist, ignoring the curious looks from a middle-aged couple passing in the other direction. There was a buzzing, bubbling sensation centred in her stomach and spreading out to the rest of her body. She slowed down and concentrated on her breathing. The last thing she needed was one of her passing-out episodes here. But this was a different feeling from the weakness and nausea that usually signalled one of them. Her head was clear but she felt like she'd swallowed a bucket of fizzing bouncy balls. She drew level with the open door of a coffee shop and slowed to a stop. As the smell of toasting bread and frying bacon lassoed itself around her senses, she realised that she was ravenous. It was six in the morning and she hadn't eaten anything since lunchtime the previous day. She checked her ticket. There was around an hour to kill before her flight was called. Just as well because if she didn't get something to eat right then she might bite someone.

She went in and ordered a bacon roll and coffee, adding a half-litre bottle of fresh orange juice to drink while she waited. The waitress raised an eyebrow when Amber gave her a fifty, but handed over her change without comment. Amber wanted to tell her to keep it, but was so gripped by hunger she didn't want any extra conversation slowing down the arrival of her food.

Sitting at a table by the window, she gulped down her orange juice. It was the best orange juice she had ever tasted, sweet and sharp and delicious. Why had she never had orange juice like this before? All orange juice should be this good. She wiped her chin and watched the people coming and going outside. Most of the shops still had their shutters down. At others, uniformed workers braced themselves for another day of counting change and mopping up spillages. She'd had plenty of jobs like that. The combination of boredom and backbreaking work was hard to like and the pay was always crap. Jobs like that should be compulsory for everyone, she decided. For at least a year. Like national service. It could be called national service-industry service. The more she thought about it, the more obviously perfect the idea was. Everyone should do their bit then no one would have to do it for long, unless they wanted to. It was only fair.

She thought about Beth. That girl had certainly served her time. Amber wondered if she would be alright. Would she manage to escape from the bizarre fantasy life she'd made for herself or would she just build another, even stranger version? Now that Helen was gone, she'd have to start again from scratch. Nothing Amber could do about it now. She was still kind of angry with Beth for dragging her along to the hospital but she couldn't blame her for not understanding how things were with her and her mother. Not many people would, and given Beth's own history, it wasn't surprising she'd tried to make things better, in her own way. She was obviously mad as a bag of ferrets, but there was still hope for her. If she could get her act together. Amber silently wished her luck and drained the last of her juice.

Food had never tasted so good. She groaned out loud as the first mouthful hit her taste buds and lit up her pleasure centres like a whole hillside of Christmas trees. The roll was fresh and a good size, the butter thick, the bacon came from a pig so tasty it had to be breaking some kind of tastiest pig in the world record. She hunched over the table, gripped the roll in two hands and gave it her full attention. The shops, the airport, the rest of the world, paled into the background. As the first pleasure rush subsided, she became aware that the waitress was watching her, kohled eyes wide under her black fringe. She had a small hoop through one slightly aristocratic nostril.

'What?' asked Amber with her mouth full.

'Sorry, nothing. Just . . . customers don't usually enjoy their food quite that much.' The girl sounded slightly wary but also amused.

'You're kidding?' This was beyond understanding. What was wrong with people? She took another bite. This bacon roll was plainly the food of the gods.

'You must've been really hungry,' said the girl.

'You have no idea,' replied Amber. Her roll was nearly finished. She wondered whether she should order another. But could it possibly be as good as this one? 'Did *you* make this?' she asked the girl, who was still lingering.

She smiled. 'Well, yeah. It's just a bacon roll.'

'Don't say that!'

'No?'

'No!' Amber stifled a belch. 'This,' she brandished the remains of the roll in her hand, 'is better than sex.'

The girl laughed. 'If you say so,' she said, and went back to wiping the next table. She had good hands, Amber noticed, small and quick with black nail varnish and a thick silver thumb ring. Her uniform of black trousers and short-sleeved red blouse was a size too small and pinched her flesh into creases at her waist and the top of her thighs.

The girl stopped what she was doing and looked at Amber looking at her. 'I'd have to disagree though.' She fingered the silver pendant that hung at her neck on a leather thong and smiled.

Amber swallowed the last bite and sat back licking her lips. 'It'd have to be shocking good sex to beat that bacon roll.'

The girl's smile widened and she held eye contact.

'What's your name?'

'Wendy.'

'Hi, Wendy.' Amber looked at her watch. 'I don't suppose . . .' She broke off and started laughing. Was she seriously flirting with this girl? There *was* something about her. Wendy reminded her of herself, so many years ago.

Wendy's smile faltered. She looked confused. 'What's so funny?'

Amber shook her head. 'Sorry. Don't mind me. I've not had any sleep is all.' She pushed her empty plate away and stood up to go. 'Well. Thanks, Wendy, for the sexiest bacon roll in the known universe.' She leant forward and planted a kiss on Wendy's lips.

Wendy flushed and took a step back. 'Hey!'

On impulse, Amber delved into her bag and pulled out a bundle of notes. She held out the money. 'Take it. I've got plenty more. Go on. Let me do something nice for you.'

Wendy's hands stayed by her sides but her mouth dropped open as she stared at the wad of money. 'You taking the piss?'

'No. Honestly. Take it. No strings attached. Think of me as your fairy godmother.' Wendy still looked reluctant so Amber grabbed her hand and stuffed the money into it. 'And, please, close your mouth, sweetheart.'

Amber walked back into the main concourse, turning to blow a kiss to Wendy who raised a hand and gave her an uncertain wave in return.

216

If things had been different she could have taken things further. Wendy exuded a carefree and generous sexuality she found almost irresistible, and it had been obvious the interest was mutual. But now was not the time.

She couldn't remember when she'd last had sex. Technically, if she counted John, it was only a matter of hours. But she didn't count John. That wasn't sex, that was work. She hadn't had proper, actual, just-for-fun sex since she'd gone professional with it. Hadn't had the time, energy or inclination. And before that, she hadn't had the brain-melting, hallelujah chorus type for years.

Had her last time already come and gone? Now there was a thought. Everyone made a big thing about the first time but what about the last? That last person wouldn't come with a caption, announcing their status. There was always the possibility that the last one could end up being the Last One. Wendy could have been the perfect ending but that was one opportunity she'd have to let slide. Shame.

Nothing could dent her mood right now. She swung her bag as she bounced along. A boiler-suited guy driving a floor polishing machine glowered at her as he droned past. She was obviously looking way too pleased with herself. But fuck it, she was done with putting a face on it for other people's benefit. She looked at the expressions on the faces of the people walking by. Either harassed or zombied seemed to be the off-the-peg choices around here. It was a lot like a hospital in that respect. Well, they could shove it up their collective arses and swivel. She wasn't insisting that others felt the same as her, wasn't going to get all evangelical on them. They had every right to be miserable bastards. As long as they respected her choice not to be.

She could admit it was perverse to feel this way given the night she'd had, but having life on a short lease had changed the way she looked at things. Even death itself stopped being anything to get worked up about. It would be impossible to carry on at all if she let herself be terrorised by what was ahead of her. It was ahead of everyone else as well. The only difference between them and her was that they pushed it away, pretended it wasn't happening. But in trying to protect themselves from the darkness, they risked missing the light. She didn't blame them. It just wasn't an option for her.

The departure lounge was quiet. Most of the waiting passengers were business types, fiddling with their blackberries and laptops. She bought a newspaper and sat at the end of a row of seats and flicked through the pages, stopping to read an article about NASA plans to send a monkey to Mars. The trip would take five-hundred and twenty days and the poor bugger wasn't expected to make it back alive. The point, apparently, was to study precisely how he died. Radiation poisoning was the most popular bet. There was a picture of the monkey sitting in his little nook inside the rocket with a long-suffering look on his face that gave Amber goose bumps. She closed the paper and looked up at the screens. Surely it was about time she was gone?

When the call came for the flight to New York to start boarding, dawn was stealing across the runways. Service vehicles buzzed around the bodies of the jets and long caterpillars of luggage carts crawled back and forth from the terminal. She was really leaving. Not much could get in the way now, short of terrorists or engine failure and she was happy enough to play those odds. She felt exhilarated knowing she would never again set foot on this particular piece of the planet. She felt light, almost as if she might lift up into the sky herself without any extra help. As she walked across the tarmac towards the plane, streaks of sunlight edged its wings with gold.

TWENTY-THREE

bollocks, bollocks, bollocks

Beth stood for a while looking at the security desk. That was that then. Mission accomplished. She could go home now. After a few moments, she noticed the security staff watching her curiously, two of them leaning in and talking to each other in low voices. It really was time to go. She turned and started walking away, back towards the escalators. She didn't see the person standing in her way until she had almost collided with her. Muttering her apologies, she went to step around, but the woman moved to block her path again.

'Not travelling today?' she asked.

It took Beth a few seconds to place her. DC Chan. She'd swapped the suit she'd been wearing in the station for jogging bottoms and a baggy jumper. Her hair hung loose from under a shapeless woollen hat that reminded Beth of her gran's tea cosy. She glanced around. No sign of DS Page. 'No, I'm going home. Unless you're going to arrest me?' She could think of worse things right now. 'If you're willing to let me sleep in the station, then fine by me.' She extended both arms towards Chan, wrists turned up.

'What would I be arresting you for?' Chan glanced down at Beth's arms as if she found them puzzling and vaguely embarrassing.

'You tell me.' Beth lowered her arms. Was this a trap? She tried to shake off the fatigue that was clouding her thinking. She didn't really want to end up in a cell if it could be avoided.

She knew there was a long list of charges that could be brought against her. They could take their pick. It would be best to play dumb until she figured out what was going on here.

'I'm not going to arrest you. Unless you'd like me to?'

If this was a trap, she couldn't figure out how it worked. Chan didn't sound like she was lying. Her expression was open and she sounded friendly but it would be foolish to let her guard down. Beth had never had a problem with the police but recent events put her and them on opposing sides. 'No. Thanks for the offer and everything, but I'll pass.' She started walking and the detective fell into step beside her.

'Mind if I walk with you?'

'Knock yourself out.'

They rode together in silence down the escalator, walked past the check in counters and ticket desks and out into the dark. How long could one night last? Beth wondered. It had been a long time since she'd deliberately stayed up all night to see the dawn. Today's was surely well overdue. Perhaps it was going to stand them all up, leave them stranded on the edge of the night, stealing glances at their watches and trying not to look conspicuously disappointed.

'Been a long night, hasn't it?' said Chan, reading her thoughts.

A handy talent for a police officer, thought Beth, as they walked towards the car park. She'd definitely have to watch what she said. Maybe it would be safer if she asked the questions herself. 'So, did you lot get Murdoch and his glamorous assistant?'

Chan nodded. 'Yeah. We got them.'

'And will you be putting them away?'

'I can't see them wriggling out of it in a hurry, considering the amount of gear they were caught with. Not to mention shooting that monkey.'

'What?' Beth stopped and stared at Chan, not sure if she'd heard what she thought she'd heard. 'Did you say *monkey*?'

'Yeah. Some joker in fancy dress got in their way when

they came after you out of the club. Got shot in the foot. He'll be okay. Told one of our guys he was trying to help, apparently. Know him, do you?'

'Yes. I mean No. I don't know him.' So he *was* in the hospital. Beth thought back to the chip van's exit from Junction Street. The bang she'd put down to the van backfiring must have been Monkey Boy getting himself shot. But what sort of an idiot would put themselves in that kind of danger for someone they didn't even know? The same sort as her, she realised, answering her own question. They could form their own club.

'Have it your own way,' said Chan with a shrug.

They started walking again. Beth realised that she'd have to pay for her parking if she wanted to get the van out. Changing course towards a pay point machine, she dug in the pockets of her jeans for change. Twenty pence and button. She was sure she must have more than that but was reluctant to start unloading her coat pockets in front of the detective, stuffed as they were with stolen money and a monkey face.

'Here, let me.' Chan fed the extortionate fee into the machine and handed Beth her ticket.

'Thanks. See you then.' Beth took the ticket and walked off while Chan was paying for her own. She headed for the van, still expecting Chan to drop the pretence and slap the cuffs on her. But she made it without being stopped. She climbed in and turned the key. The engine hawked and spat but refused to catch. She tried a few more times then rested her head on the steering wheel. Bollocks, she thought. It seemed so exactly the right word she said it out loud. 'Bollocks, bollocks, bollocks.'

'A three bollock situation, eh?' Chan spoke through the open window.

Beth turned her head to look at her but hadn't the energy to lift it from the steering wheel. 'At least three. Probably more.'

'I'm surprised you got as far as you did in this thing.' Chan inspected the destroyed wing mirror. 'And almost in one piece.' She patted the bonnet as if comforting a sick animal, then twirled a set of car keys in the air. 'Give you a lift back to town?'

Beth lifted her head and narrowed her eyes.

'Up to you. I'm going that way anyway. But I'm not going to twist your arm, honest.'

She was too tired to argue and Chan was so persistently likeable it was wearing her down. 'Yeah, okay. Thanks.' She climbed out of the van and followed the other woman along the row of parked cars until she stopped at a neat black Mini. They got in.

When they had cleared the barriers and taken the exit towards town, Chan broke the silence. 'Did your friend get away all right then?' she asked.

Beth considered the question. It sounded like an innocent enquiry but it could easily be another trap. 'I don't know what you're talking about,' she said and stared out of the passenger window. Chan was trying to trip her up, get her to say something incriminating so she could arrest her anyway.

Chan let out an irritated sigh. 'I told you. I'm not interested in arresting you. I'm not even on duty right now. Whatever you say will *not* be used in evidence against you. Okay?'

Beth hesitated. She hadn't expected that. She looked over at Chan. Her right hand rested on the steering wheel while the other was hooked over her left shoulder, pressing and kneading the muscle. She took her hand away and stretched her neck to the side. Beth heard something pop and Chan let out a groan.

'I've had a very long night,' she said, her eyes still on the road, 'and to be honest, I've taken about as much bullshit as I can deal with. So can we just cut the crap?'

Maybe sometimes, thought Beth, when someone looks genuine and sounds genuine, then what's coming out of their mouth actually might be the truth. She decided to trust her instinct. 'Yes, she's gone.'

'Good.' Chan was emphatic.

'You're pleased about that?'

'Why shouldn't I be? We got the bad guys. Admittedly, some might disagree about leaving it there. There's quite a few charges we could bring against your friend, if we tracked her down. Personally, I think we'd be wasting our time and resources. Good luck to her, I say.'

'And what about me?' She was glad no one would be chasing Amber but did that mean she would be the one who answered for everything?

'You're going to have to come in to the station sometime in the next few days to answer some questions.'

'I see.' Beth closed her eyes and wondered if that meant she would be going to prison, and if so, for how long.

'But I think, under the circumstances, we can swing it so no charges are brought.'

Beth opened her eyes again. 'What circumstances?' Whatever they were, she was in favour of them. But she held her relief in check until she knew exactly what they were.

'Did you not wonder why we weren't all over the club, asking questions? Or why you two weren't picked up straight away when you were driving the most conspicuous getaway vehicle in the world, ever?'

'Well, yeah.' Beth thought back. 'I did. I guess I just put it down to incompetence.'

Chan laughed. 'Your faith in modern policing is truly touching.'

'Sorry, I didn't mean you personally, just y'know, generally. What was the reason then?'

'Page was in charge of the operation. He called all the shots.' Chan gave a wry smile and threw Beth a sideways look. 'But not anymore.'

'Really? Has he been taken off the case?'

'Kind of.' Chan glanced out of her window as if someone

might be hanging around eavesdropping at fifty miles an hour. 'We're not supposed to talk about this sort of thing. To anyone. Ever. Personally, I think the whole culture of secrecy thing just makes it worse. That said, if you repeat any of what I'm about to tell you, I promise I will arrest and charge you with every remotely illegal thing you've ever done, and some you've only ever dreamed about. Understand?'

Beth nodded. 'Got it.'

Chan sighed and rolled her shoulders. 'Page was working both sides. Doing a spot of freelance, if you like. They used to call it a protection racket. He's not talking much right now but we've got a pretty good picture of the set up from his pal, Big Fry.'

'Big Fry?'

'Yeah. Colin Aloysius Fry. Big as in not small. One of the bouncers at the club. We picked him up near the airport, trying to disentangle his car from a tree.'

Beth checked her mental image of the guy who'd tried to run them off the road and made a match with the bouncer who'd admitted her to the club. Snap. Maybe it was just exhaustion, but her head hurt trying to figure out how it all fitted together. 'Could you start at the beginning please?'

'John, the guy with the sunroof in his head, you remember him?'

'Yeah.' Beth thought back to the moment John had walked into the shop, what seemed like years ago now but was really only a few hours.

'He was on his way to sort out terms with Page, for derailing the police operation on Murdoch, when he had his little mishap. Fate, or whatever you want to call it, got in the way.'

'It does that.'

'After that, Page was winging it. He had to appear to be running a regular investigation, questioning you and so on, but in fact he was trying to figure out why you were covering for the other girl.'

'He knew about her all along?'

'Must have seen the whole thing while waiting for John. The accident, your friend. The lot. No one else knew about her because the CCTV covering the street wasn't recording. We think Page somehow arranged that, so he wouldn't show up on the film himself. He stalled the investigation until he worked out why you were lying. When the two of you made your exit, and there was no choice but to detain Murdoch with the gear, he realised you must have the cash. He couldn't resist the temptation of some easy money and sent Big Fry to collect. We'd had our suspicions about Page for a while but had to wait for him to make a mistake. And that was it. So really, we have you and your friend to thank for that.'

'And that's why you're not arresting me? Gratitude?'

'Well, I personally think it would be rather rude. But that's not the only reason.'

'What else is there?'

'You don't remember me, do you?'

'Small chips and a pickled egg.'

'Yeah. Okay,' said Chan smiling. 'You have a pretty good memory for matching faces to food. But I'm talking further back than that.'

Beth searched her memory. Nothing. She couldn't remember seeing Chan in any other setting than the Deep Sea and tonight in the police station. 'No, sorry, you're going to have to help me out here.'

'Before I transferred to CID, I was with Traffic. Couple of years back, I was at the scene of a particularly nasty head on collision. Van and a car.'

They sat in silence. Beth saw the road rushing towards them through the windscreen, the white line racing in, seeming to hit her right between the eyes and force its way into her brain. Did all roads lead back to that night, that split second two years ago? Was everything that had happened tonight connected to that single point? It was like a black hole pulling everything else in towards it. She looked over at Chan in disbelief. 'You were there?'

'First on the scene. Found you by the verge. I never forget a face. Recognised you working in that chippy when I first transferred here a year ago.'

'And what? You've been keeping tabs on me?'

'No. I just really like pickled eggs and they're hard to find these days.' She smiled then looked serious again. 'Look, I don't know how you managed to get mixed up in all this tonight, and I don't want to know, but I reckon it's high time life cut you a break. So here's some friendly advice. When you come into the station, you know nothing about any drugs or any money. Nothing. You were just giving a friend a lift. If you stick to that, there's not much they can do.'

'But what about Murdoch and Ryan? Won't their story contradict mine?' They had no reason not to tell the police everything about her involvement with Amber, the way she'd stalled them while they waited on her bringing the coke, the penguin incident, all of it.

'Talking about you won't help their case any, so they won't bother. At the moment they're saying nothing at all, on the advice of their lawyer. As far as I'm concerned, you're in the clear.' Chan put the hand-brake on and Beth noticed with a start that they were back on Junction Street. The first glimmers of morning light stumbled along the street, tripped over the rubbish bags and leant weakly against the buildings.

'Thanks. For everything,' said Beth. There wasn't much else to say.

'It's nothing. Just do me a favour and stay out of trouble from now on, will you?'

'I'll do my best. Thanks for the lift.' She got out of the car and watched as Chan did a tight U-turn and accelerated away, one hand raised in farewell. Beth lifted her arm and waved back, then turned towards home.

The dawn was grey and tissue thin, like it could be wiped away and underneath, the night would still be there, neon reflecting from the wet black street, making multi-coloured

226

raindrops. Junction Street came properly alive only in the dark. It got through daylight hours wearing shades and moving awkwardly. Beth was cold and tired. She felt like she had lived a decade in a single night. Her legs were unsteady, as if she had just returned to land after a long sea voyage.

Her flat was on the top floor, on a corner overlooking the main intersection. At street level, the bottle green paint on the communal door was chipped and often splattered with the previous night's mistakes and accidents. As she approached, fumbling in her pocket for the keys, she noticed that it appeared to have been spared this time, but there was something pink lying on the stone step. She stooped to pick it up. It was a very bent and sorry looking pink, fluffy halo. She put it on her wrist and put the key in the lock.

Once inside, she sat by the window and watched the street slowly rouse itself. Being Sunday, it was in no big rush. The shops were still shuttered and most of the higher flats still had their curtains drawn. A street sweeper van droned by, sucking up pizza crusts and fag ends. Pigeons patrolled the remains, eyeing the gutters sideways.

She needed to sleep. She couldn't sleep. She needed to think. She couldn't think. Her mind trailed round in uneven circles. She emptied her pockets onto the coffee table: two bundles of used notes and one monkey mask. She counted the money. There was more than enough to pay her rent arrears and put a deposit down on somewhere new. She'd start looking tomorrow.

A half-empty bottle of Jack Daniels winked at her from the floor. She went to the kitchen to make a cup of tea. The place felt stale and unlived in, as if she'd been gone for months and it had lain empty, gathering dust. It was hard to believe she had woken up here yesterday, had come and gone to the hospital, to work, just like any other day. It came to her forcefully that this was no longer home. In fact, it was somewhere she couldn't even spend another night.

A bed and breakfast would do until she found somewhere

else. She wouldn't need to pack much. The last items she added to her suitcase were the monkey mask and the halo. Something told her they belonged together. She closed the case and did up the buckles.

She stood by the bay window and took a last look out over Junction Street, watched the traffic lights cycle from red to green. The floorboards under her feet seemed to roll gently, as if on a rising tide.

TWENTY-FOUR

cleaning this trombone, and wondering

Sometimes you just want your mum. Doesn't matter how old you are, how grown up, how self-sufficient. Sometimes the only thing that makes you feel better is a hug from your mum. Even if she's now smaller than you and a little doddery, it somehow still feels like it did when she scooped you up into her arms after you'd fallen and skinned your knees on your fourth birthday. That's how it is for me anyway. When I got out of hospital, it was my mum I wanted.

Davey came to collect me. I'd given them his number on the Sunday and he arrived in the afternoon, unshaven and smelling worse than I did. Pretty impressive considering I'd been marinating in my own sweat inside that hairy costume for most of the previous night. 'What the fuck?' he said, and stood staring at me. 'Shot? You got yourself fucking shot? I do three tours of duty in Iraq and come back without any holes in me. But you! I leave you alone for five minutes and you end up like this. You stupid, stupid bastard.' He sat on the side of the bed and punched me in the chest, quite hard. We sat in silence for a while.

Davey was discharged from the army with PTSD when his patrol was almost wiped out and three of his mates killed. He didn't speak for a year after he was shipped back and could only sleep in half hour bursts before he'd wake up sweating and shaking. He still has flashbacks. He's never told

229

me all the details and I've not pressed him to but I should have realised this would be hard for him, should have got my sister to pick me up. I didn't make the connection. It's obvious now, of course: guns, bullets. Duh. He's right, I am a stupid bastard. 'Sorry mate,' I said.

He sniffed and coughed to clear his throat. 'Oh, you will be. Don't you worry.' He stood up and clapped his hands together. 'Right, we busting you out of here or what?'

They kept us hanging around till the end of the day, checking stuff and re-dressing my foot but eventually they let me go. I have to wear a medic alert wristband now in case I need another emergency operation; it'll warn people about my allergy to anaesthetic.

Davey knew the way to my mum's house and drove me straight there. Mum has kind of adopted Davey as well. She's like that, always the one to nurse a bird with a broken wing, or foot, as the case may be. After she'd filled him with tea and sandwiches and extracted promises from him to look after himself and come back soon, she made a bed for me on the sofa, propped up my foot with cushions, tucked me in with blankets and kept the tea and biscuits coming. I ended up staying a few days, watching box sets of old TV shows and generally being made a fuss of. My sister came to visit, without the kids. She said she didn't trust them not to sit on my foot by mistake and anyway they'd been far too interested in getting a look at my wound. The eldest wanted to know if he would be able to stick his finger through the hole. He's a nice lad, just curious, which is great. All the same I was relieved she didn't bring them, not least because I got a whole batch of her fairy cakes to myself.

But after three or four days, I felt it was time to stand up and be a man again. Whatever that turns out to be. Unfortunately, it's not something that can be tackled lying on your mum's sofa, watching telly and getting fat. Shame that, but it's a fact. So, I went back to the flat, back to my grown up life, to try and figure it out.

Apart from getting shot, in some ways the experiences of that night have been good for me. First thing I did was have a clear out. I went through the flat with a black bin liner. In went the framed photo of me and the fictional Zoe on holiday, then the few items of disputed ownership she'd left in the kitchen, things that never got used anyway: egg slicer, waffle maker, deep fat fryer. There wasn't all that much, barely enough to fill the one bag, but the effect on how the flat felt was huge. I even junked the bed, not realising it takes time for a new one to be delivered, so I'm sleeping on the couch for a while, but that's fair enough. I'm really glad I met Zoe again. Not glad to see her such a mess, but because it made me realise I'd been moping for someone who never really existed. For two whole years.

That's what made me hesitate before starting to look for Beth, if that's her name. I could have misheard after all; I only heard it once and that was second hand. What if I've simply transferred my unrealistic affections from Zoe onto her? I know nothing about her. She may not even be a nice person. She could be a complete psychopath. But no amount of talking to myself in a sensible voice makes any difference, she's still there in my head.

I find myself thinking about her at odd times of the day, like now while at work and supposed to be cleaning this trombone, and wondering if I'll ever see her again. The odds aren't good.

'Oi, Limpy! Want a cup of tea?' Davey calls from the back room.

'Would you please stop calling me that?' Davey's been having a great laugh since I came back to work. I've been Limpy, Lefty, Hop-along Cassidy and once even Richard the Third when he was feeling a bit literary.

'Sorry, Limpy,' he says and goes to make the tea.

Another change in the last couple of weeks is that I've talked to Davey about cutting my hours in the shop. I'm thinking of going to college or uni after all. I've still to check

231

out my options locally but I'm thinking occupational therapy, hoping to specialise in music therapy eventually. And not because of Zoe's criticism of me as some kind of no-brain drifter, although I did think that was unjustified. It's more that getting shot, even in the foot, made me think about how temporary life is and whether I could do something useful with mine, with my theories about music. All that sort of *What am I for?* stuff. Maybe after I've studied and figured some of it out, I could help more people than I can by selling bongos to stoned students and locating rare vinyl for collectors.

I thought Davey would have a problem with it. Thought he'd take the piss, like he usually does. But he surprised me. 'Was wondering when you'd get off your arse and do something,' he said. 'You've been hanging around here making the place look untidy for too long. Frankly, you've outstayed your welcome. And to be honest, the only thing I liked about you was that you didn't go around getting shot. So you've blown that, haven't you?' What he means is that I have his blessing and that he'll kind of miss me. There's no way he's going to say anything like that, but I understand him well enough, and he knows I do, so there's no need to go embarrassing ourselves. I'll still do Saturdays and the odd afternoon when I can.

So I've got a lot to think about but even so, Beth with her guarded eyes and lanky body, the way she almost smiled at me, is still taking up at least half of my head space.

The police, when they interviewed me in the hospital, wouldn't tell me whether they knew if she was alright. Wouldn't tell me much about what went on that night at all. 'We ask the questions, sunshine,' one of them said. They asked me why I got in the way of the two men they had later arrested and whether or not I knew the driver of the chip van. I was completely honest and told them I'd talked to Beth in the chip shop, and that I'd been going back with flowers to apologise for what I'd said and to thank her for the free chips. They looked at me pityingly, shook their heads and complained about the paperwork they were having to fill in on such blatant idiocy. When they'd finally accepted that I really did know nothing and wasn't just playing dumb, they left with a warning about keeping my nose clean and maybe giving the monkey suit a miss for a while.

That's not going to be a problem. The hospital gave me a bag with what was left of it, all cut up and missing the head. I took it back to the shop yesterday. You wouldn't believe how much a replacement monkey suit costs these days. I'll need to work a few more weeks full-time to pay it off before I do anything else.

Of course I tried to find her. I was still walking with a stick but I hobbled back to the chip shop the next Saturday night. I didn't know if she would be there. For all I knew, when she drove out of the street that night, she wasn't planning on coming back at all, or something could have happened to her. But I had to try and that was the only lead I had.

A heavy guy with Elvis hair was wiping the counters down. A much older woman who looked like she could be his mother stood with her arms folded at the till. She was all in black and had hard black eyes. Looked like a fairy tale witch. Like she was on the lookout for children to kidnap so she could fatten them up then shove them in the fryers.

'I'm looking for Beth,' I said, speaking to Elvis.

He looked up, suspicious. 'Friend of hers, are you?'

'Yeah. Is she not working tonight?'

'Not tonight. Not any night. She quit.'

'Really?'

'Yeah, really. Didn't work her notice either. Can't get the staff these days.' He sounded disgruntled but not really angry.

'I don't suppose you know her address?'

'Course I do. But I'm not telling you. For all I know you could be a nutter. A stalker or something.'

'I'm not. Honest.' I smiled, trying to look sane and un-stalkerish.

'Well, you're not exactly likely to admit it. Are you?'

'Fair point.' I stood for a bit wondering what to do. If they weren't going to give me an address then there wasn't anything I could do. I ordered a bag of chips, being careful not to catch the witch's eye while I paid for them, and left.

So that was that. At least I know, if she was able to quit her job, that she's still in one piece. That's something.

I go through to the back to get my tea. Davey's already finished his. I think he has an asbestos throat. We're getting into a heated debate about optimum tea drinking temperature when the bell on the door rings. I go to reach for my stick. 'Relax. I've got it,' says Davey, and he goes through to the front shop.

I switch the radio on. I should know better really because I'm cursed when it comes to radio playlists. No matter which station I pick, the DJ has had access to what's going on inside my head and translates it into the cheesiest songs ever written. It's like the radio is mocking me for having mass market, standard issue emotions, when I'm truly suffering. It doesn't help. I swear, for months after Zoe left, every time I was within earshot of a radio, I'd catch a blast of *I ain't missing you* or *What becomes of the broken hearted?* or something like that. Today I get *Waiting for a girl like you* so I twist the dial and get Lionel bloody Ritchie giving it *I wonder where you are and I wonder what you do, Are you somewhere feeling lonely* . . . Oh bugger off, Lionel. I switch the damn thing off.

Davey slams back into the room. He's red in the face and obviously angry. 'That Fender. You know the sunburst one? Really fucking quality guitar?' I tell him, yes, I know the one. 'Someone wants to just . . .' he tails off, as if he's having trouble with the next word. He takes a deep breath and manages to spit out, 'buy it. Just . . . buy it.' He says it the way you'd expect him to say *burn it* or *use it as a toilet seat*.

234

'I'm not seeing the problem here,' I say. 'You are running a shop. People wanting to buy things would generally be a good thing. No?'

'You don't understand! They won't even check the action. They're trying to hand me this big bundle of notes and have it bagged up. It's just wrong. I mean, a guitar like that deserves someone who'll play it. It's not an ornament.' He throws his hands up. 'I can't do it!'

'Tell you what, mate,' I say, handing him an empty sandwich bag from the clutter on the desk. 'Why don't you just stay back here, breathe into this for a few minutes and I'll deal with this one. Okay?' I leave him pacing around the back room, making explosive outraged and disgusted noises.

When I get through to the front there's someone crouched down next to one of the boxes of records, rifling through them. She hears me and looks up and her mouth falls open. 'You!' she says and we just stare at each other for a bit until she starts smiling.

'You're okay?' I say. Pretty lame, I know, but at least it's better than the *small world* that's knocking around my head.

She laughs and straightens up. 'I'm okay. Yeah, I'm fine.' She looks at my stick and bites her lip. 'What about you?'

'Oh this? I don't really need it anymore. I just reckon it looks cool,' I lie. I still need the stick to keep the weight off the foot when I'm walking but it's not really that sore. I'll not be needing it for much longer.

'I heard what you tried to do. That was pretty stupid.'

Coming from her, it somehow doesn't sound like an insult. 'Stupid is one of my specialities,' I tell her.

She frowns. 'No, really, you were lucky those guys didn't kill you.' She pauses, seems to be trying to gather herself to do something she's scared of, like jumping off a cliff. When she eventually speaks it comes out slow and deliberate, each word laid down like a footstep across a high wire. 'But as

235

well as stupid and lucky, what you did was also incredibly brave and kind. So, thank you.'

I can feel myself going red and am trying to resist the urge to say something daft to cover my embarrassment.

'And thanks for the flowers too. That was a lovely thought.'

'Aw, shucks,' I say in a cod cowboy accent. 'It weren't nuthin.' But I'm still red as a post box.

So we stand there for a while and I realise I'm just grinning at her like an idiot. I give myself a shake. 'You want to buy the Fender then?'

She nods.

'You play?'

'Yeah. But not for a long time.'

'My boss is having a hairy canary that you don't want to check it out before you hand over your cash. Is there a reason you don't want to?'

She sighs. 'It's complicated.'

'Tell you what,' I say. 'You can explain it to me over a drink, if you like.' She's looking unsure. 'Or a coffee. Or we could just walk. Whatever you fancy.'

'I could use a drink actually.'

So I shout through to Davey, who grunts something unintelligible back, and we're actually walking along the road together, heading for one of the old-man pubs that still survive around the area. Neither of us is leading, we're just aiming for the same place without debating it, walking past the Irish theme pub and the swanky new vodka bar. The place we choose is dim and kind of grubby but comfortable. We order a couple of pints and sit in the back room.

Although this is the first time we've properly met, it's like we've known each other before. She tells me about the band she used to be in and what happened to them, and why playing the guitar again is such a private thing. She can't just pick one up and play, not in public like that.

'Fair enough,' I say. 'Don't worry about Davey. I'll put the guitar aside for you and you can pick it up tomorrow morning.'

'When do you open?'

'Nine-thirty. But you can trust us. We won't sell it to anyone else before you get there. Promise.'

'No, it's not that. I just think I've wasted enough time already.'

'Okay. Nine thirty it is. So . . . you going to tell me the whole story about that night then?' She seems, as far as I can tell, like a fairly level-headed person, not someone who gets chased from strip bars by gunmen very often. Of course I'm curious about how she ended up in that situation, but mostly I want to keep her here a bit longer.

She drains her pint. 'Perhaps another day for that story.'

'Another day?' I seize on her wording, hoping she means she'd like to see me again, deliberately, not only if we happen to bump into each other.

'If you like?' She seems unsure of herself, twisting her beer mat around in her hands.

'I like. I like very much.'

She looks right into my eyes as if I'm a curious animal she's never seen before. Talking monkey maybe. But her eyes are totally amazing, dark and shining, liquid. Oh shit, she's not going to cry is she? I reach out and put my hand on her arm, the way you'd put a finger under your nose to stop a sneeze, hoping to steady her, and somehow stop her detonating.

She blinks a few times. 'I'm sorry. I'm okay. It's just. I don't know. This is all so easy.'

'Easy?' I'm not sure how to take that.

She's got a look of concentration on her face like she's searching for the right words to express something and it's not about me, or at least not directly. 'I thought my life was simple before, no complications. But it was so hard and I didn't even notice. There was nothing easy about it. Not like this. Having a pint with a friend. Talking about stuff. It's all so obvious and straightforward. I've been so stupid.'

'Ah now, c'mon. You're on my patch there. Stupid is my territory. But I tell you what, how about you can have dumb?

Or I could do you a good deal on idiotic? Ten per cent off moronic?' I know I'm blathering and maybe I should be more sensitive, try to draw her out and ask the right questions, get to heart of her problems, but it doesn't feel right. For either of us. Not now. Not yet. So I'm putting my money on blathering and making light of things that weigh too much. There's time enough for everything else. Right now, at this moment, a reduction in gravity is what's needed.

She's smiling again, and that really is something.

TWENTY-FIVE

possible universes

It would be great, wouldn't it, if it all worked out happily ever after? All the loose ends tied up, the baddies served their just deserts and the heroes sailing off into the sunset. No matter how clever and sophisticated we think we are, we still want those stories. Our childish hearts cry out for them because the real world doesn't work out that way.

Take this scene. It's so chocolate-box, rosy-glow perfect that it can't possibly be real.

Christmas Day. Altogether there are nine of us, six adults and three kids. The grownups, and to my own surprise I'm including myself in that group, are sitting around an oval table covered with a white cotton cloth trimmed with red and green. It's spotted with dots of gravy and wine and scattered with the torn remains of crackers; the aftermath of Christmas dinner. There's a slightly lopsided centrepiece, made by one of the kids, from pine cones and sprigs of holly with a little gold-painted saucer in the middle, holding a red candle that smells of oranges and cloves. The air itself seems shot through with gold dust.

I'm sitting right in the middle of it all and even I don't believe it. I keep thinking I'm going to wake up, or the house is going to explode, or fall into a pit. How did I get here? I think about the way I spent my last few Christmases, in bed with a bottle of anything that promised a fast route to oblivion,

239

trying to miss as much of the day as possible, not even switching on the television because of all the fake jollity and sentiment. Now cut to this. A scene so well-worn you'd be forgiven for wondering when Tiny Tim is going to show up. For a moment, the sense of dislocation is so extreme my head spins and I feel a little queasy.

I can't say exactly why, but although this scene could definitely be used to sell mince pies, there's nothing fake about it. Like a tricky spot-the-difference puzzle, I'm looking for the discrepancies between the forgery and the real thing. Eventually I realise it's something felt not seen and it's me that feels different. I feel full, and not just my stomach, the whole of me from my fingertips to the ends of my hair feels three-dimensional. Maybe other people feel like this all the time but it's a new one on me. And I've not even had a drink yet.

There's George, a bit flushed from the couple of whiskies he's had, still wearing the pink paper crown from his cracker and wiping tears of laughter from his eyes. With his new beard and the crown, he reminds me a little of Kubrick. That's what Davey christened the monkey mask that now sits, stuffed with old sheet music, in the window of the Music Box with a pink fluffy halo balanced on his head. I have an urge to reach over and pinch George to check he's real. We've hardly been out of each other's company since that day I bumped into him in the shop and I still find myself pressing a finger into the side of his face or leaning my head on his shoulder to breathe in the smell of him, just to get that reality hit.

It's hard to believe we've only been together about six weeks. Everything happened really fast after we demolished my mental block about the guitar.

I'd taken it home and leaned it up against the wall but hadn't managed to actually play it, just stared at it a lot. A couple of days later the doorbell rang. The only person I'd given my new address to was George.

'Morning,' he said, walked past me into the flat and looked at the guitar, 'So. Have you?'

I shook my head.

'If you don't play that thing then I will.'

'But you can't play guitar.'

'Exactly.'

'Okay. I'll do it. I promise.'

'Do it now.'

'I can't. Not just like that.'

'Come on. Enough of this putting it off. It's only going to get more difficult the longer you leave it. Pick it up right now and play the first thing that comes into your head. Doesn't matter if it's good or bad or indifferent. You'll have done it, and then you can go on and do other things, better or worse or more indifferent. But you have to get past this first.'

He picked up the guitar and handed it to me. 'It's time.'

So I took it, sat on the bed and laid it over my knee, drew my fingers across the strings, quietly adjusted the tuning keys. It had a beautiful sound. The action on the strings was smooth and flowing like it wanted to be played. I tried a few chords. God, it was gorgeous. And then I was playing before I even realised I'd decided to start. It was only when I came to the end of the song and George clapped, laughed and said, 'There. Better?' that I came out of the trance.

I nodded, still dazed. Then he leant his face to mine and kissed me.

'Much better,' I said and kissed him back. It seemed like the best and only thing to do. He raised his eyebrows and grinned. I gave him a gentle shove and he toppled onto the bed.

'If this is the effect playing the guitar has on you, then I definitely think you're going to need an awful lot more practice. But, it's okay, I am prepared to help. At great personal cost, you understand, but you can count on me.'

I kissed him again.

'I mean, it's a dirty job, but someone's got to do it. I'll just have to man up and struggle through it somehow. It'll be hard work but I can do it. Or die trying.'

I grabbed his face and squeezed, puckering his lips out and making it impossible for him to keep talking. I leant down and looked into his eyes. 'Will you please shut up?'

There's his mum, Pauline. She's throwing the joke from her cracker at him, pretending to be cross because he's laughing at her for messing up the punch line. She's a tiny wee bird-like woman with white hair who wears her glasses on a beaded chain round her neck and has a slight shake in her hands. Hard to believe she produced a big hairy lump like George but what she lacks in size she makes up for in warmth. When we first arrived, I was almost rigid with nerves at meeting George's family, and on Christmas Day as well (no pressure there!) but she just took my arm, hauled me through to the kitchen and blethered away, breaking off every now and then to have a boogie to her new *Best of Kirsty McColl* CD. She has this huge collection of music by female singer-songwriters. I'm already invited over one night to have a rummage.

There's Davey, looking ferociously clean-shaven as if to offset George's extra hair. Both his head and face are that bluey-grey stubble colour. He'd look quite scary if you didn't know him but he's one of the gentlest people I've ever met. True, he could kill you with his bare hands, but he really, really wouldn't want to. Once George had explained to him that I wasn't going to use the Fender as a coffee table, and why I hadn't wanted to try it out in the shop, he's been great. In fact, we get on so well I've agreed to take over George's hours in the shop when he starts college. Davey thinks I should get professional help for the flashbacks but I'm not convinced. I've said I'll think about it. One thing at a time. This talking to people lark is still new to me. I don't want to go too far in that direction and end up like one of those creepy folk who go on about being in touch with themselves. There are limits.

Davey doesn't go to his own folks at Christmas any more.

They're an army family and his dad's very Old School. 'If I wanted to spend time being told to pull myself together I could do that any day of the year. I'd rather it wasn't today,' he said. He's chewing contentedly on a mince pie and playing Jenga with George's niece, Marcy, who's about eight. She's wearing a long flowing white dress and earmuffs made of dark coils of hair. Princess Leia is, I think, about to triumph yet again. George got them all costumes for Christmas presents, along with a box set of the original Star Wars trilogy. The two younger boys are dressed as Darth Vader and Luke Skywalker. Luke is currently running for cover pursued by a furious Darth, shouting, 'No one wedgies the Dark Lord and lives!'

George's sister, Diane, is no-nonsense and energetic, and could plainly run a small country in her spare time, if she had any. As it is, she and Rob, her husband, run a small bakery shop so, with the kids, that doesn't leave them much time for anything else. Rob is a big shapeless guy, balding and kind of serene. I wonder if he's a Buddhist. He's got that sort of calm contentment. He doesn't talk much, seems happy to let Diane talk for both of them.

I don't say much either. I'm not so much calm as simply mesmerised by everything. I keep telling myself that just because it looks like a story doesn't mean it's not real.

It's getting late. Diane and Rob round up the kids and get them settled upstairs. Shortly afterwards, Pauline yawns and announces she's going to bed too. 'You're going to have to fight over who gets the fold-down, the couch or the floor. Just remember to blow that candle out before you turn in,' she says before kissing everyone and padding off upstairs. I watch the tiny flame and listen to the talk around the table.

Davey is deep into one of his theories. Rob is nodding and frowning as if he can't decide whether what Davey's saying is incredibly clever or mind-blowingly stupid.

'What I'm saying is that there's no middle of anything.

You're always at the beginning and the end at the same time. The beginning of the end or the end of the beginning. It's all circular. The end of one second and the beginning of the next are constant, and infinite.'

'Wow,' says Diane, 'that's deep. Did that come out of your cracker?' She laughs and refills everyone's glasses, giving me a brief curious look when I put my hand over mine and shake my head. My glass of wine from dinner is still almost full. Perhaps it's only the novelty of seeing Christmas sober, but drink doesn't appeal today.

'Don't mock the man, Diane.' Rob is smiling, apparently relieved Davey seems to be saying something he can latch on to. He puts his elbows on the table and leans forwards. 'But if we exist in an infinite number of possible universes then there must be one in which there are not an infinite number of possible universes. So how would we know if this one is it?'

Davey frowns and sits back to digest this. George laughs, 'Oh, you're good, Rob.' He lifts his glass to salute his brother-in-law. 'I'm impressed though, Davey. It almost sounds like you've thought this one through. But isn't it a bit of a deviation from your sex and chips theory of humanity?'

'Not necessarily,' says Davey warily. 'And if I had any idea what you were talking about, I'd be able to tell you exactly why that is.'

I kind of zone out while George is telling everyone about the last World According to Davey theory. I'm still thinking about what he was saying about beginnings and endings. Obviously I've thought a lot about that night. There had to be a specific moment or a single choice that set in motion the chain of events that brought me here. Was it giving George a replacement bag of chips? Covering for Amber? Not letting go of that fire escape? Or something further back? Or, and this is where it really starts messing with my head, maybe the choice wasn't even mine but part of someone else's chain:

Amber's or George's or Helen's, or another person I don't even know. Where does one story end and another begin? And can there still be an end when you don't know where it started?

There are an infinite number of ways in which that Saturday night could have turned out differently. But it didn't. The chances against my being here now, in this room, with these people, are cosmically massive. But I'm still here.

My head is starting to spin so I force myself to focus on what people are saying.

'It's all completely random though, isn't it?' says Diane.

'Well, yes, in a way,' replies Davey. 'But if it is, and we're the result, then what does that tell us about the nature of randomness? As a force?'

'Use the force, Luke!' says George, picking up one of the kids' discarded light sabres and waving it around.

I feel hot and dizzy. I stand up and excuse myself and go to the bathroom to splash cold water on my face. I sit on the edge of the bath and feel the hard plastic shape in the side pocket of my combats. I've been carrying this thing around for days now and I keep putting it off. I can hear voices coming from the sitting room and wonder if I should go home after all. Perhaps this is something I need to deal with on my own. The thought reminds me of Amber and I wonder what she'd say. Probably she'd tell me to stop being an arse and get on with it. Then I think about George and know that I want to be with him tonight, whatever happens. I've got a lot to learn about sharing my life with another person, but I'll wear my L-plates for as long as it takes. I stand up and take the thing out of my pocket. It's time.

I follow the instructions carefully and manage not to pee on my hand then put the cap on and place the tester behind me on the cistern. I wait. I'm not going to turn around before the two minutes are up. I need to be sure about this. The second hand on my wrist watch circles the dial twice and keeps going. I turn around and look in the little square window which gives the result and there it is, a thick unmistakable blue line.

And so you're here.

Hello you.

TWENTY-SIX

take a picnic

I'm not going to describe all the places I've been. Get off your arse and go and see them yourself. I'm not your fucking tour guide.

I will tell you I've seen all the places in my alphabet and plenty more besides. And I wish I could say it's brought me a sense of fulfilment and completeness or that I've reached some level of inner peace. But it hasn't. If anything I'm angrier, less accepting of the way my life has been and what's still to come. Seeing the world has made the thought of leaving it so much harder. I was more philosophical about everything before I set off, when I was still working back at the club. It's not the end itself that's getting to me, it's the fucking unfairness of it. And the fact that I'll never have any answers. When did this start? Why did it happen to me? Was it all coded in my DNA before I was even born? I feel I have lived a very short time and it's just not *enough*.

It's a beautiful morning as I leave the small apartment I rented about a month ago near Upper Haight. I came back to the States for only one reason. Here, it's easy to get hold of what I need for the pain. After I set off, my symptoms faded and for the first year I almost let myself believe that the doctors could've been wrong and I could outrun my diagnosis. But it caught up with me eventually and now it's either deal with

247

the situation myself or go into hospital and that won't be happening. Within a few days of arriving, I managed to secure a good stock of Fentanyl patches. Frank, the guy I buy from, is reliable and very obliging, especially when he realised money isn't a problem. Yesterday he brought me a bunch of lozenges and raspberry flavoured lollipops called perc-o-pops. They have the same stuff in them as the patches but work quicker. 'Welcome to America,' he said. 'Dontcha just fucking love this country?' I don't mess about with them, just use them the same way they would in a hospital, but having my own supply saves me having to go anywhere near a doctor. Last night I had the best night's sleep I've had in ages. This morning I feel relaxed, loose-limbed and easy, walking in the sunshine in search of a quiet café for breakfast. I guess life could be worse.

After two years of almost constant travelling, it's nice to stop in one place for a while. No matter how strange your life becomes, if that strangeness goes on long enough, it becomes ordinary. I like this place. San Francisco is a city of neighbourhoods, all jammed up next to each other, each with its own personality. This means the city is riddled with grey areas, in-between places that exist on the edges. Kind of like Junction Street. It makes me laugh now to think how much time and effort I spent trying to get away from that place, when it turns out it's exactly the kind of place where I'm most comfortable.

Nights when I can't sleep and have the energy, I go out and visit a few bars. Usually I end up talking with someone. I recommend talking to strangers, especially in bars after a few drinks. These days I listen more than I talk. People tell me stuff they probably don't tell anyone else. I must have one of those faces. Some of the stories I hear make my life read like a fairy tale. Others are more about what hasn't happened – longed-for events that never took place. In my mind now, all the stories overlap and merge into a kind of music. It's like the organ music they play at fairgrounds, sad

248

and spooky and slightly off-kilter. Most of life is like that, I think.

I sit at the back of a dimly-lit, laid-back little café with a coffee and a toasted bagel and read one of the newspapers. It's warm in here so I slip off my hat. I've more or less given up on the wigs now. I continued to wear them for the past two years, mostly because wherever you are in the world, bald women attract such a lot of attention. Funny, I could walk around in a sparkly bikini and not get noticed as much. How do bald men manage to look so inconspicuous? I don't let it bother me though. When I tune in, I can feel people's stares crawling all over the skin of my head, like insects. I recognise the sensation from my days at the club, although now it's concentrated on a different part of my anatomy. It's not a problem. I learned long ago how to tune out.

A studious-looking boy of about twelve comes up to me and taps me on the arm. 'Do you have cancer?' he asks, blinking behind his glasses. He doesn't look malicious, just curious. His mother is standing at the counter, waiting for the waitress to add up their bill. She's frozen to the spot, her eyes widening in horror as she overhears her kid. She's wondering whether or not she can get away with pretending he doesn't actually belong to her. I'd be proud of him. If you want to know something, you can do a lot worse than ask a question.

'Yes, I do,' I tell him with a smile.

'Are you going to die?'

The kid's second question causes his mother to choke on thin air and press a twenty dollar bill on the slow-motion waitress, muttering, 'Keep it, just keep the change. No, really.' But the waitress is one of those dogged types who does everything properly. Slowly and properly. 'Ma'am. If you'll just be patient . . .' The mother glances over to our table and chews her lip.

I look at the boy again. Is he likely to get upset? No, I doubt it. 'Yes, I am.'

The boy blinks again. 'When?'

'Well, I'm not exactly sure.'

'Soon?'

I laugh. 'Well not right now this second, if that's what you're asking. But probably quite soon, yes.'

The boy's mother eventually succeeds in paying their bill, comes over, grasps the boy's wrist and begins to haul him away from my table. 'I'm so sorry,' she says. 'I don't know why he says these things. I hope he didn't upset you.'

'Not at all.'

'Chester, apologise to the lady.'

The boy mutters something into his chest.

'No, no. Really. I mean it,' I say. 'Not a problem.' I raise the boy's chin with the edge of my hand while his mother watches anxiously. 'Never be afraid to ask. And may your questions all have answers. Okay?' The boy nods and allows his mother to lead him out of the café.

The bell dings behind them as they leave and at the sound, like the next round of a boxing match, someone new sits down next to me. 'I'm sorry,' says the old woman, 'but I couldn't help overhearing.'

'Don't be, please.' I begin to gather my things together, pull my hat back on and unfold my coat from the back of the chair. I have to be careful with old people. They can be forceful with their sympathy and always have an endless stock of cancer stories.

'No, honey. You misunderstand me. I'm not sorry about your cancer. I'm not even sorry you're dying. Happens to us all, doesn't it, hmm?' She puts her head to one side and her eyes twinkle. Now I look at her a bit closer, I notice she's not your standard issue little old lady. She's firing on more cylinders than a lot of folk ever manage.

'Oh. Okay, then. What can I do for you?' I ask.

'Just take one of these. You might want to put it on your bucket list,' she says, and hands me a postcard with a picture of a rugged looking island surrounded by bright blue sea.

'Bucket list?'

'Things to do before you die.'

'Oh right.'

'I guess in your case, you best get there in a hurry, huh?' The old lady doubles over with laughter, then nudges me in the arm with a sharp elbow. What is this old fruitcake on? Not that I mind. In fact, it's great.

'Can I get you a coffee or anything?' I ask.

'Can't stop. I've got to get rid of the rest of these.' She brandishes a handful of postcards.

I read the text on the one I'm holding. *Angel Island Nature Reserve.*

'Ferry goes out from the Bay three times a day. Only takes a few minutes. You should go. Been a lot of different things, that island. Prison, quarantine facility, immigration centre, military base. But now it's a nature reserve.' She scoots around the café, giving out a few more postcards. 'It's also real pretty,' she says to me as she leaves. 'Take a picnic.'

The ferry docks at the edge of Ayala Cove and the passengers disembark, pushing bicycles, hoisting rucksacks, talking in loud outdoors voices. They head for the white clapper-board buildings that house the Visitor Centre and Segway Tours or stake a claim to one of the half dozen picnic tables dotted around.

I walk up the pier and take one of the tree-lined coastal trails. I walk for about twenty minutes then stop next to a rocky outcrop and look back towards San Francisco. The Golden Gate Bridge stretches across the water like an optical illusion. I've seen that bridge so many times in movies, getting trashed by Godzilla or aliens, having planes flying under it, getting blown up or knocked down, it's slightly weird to see it in reality. Like I'm playing the part of myself in the disaster movie of my life.

I leave the path to turn inland and climb uphill. After a while I find a stretch of grass partially sheltered by some

251

tough looking shrubs and squat trees. I take off my coat, spread it out on the ground and sit down. The grass is coarse and seems to be all that's holding the soft sandy ground together. I did bring a picnic, a banana I picked up on my way to the ferry, but I don't fancy it right now. My appetite is patchy these days and the pain is back. Lately, the battle between the pain and the pain killers has turned into an arms race, weapons proliferating on each side. I can feel the pain twisting and growling along my nerve fibres, testing for weaknesses, like a hungry dog in a fragile cage. It's only a matter of time before it breaks out. I take a swig of water from my bottle and reach into my pocket for one of Frank's magic lollipops. I twirl it between my fingers and listen to the waves breaking on the beach and the cries of gulls overhead. Today should be pain free, I decide. I slip the lollipop into the side of my mouth, lie down and wait.

Not sure how long it's been. A clean wind breathes through the grass around my head. The pain changes character, the dog curls up and goes to sleep, its breath falling into time with the respiration of the grass. I am aware only of the familiar tensed presence under the skin of my back, huge and constricted, like phantom limbs pushing to get out.

The sky is the kind of blue that goes on forever. I lie very still and stare into it without blinking. The blue is so intense it's magnetic. It is both question and answer, and more – an invitation. The strength of it reaches down to me, passes through the open windows of my eyes and locks into my brain. Then it pulls, and it keeps pulling until something tears and my whole self is turned inside out through the channel of my skull and I am born again into the air. I arch and flex my new wings and know that this is where I now belong. This is not the end.